Stanislas M. Yassukovich was born in Paris of a Russian émigré father and a French mother. The family went to America in 1940, and Stanislas was educated there at Deerfield Academy and Harvard College. He served in the United States Marine Corps and then moved to England in 1961, where he pursued a distinguished career in the City of London—becoming known as one of the founders of the international capital markets. On retirement, he moved to the Luberon region of Provence in Southern France, and he now lives in the Western Cape, South Africa. For services to the financial industry, Stanislas was made a Commander of the Order of the British Empire. He is a Fellow of the Royal Society of Arts and a Freeman of the City of London. His previous works, Two Lives: A Social and Financial Memoir, Lives of the Luberon, James Grant, a novel, and Short Stories, a collection, were published by Austin Macauley Publishers in 2016, 2020 and 2021. Stanislas is married to the former Diana Townsend of Lowdale Farm, Mazoe, Zimbabwe, and they have three children: Tatyana, Michael, and Nicholas.

To Angela Frater

Stanislas M. Yassukovich

THIRD COLLECTION OF SHORT STORIES

AUSTIN MACAULEY PUBLISHERS™

LONDON * CAMBRIDGE * NEW YORK * SHARJAH

A CIP catalogue record for this title is available from the British Library.

ISBN 9781035808816 (Paperback)
ISBN 9781035808823 (ePub e-book)

www.austinmacauley.co.uk

First Published 2024
Austin Macauley Publishers Ltd®
1 Canada Square
Canary Wharf
London
E14 5AA

I owe my inspiration as a writer of fiction to the people, places, and events a cosmopolitan and varied life has provided. To be fair therefore, I should acknowledge and thank my parents, teachers, employers, and life's coincidences as responsible for this boon. The more I indulge in backward glances, the more I appreciate how fortunate I have been. As in any evocation of memories, I add considerable embroidery to their underlying pattern, and heavily disguise the characters—many of which are outright inventions. I am grateful to my grandson Boris Duke for the cover concept. I am most grateful to many friends who encourage me to keep writing. My relationship with my esteemed publishers Austin Macauley suffers from the great geographical distance between us. But, as in my past publications, they have made every effort to overcome this, and to cope with my digital inadequacy. I thank them.

Table of Contents

A Morganatic Marriage

"Mama! Mama! Eveline… look! Antoine has fished almost 20 crayfish and he has given me half for helping him!"

So cried little Clara, as she rushed, glowing and breathless, through the kitchen door.

"And what have you done to help him?" said a statuesque, blonde lady, who was called Madame at home, now standing next to Eveline, the cook, at the kitchen table.

"*Ah! Des écrevices*!" exclaimed Eveline in admiration.

Clara flopped down on a chair at the table, having dumped her crayfish on its crowded surface, wrapped in pages of *Le Monde*.

"Well," she explained, "I stood on the bank to make sure Antoine wouldn't fall in the stream!"

"I must put those straight in boiling water," said Evaline, gathering them up. "Then I will grill them in their shells and the meat will lift out easily."

"And what would you have done if Antoine had fallen in, my treasure?" asked Madame, looking at Clara's dirty hands.

"I would have saved him—I'm a much better swimmer than him." Clara went to the sink and started washing her hands—standing on tiptoes.

Sophie, a thin and severe woman in her fifties, was sitting at a sewing machine table in a little alcove of the kitchen. Whilst continuing to work the pedals of the Singer and without looking up, she said, "*Ecrevices* are not fish, my dear Clara, so they are caught—not fished."

"Sheer pedantry!" said Madame. This lady, Clara's mother and named Tatyana, dominated the animated scene in the kitchen through sheer presence, rather than maternal authority. In her 40s, she might have been under 30, but for a complexion which showed signs of make-up use—although it was now clear, and her blonde hair was dressed informally, gathered on the top of her head. Her modulated voice and measured movements would certainly suggest stage training to the cognoscenti.

Clara, a ten-year-old in constant motion, with freckles and pigtails, was drying her hands on Evaline's apron, as the cook poured boiling water over the crayfish in a large bowl. She said, "Antoine has asked again, Mama."

"What has he asked again?" said her mother.

"You know—his Mama wants us to come to dinner."

"Well, you must tell Antoine to thank his mother for her kindness but explain once again that I do not go out. M and Mme Le Grand—and Antoine, must come here to dinner."

"But she wants us to see their house—and she says we can come before Papa arrives."

"What tact!" said Madame.

"And kindness," said Sophie, still sewing away on her Singer. "Why must you persist with this silly complex?"

"You know perfectly well, my dear Sophie—I will feel less awkward here in my home."

There was a knock on the open kitchen door and a gentleman wearing a straw boater and carrying a cane walked in. He was elegantly dressed for the summer climate and had the manner of a *boulevardier*—slightly stooped, with thinning, reddish hair—wavy and worn rather too long around the temples.

"I knew I would find you here," he said as he walked over and kissed Madame's hand. "Tanichka! You are as beautiful in the kitchen as you always were on stage!"

"And still flattered insincerely—you might add," said the object of his compliment.

"Look here, *M le Comte,*" said Eveline, pointing at the bowl with the crayfish.

"Ecrevices!" he said, licking his lips.

"Antoine and I caught them," said Clara, as the count walked over and kissed her forehead.

Sophie had stopped sewing and was looking at the visitor.

"There is a button loose on your sleeve. *M le Comte*," she said, quietly.

"What Eagle eyes you have, my dear Sophie," said the count, as he shook her hand.

"I was not a dresser at the theatre for 20 years, without being able to spot a costume fault. Take off your jacket, please—and I will sew it back on."

The count took off his tan-coloured, light jacket to reveal an embroidered waistcoat, handed it to Sophie and sat down at the kitchen table. Evaline brought him a glass of sherry. Clearly, he was a regular visitor.

"You'll stay to luncheon?" asked the lady of the house.

"With crayfish on the menu—need you to ask?" replied the count, sipping his sherry and almost smacking his lips.

Clara was determined to press her case. "*Oncle* Pierre, please tell Mama she can go to dinner at Antoine's house. I'm invited too and I want to see their house."

"Clara, darling—you must forget this—Uncle Pierre knows full well why it is awkward for me." She turned to the count.

"Pierre—let's go to the drawing room, Sophie will bring your jacket."

The two went from the kitchen through a short passage to a comfortable room furnished largely with wicker furniture. They were in one of those houses typical of the Normandy coast and although often referred to as cottages by summer residents of Trouville-sur-Mer, they were commodious houses with half-timbered, stucco sides and hip and mansard roofs in grey slate. Clearly built for a summer residence, the rooms were large and well-lit from windows looking at the sea.

There was an unmistakable taste of Russia in the décor of this example, with dozens of family photographs scattered about and an icon in a corner with a candle burning before it.

"So, when can we expect Vladimir Vladimirovich," asked the count, as they sat down, and he waved his gold cigarette case.

"Of course, you can smoke," said Tatyana (called Tanichka as a form of endearment). She continued as Pierre lit a Russian cigarette. "I haven't checked to see if the race meeting at Longchamps is over—if it is—he'll be here shortly. The Casino is always open."

"Come, Tanichka! You know he's not really a gambler."

"Yes, I know. People who are not drinkers drink when they are unhappy. Vladimir is not a gambler, but he gambles because he is unhappy."

"If he's unhappy, it may be because you are unhappy. And you have no cause to be—do you think of that?"

"My dear, I think of it all the time. Maybe unhappy is too strong a word. Maybe I'm just uncomfortable. I don't mean with all this." She made a sweeping gesture to indicate the house and its venue. "I mean because of my awkward position. Clara wants me to go and dine at her friend's house. But you know what it's like. They don't know how to deal with me. As good republicans, they don't know if they should curtsey—call me 'Your Imperial Highness' or just fawn over *Madame la Comtesse*. I must explain I'm not an Imperial Highness, I'm not even really a *comtesse*. All right, the Tzar made me one when I married his younger brother, but I'm just Tatyana Biel, an actress. In fact, you are supposed to call actresses Mademoiselle even when they are married. Isn't it funny—they call opera divas 'Madame' when they are not married."

"But Tanichka, you knew all this when you married Vladimir. And even in republican France, they know about morganatic marriages. And you are hardly lacking in social status. Biel is a noble name in Poland."

"As the people in the Imperial household reminded me. I know all that—but my family have always been proud to be part of the untitled nobility, the *Szlachta*. They were unhappy when I went on the stage. They were even unhappier when I married a Grand Duke. And now they don't like it that I'm called a countess. And how often we discussed these questions when we decided to marry! But Vladimir promised we would lead a quiet life, retire from society— he looked forward to it; he said he was happy to be out of the Imperial entourage."

"But for Vladimir, this *is* a quiet life." The Count got up and walked to the French windows. He did not like to contradict Tatyana. He continued-

"Even in Paris, you are not over-lionised. Vladimir goes to his club. You have some of his friends for a quiet dinner—even me, very often—how I enjoy those friendly dinners! Sometimes you have old friends from the theatre. Vladimir loves it. It's informal. And little Clara catches crayfish with her bourgeois friend here in Trouville and goes to the Lycée in Paris where no one knows she is the daughter of a grand duke. Yes, she is called Mademoiselle de Biel but there are other girls with a *particule*. You must realise that it is all relative. Compared to the Imperial court, you live a simple and peaceful life. And what about when you were a celebrity? A member of the *Comédie Française,* with all of Petersburg society at your feet with your performances of Molière at the Bolshoi? Were you not lionised, pursued by your admirers—male and female? Are you not at peace now—even with a highly placed husband?"

"But that was different," replied the countess. "I was myself, a famous actress—and I had worked hard to become that. I accepted the price of fame. What am I now? A partner in a morganatic marriage—the object of my husband's fall from grace."

She rose and began to walk about. Now both were pacing around the room—each thinking of their side of the discussion.

The count stopped and turned to Tatyana, "Do you want to hear something silly? It puts all this nonsense in perspective. You know Clara confides in me?"

"She adores her Uncle Pierre who she sees more often than her father." Tatyana sat down again with a frown.

"Well, apparently her friend Antoine told her some time ago that his parents were not sure they should receive you because you were an actress!"

"How charmingly old-fashioned! It goes back to the days when actresses were assumed to be prostitutes, as well. I suppose when they heard I was a countess, I was acceptable."

Sophie entered the room with Pierre's jacket, followed by a skipping Clara, who took it from her to put it on her uncle—who, of course, wasn't really her uncle.

"Lean back, *Oncle* Pierre," she said, "I want to put it on you."

"Thank you, Sophie—and Clara," said Pierre. "Would you both like to inspect me again to see if there is nothing amiss with my costume?"

"Monsieur le Comte is always impeccable," said Sophie.

"I never noticed the button," said Clara, frowning.

"And Sophie is always tactful," replied the Count.

"Can you smell the crayfish?" cried Clara, taking her mother by the hand.

As if on cue, Evaline entered and said, "*Madame la Comtesse est servie.*"

As they passed into the small dining room, Tatyana said to Pierre, in a near whisper-

"She makes these formal announcements because you are here. It's usually just 'lunch is ready'."

"You must allow her the treat," said Sophie, who overheard, "you know how Eveline brags in the whole neighbourhood that she works for a countess."

The four sat down at the table—Clara tucking her napkin into the collar of her gingham frock.

"Oh, goody!" she exclaimed.

The crayfish were brought in by Evaline with a proud flourish. They had been grilled and then lemon butter added. There was a steaming bowl of rice and another of leaf spinach. Pierre opened the bottle of Chablis Evaline had placed in a wine bucket with ice.

"Can I have some with water?" asked Clara.

"Not too much," cautioned Tatyana, as Pierre poured some wine into Clara's glass, adding water from a jug.

The consumption of the crayfish and its supplementary dishes produced silence and pleasant concentration for a while. When Evaline came in with the cheese, a chorus of compliments greeted her. The count was thinking to himself: *'here we are, like a normal family, with a close family friend and even the lady's maid at the table. Far from all the nonsense of Imperial Highnesses and God knows what fuss. Why can't Tanichka appreciate it?'* With the thought came another idea—which he spoke out-

"I have an idea. Clara wants to see Antoine's house. Why not ask him to ask his mother Madame Le Grand if she would be happy to receive me as Clara's escort in your place, Tanichka? They know me—we have met on several occasions around town."

"Oh yes!" exclaimed Clara. "What a lovely idea! Please, Mama—can I tell Antoine?"

"I think the idea is you *ask* Antoine—not *tell* him!" observed Sophie.

"You always correct me, Sophie," said Clara, "But I don't mind."

"You will explain that your mother is most grateful—but she does not go out," said Tatyana, who thought to herself: *'I'm sure the Le Grands will be delighted to entertain the Comte de Chambord.'*

And so, this complexity of social life in Trouville was successfully negotiated and some few evenings later, Pierre found himself walking along the esplanade the short distance to the Le Grands, with Clara dressed in her best frock and wearing a light green cloak. It was a balmy summer's evening with the blues, greys and whites of the sky, sea and sand illuminated by a pink setting sun. Pierre fully expected Clara would take advantage of this time alone to ask him questions on family matters which her mother answered poorly or evasively. And he had not long to wait.

"Why is Papa away so much, *Oncle* Pierre? I know he was once a very important person—Evaline sometimes calls him something high, but I thought he was retired so he could spend time with us—doesn't he love us?"

"Of course, he loves you dearly, but you see he has interests and occupations which he thinks your mother might not enjoy."

"Do you think if I had a brother he would be more at home?"

"No, it's not that at all. You must understand he grew up in a very different world. He hardly saw his parents, but they still loved each other."

"Antoine says he was not supposed to marry Mama."

"Antoine talks nonsense—as many 15-year-olds do. Your Papa married your Mama because he loved her, and she loved him—and they still do—love each other."

'*I'm not doing this very well,*' Pierre thought to himself.

He handled the dinner better. When Antoine took Clara to his room to show her his collection of shells, he explained to Mr and Mrs Le Grand that Tatyana felt awkward and embarrassed in society as the morganatic wife of a grand duke of Russia. He suggested they accept her invitation to dine. They would see how simple and easy a life she led here in Trouville—with no ceremony. She would relax and all could look forward to a comfortable friendship. His mission accomplished; Pierre was able to turn the conversation into general matters.

Of course, this included references to the tensions in Europe. The recent wars between Greece and Turkey had done nothing to ease the Balkan situation. The Austro-Hungarian Empire seemed increasingly fragile—nationalist movements were courting danger and the Slavophiles in Russia were too eager to support them. "Will there be war?" was asked more often at dinner tables and the question was bound to come up on this evening. The count was ambivalent, but M Le Grand was pessimistic.

"The Kaiser is a military fanatic," he opined. "He is looking for an excuse to go to war."

"What will Viviani do if he does? We are allied with Russia, don't forget," said the count.

"And the Tsar is a cousin of the Kaiser," remarked M. Le Grand. "How can they fight each other?"

"Ah—that will be of no avail if Russia has to support the Slavs of Serbia," the count mused almost to himself.

When the children re-joined the company, the conversation returned to banalities and M Le Grand ordered a carriage to take Clara home and Pierre back to his cottage, a *demeure* which answered more readily to that description.

Some few days later, Clara and the whole household were in a state of excitement following the receipt of a telegram announcing the imminent arrival of Vladimir Vladimirovich.

"What can we give *Son Altesse Imperial* for dinner?" asked Evaline, who was the most excited of all.

"Evaline, you can do him the favour of just addressing him as 'Monsieur'—as I have often asked you," said Tatyana.

"But Madame—a Grand Duke! I cannot help it!"

"Try, Evaline, try! He hates formality."

When Vladimir arrived, he picked up Clara, swung her round and round and then kissed her tears of joy. He enveloped Tatyana in the closest embrace, kissing her lips, eyes and neck. He then kissed Sophie's hand and went into the kitchen to receive Evaline's deep curtsey to which he responded by kissing her shoulder. Whether Evaline appreciated this ironic reversal of the Russian custom of servants kissing their master's shoulder, is very doubtful.

A new arrival in a room can make waves like a diver in a swimming pool where the occupants are merely standing or treading water. Vladimir was no exception. Taller than his wife, broad-shouldered, powerful of figure but displaying gentleness in his gait and movement, his features were regular, in a face clean shaven under black hair streaked with grey at the temples and worn short in a military style.

In profile one could see the shortish, almost pug nose common in his family—said to stem from Paul Ist. Having come straight from Paris, he was dressed formally in a grey morning coat and salt and pepper trousers. Regardless of how much he might seek anonymity, Vladimir was one of those people one notices immediately, in any context.

That evening, after the *boeuf bourguignon*, which was Vladimir's favourite, Tatyana and Vladimir sat on the terrace facing the sea, enjoying the gathering dusk, the rising moon and the sound of a gentle surf lapping a silvery beach.

"I hope de Chambord has kept you company and you haven't been too lonely," said Vladimir.

"Oh, yes and he took Clara to dinner at the Le Grands. She so wanted to see her friend Antoine's house."

"You didn't go, Tanichka?"

"No, dearest—you know I feel awkward with people like that. They are very nice people, but I cannot be at my ease because I sense they are not at their ease. They don't know how they should treat me."

"My darling—we have been over this so many times. If you will act natural, they will act natural."

"But the problem is—who will act natural first! The other day, old Lady Smithson—the English should know better—started a curtsy, then realised she shouldn't; I stuck out my hand, she wouldn't take it; then she finally stuck hers out when I had dropped mine. It was like business on stage—but unrehearsed."

"Perhaps we should put an announcement in the *Journal*: 'The Countess de Biel respectfully requests that you treat her like any ordinary countess, as she regards herself as ordinary.'"

"You are joking."

"Of course, I am, but I am also brooding—but on something more important than protocol confusion." Vladimir got up and lit a cigarette. He leaned on the balcony of the terrace and blew smoke out to sea.

"Pierre says you are unhappy," Tatyana spoke very quietly—as if she feared Clara might hear her in her room above the terrace.

"I've been rather unhappy for some time," said Vladimir, still looking at the sea. "And I am an idiot for not thinking about it sooner—when I could have adjusted better. It's very simple. I am unhappy because I don't have a job and I am not allowed to have one. Why should I be different from a cobbler or a carriage maker? If they can't ply their trade for some reason, they are unhappy. But—and this is the issue. If the cobbler can't make shoes, he can become a tailor and the carriage maker can build houses instead. My job was being a member of the Imperial family. I understand I don't have that job anymore—but I'm not allowed to have another job."

"You should not have married me," said Tatyana very quietly—almost in a whisper.

"Nonsense! If I had not married you, Tanichka, I would have died of love. I would rather be a bit frustrated than dead."

"You could have made me your mistress."

"Certainly not! I would not insult you. I wanted a wife—a child."

"And I only gave you a daughter."

"Clara! The light of my life next to you—how can you say 'only'?"

19

"Why are they so unreasonable? The dynasty won't fall if a member of the Imperial family has an ordinary job."

"It's a question of setting a precedent, my poor Tanichka. If I was in Nicky's shoes, I would do the same thing. His is a terrible responsibility. He has to protect the dignity of the family because he has to protect Mother Russia."

"It's stupid!"

"The world is a stupid place, my sweet Tanichka."

The moon was full and now bathed the sea in a silvery glow. Along the Esplanade, lights flickered, and one heard only faintly the occasional strain of music. There was a hum of silence and a warmth of peace, despite a refreshing evening coolness. The couple now shared the silence and Vladimir took Tanichka's hand in his and raised it slowly to his lips.

Next morning at breakfast, Vladimir announced he planned to lunch at the Casino. "I'm sure to see de Chambord there."

"Oh, can I come with you Papa?" said Clara.

"No, my sweet—no young ladies are allowed," explained Vladimir.

"It's not fair! Dogs are allowed. *Oncle* Pierre told me so."

"But they have to be kept on leads. Would you like to be on a lead?"

"Oh, you are funny, Papa!" and Clara got down from table and ran to hug and kiss her father.

"I'll tell you what," said Vladimir as he gently disengaged himself—"it's a fine morning, let's walk on the beach you and I—and you can show me where you and Antoine caught those crayfish you wrote me about."

"Clara wrote you a letter?" asked Tatyana, "What a clever girl!"

"Sophie addressed and posted it. You owe her for the stamp, Mama," said Clara, proudly.

"It's a present," said Sophie.

For their promenade, it was low tide and the two had firm sand to walk upon, occasionally skipping nimbly to avoid an incoming wave. Clara ran ahead and then back and forth, filled with unspeakable joy. Vladimir spotted a youth standing at some distance and watching them.

"Isn't that your friend Antoine?" asked Vladimir. "Why doesn't he come and greet us?"

"He's too shy, I'm sure," said Clara, waving at her friend.

Vladimir thought to himself: '*Funny how everyone avoids me—even a 15-year-old lad. Do they think I will eat them? Send them to Siberia? Is it that old*

French expression: "scratch a Russian and your find a Tartar"? I suppose this is part of my exile. My poor Tanichka! She suffers much more than me from this dépaysement.' Still, his time alone with Clara made up for everything. Her happiness was a balm.

"Don't lose too much!" said Tatyana, as Vladimir left for the Casino, with hugs and kisses from Clara.

"Oh, I don't think I will play," he said. "I'm just looking forward to lunching with de Chambord, you know—boys like to have a gossip, like the ladies. Also, I did rather well at the races at Longchamps—that's a sign to stop betting for a while."

The Casino Barriere at Trouville was an imposing building in the Edwardian style, no doubt much visited by the then Prince of Wales and so perhaps better described as Victorian. Vladimir quickly found the Comte de Chambord, who had fully expected him when learning of his arrival in Trouville. They were such close friends they often anticipated each other's movements with no pre-arrangement.

With feigned surprise and much pleasure, the *maître d'hôtel* bowed and scraped, *"Altesse! Monsieur le Comte!—*I have your favourite table."

Waiters dashed about, others lunching nearby stopped and stared; Vladimir frowned, and Pierre smiled.

"What a lot of fuss," said Vladimir.

"You would appreciate it if you were a famous tenor or actor," said Pierre.

"Maybe I should try the stage. I could play opposite Tanichka."

"I can just see the reaction at the Winter Palace when they see the playbill!"

They both ordered oysters and a *blanquette de veau.* A bottle of Veuve Cliquot had arrived 'with the complements of the house,' but Vladimir sent it back and ordered a Meursault.

"Now, let's get down to business," he said.

"You mean discussing whether Tanichka is happy?" suggested Pierre, twiddling with a bread roll.

"Don't eat that, they'll bring buttered brown bread with the oysters—an English habit—its full of them here—but, yes, I am worried about Tanichka, and I am not helping because I am sharing my own restiveness with her—making her even unhappier."

The oysters arrived. The count thought to himself: '*what a ridiculous situation! They each are unhappy because they think the other is unhappy.*' He began to eat his oysters.

"What excellent oysters," said the count, "Belons are always best—not too large." He paused again before speaking, "Vladimir, my dear friend, you and Tanichka are like two drunks supporting each other as they emerge from the café. Each thinks the other is going to fall."

"But we are both having difficulty adjusting to ordinary life," said Vladimir.

"But you were never going to live an ordinary life—it is not every day that a grand duke marries an actress. In any case, who lives an ordinary life? We are all exceptional—at least to ourselves. And let me remind you of something about Tanichka. Like all great actresses, she had problems coping with so-called ordinary life. She told me and I'm sure she told you. On stage in Paris, reciting the lines of Racine, they said she was foreign. In Petersburg, they said she was Polish even though her name was Tatyana. In Warsaw, they said she couldn't be Polish with a name like that."

"Her grandmother was Russian—Tatyana, née Volitzine. She lived to 95," said Vladimir.

"I know," said the count, "and I suppose they couldn't help naming her after granny who lived with the family. But my point is she has always felt *dépaysé*— adding to the stress of a theatrical career."

"Of course, you're right, my dear Pierre, but I thought I would bring her a certain security by living what some might call a simple, middle-class life. I wonder what I am doing wrong—how I can change my life to help her."

Now the *blanquette* arrived and the *sommelier* refilled their glasses, leaving them each to their thoughts for a moment.

"Permit me to give you a piece of advice," said the count, "No, that's wrong! One should not ask that of a friend. He has little choice but to agree."

Vladimir laughed. "You mean one should just give it anyway—without asking. Well, I've had advice all my life. I'm not afraid to change. Some of the advice has been contradictory. My English tutor said I should never ask the men I commanded to do something I wouldn't do myself. My German tutor said I should never do anything myself that could be done by a subordinate."

"What an interesting reflection on the different mentalities of the English and the Germans! But I am going to suggest you do something very simple."

"Which is?"

"Nothing."

"Nothing?"

"Absolutely nothing! Do not change your life. Do not change yourself. Who do you think Tanichka fell in love with, for goodness' sake? Not a grand duke, I can assure you. It was Vladimir Vladimirovich Romanov—the man, not the prince of the blood."

"Well, I must say that is easy advice to follow, at least!"

"All you have to do is to remember your married Tanichka to make her happy. You are still married and therefore she is happy. If she is happy, you are happy. *Finito*! The rest are just the frustrations of 'ordinary' life."

The two friends finished their luncheon with small talk, but with each ruminating in the back of their minds on their more substantial conversation—the giver of advice worried about its reception and the receiver relieved it might be followed effortlessly.

Some days went by, and Vladimir's more relaxed attitude had a salubrious effect on Tatyana, whilst Clara's joy at the presence of her father gave pleasure to all the household. But life—ordinary or extraordinary, does not stand still.

One mid-day, the doorbell rang, Evaline answered and then came to Vladimir's study.

"Pardon, un Comte Kotzebue demande Votre Altesse Imperiale," she said— ignoring her mistress's exhortation on a form of address.

"Kotzebue, here!" exclaimed her master. "Show him in immediately and tell Madame! He must stay for lunch."

A thin and rigid man of medium height entered the room, He was in civilian dress, rather tight, but seemingly uncomfortable to a military man, accustomed to being in uniform.

"Your Imperial Highness!" barked Count Kotzebue, snapping to ramrod attention, clicking his heels, and executing a military bow with a jerking nod of his head.

"Stop that nonsense, Kotzebue! We are comrades in the same regiment after all!"

"You are my colonel," said Kotzebue, flushing crimson.

"Well, call me *mon colonel* in French and, my dear comrade in arms, you know an ordinary soldier can kiss the Tzar on Easter morning—you can embrace an old comrade you have not seen for ten years!" And he rose and taking

Kotzebue by the shoulders, put his face to his cheek three times in the Russian fashion.

Tatyana entered and Vladimir said, "Look here is Kotzebue! Maybe you can make him stand at ease."

"Dimitri Kyrilovich! What a lovely surprise!" she said and, as he bent over her hand, she lifted him and kissed his cheek.

"Ah, finally—that is how we greet an old friend in this house," said Vladimir.

These ceremonies over, all repaired to the drawing room where Clara skipped in, was introduced to the old friend and, quite naturally, put her face up to be kissed. It took some moments for Count Kotzebue to be put at ease. As an *aide de camps* to the Tzar, he was used to a rather more formal contact with Imperial family. It was even with difficulty that he was persuaded to stay for luncheon.

"You have business to discuss, I suspect, Dimitri Kyrilovich," announced Tatyana. "I will leave until later."

Vladimir offered his case to Kotzebue and both lit cigarettes.

"Yes, *mon colonel*, I have a letter from His Imperial Majesty," said Kotzebue, drawing a sealed envelope from his inner pocket.

"I thought as much," said Vladimir taking it. "I suppose I am being stripped of some other honour?"

"I think not, *mon colonel*."

Vladimir broke the red wax seal with the Imperial crest, opened the letter and read it. A smile began to light his face. He handed the letter to Count Kotzebue. It was handwritten and very short.

"My dear Vladimir.

I fear war.

You are ordered to return and resume your command.

Mes hommages à la comtesse.

Yours as ever,

Nicky."

"Well!" said Vladimir to Kotzebue. "I suppose you knew of this?"

"I guessed it, *mon colonel.*"

"I must say, I didn't—it is a pleasant surprise, although I was never formally replaced at the *Chevalier Gardes*. Talashnikov has been doing a good job as adjutant?"

"Yes, *mon colonel*—but it's not the same—"

24

"A good man—I must keep him."

Vladimir strode to the door and called, "Tanichka, can you come here?"

Tatyana entered, pale and even trembling slightly.

"Bad news?" she said.

"Yes and no," replied Vladimir. "I'm called back to duty."

"My darling!" and she flew to his arms.

"Show her the letter, Kotzebue," said Vladimir.

Tatyana read the short letter in seconds.

"The emperor sends me greetings? Good Lord!—it's the first time he acknowledges my existence. You must thank him for that. But, my darling, I'm happy you resume your rightful place." However, the circumstances are alarming. "Tell me, Dimitri Kyrilovich, does all Petersburg think war is imminent?"

"Many do, Countess. The situation in the Balkans is so difficult. If Serbia is attacked by Vienna, the Slavophiles will insist we go to their defence."

"But what will Germany do?"

"That is the question, darling Tanichka," said Vladimir, "but let us not anticipate events; there is no war yet. Nicky is cautious—and perhaps he uses this to save some face in ordering me back. I will write a reply and we will prepare. I will go first to see the lay of the land, as they say—and you and Clara will follow me with Sophie."

"I return immediately with Your Imperial High—er, I mean my Colonel's reply to His Majesty, and I am at your orders to make whatever preparation you need. Your palace is not closed, I believe?" Kotzebue was back at attention.

"Yes—Hermann, the senior steward is there. But do nothing until you have His Majesty's instructions. I don't know when and how he wishes to announce my return—it will attract some comments. But we do nothing at all until we lunch, my friends. Let's just say to Clara, I have news from home and may need to take a trip."

After lunch, Vladimir went into his study and wrote:

"My dear Nicky,

I return at once. I salute you. I am delighted to be once more at your service.

Tatyana thanks you for your kind words. She curtsies and kisses your hand.

Yours as ever,

Vladimir."

He placed the letter into his own embossed envelope, dripped some red wax on the back, licked his signet ring and sealed it.

That evening, Vladimir and Tatyana sat once more on the veranda in the slowly fading light. The lights along the esplanade still flickered, but there seemed to be fewer.

"I suppose there will be war," said Tatyana.

"I'm sure of it," said Vladimir. "The Balkan region is a tinder box. The Serbs are the main problem. If they entice Vienna to war, Berlin will have to follow. There is a secret treaty. And I'm afraid cousin Willy has become a militaristic bully—to cover up his great insecurity."

"The Kaiser of the German Empire is insecure?" said Tatyana.

"Of course! It's the withered arm!" replied Vladimir. "And if I had suffered what the poor lad went through in stupid attempts to put it right, I would be unbalanced as well. They basically tortured him. And then imagine growing up with healthy and active relatives—like his Uncle Edward, who he hated and so he has no time for George."

"How terrible!—you are all cousins—how can you fight?"

"But we all have different personalities, my darling Tanichka. Like many handicapped people, Willy is afraid of being thought weak, so he compensates by acting as strong as possible. My brother Nicky is a sweet and gentle person. His handicap is a son who is seriously ill and a wife who is distraught. It is hardly Alexandra Feodorovna's fault that she had four daughters before producing an heir, but she is consumed with guilt because she brought the haemophilia— which is genetic and rampant in the Hesse family.

"Anyway, it comes from her mother Alice and then from Victoria. Poor Alix! But unfortunately, it is all a terrible distraction for Nicky—at the worst possible moment with all that's going on in Europe."

"Remind me—what is haemophilia?"

"Blood won't clot—an injury just keeps bleeding—particularly a bruise which bleeds internally."

Vladimir lit another cigarette, and they were silent with their thoughts— looking out at a quiet sea which lapped at the sandy shore with all the confidence and regularity which nature provides to volatile mankind.

"I'm happy to hear you speak your thoughts, my dear husband—it suggests you are content," said Tatyana, reaching for his hand.

"I have a proper job again—Nicky writes 'resume your command' so that means I won't be sitting around at Staff. I have my regiment back. But I must leave you for a short while."

"And if there is war?"

"Then you and Clara might be safer here. We must consider if the time comes. You might also go to England to the place we rented in Sussex. There is plenty of money at Barings."

Now, Tatyana rose and went to the balcony to look at the moonlit sea.

"It is so quiet and beautiful here, I wonder what's going to happen," she said.

"There will be a great change, my darling Tanichka, yes—great change."

"One thing won't change for us," Tatyana came back to Vladimir and stroked his hair. "We will love each other ''til death do us part'."

"As well it might," said Vladimir, thoughtfully, "—as well it might."

FINIS

A Rainbow Nation

Gys van der Bosch and Reginald Carter were both South Africans but hailing from two different white tribes: Afrikaner and European. They became close friends, having eliminated the ethnic divide between them on the rugby pitch at Stellenbosch University. Rugby football is a great leveller and source of lifetime friendships. With the two lads in prominent positions—Gys in the scrum and Reginald at back, the Stellenbosch 15, known as the 'Maties', had won the annual Varsity Rugby Cup two years in succession. Their friendship had intensified in the celebrations that followed each victory and been maintained thereafter.

Gys was the scion of an ancient Afrikaner family. His forbears had been contemporaries of Simon van der Stel and had owned extensive lands in the Constantia valley. Reginald was a relative newcomer; his grandfather had come from England in 1820 to set up as a wholesale merchant in Caledon. His father had gone home to study medicine in London but had returned to practice as a cardiac specialist in Cape Town.

Certainly, the enmity which had prevailed between the two white communities after the Anglo/Boer War at the turn of the 19th century had been dissipated over time. But there was not a great deal of social intercourse.

Stellenbosch University used to be considered mainly patronised by the Afrikaner population whereas the University of Cape Town was primarily English. These distinctions have largely disappeared and both universities are now very ethnically and racially mixed. Reginald's father had hoped his son would follow in his medical footsteps and Stellenbosch is known for its medical school.

Gys followed a family tradition and had assumed the management of one of its wine estates—Boschenkraal, in the Constantia valley. Reginald had not become a doctor however, despite earning a medical degree, but had chosen to become an art dealer, specialising in antiques—early Afrikaner furniture, now increasingly rare and valuable.

The two men lunched together at least once a month to discuss rugby and politics. Their wives were school friends, having attended the elite girl's school Herschel in Claremont. They lunched together somewhat less frequently to discuss a broader range of issues—as ladies do. The four played bridge together weekly alternating between their two houses.

Gys's wine estate, graced with a pure Cape Dutch mansion, was in a section known as Beau Constantia. His wife Elspeth was from another old Afrikaner family who farmed near Franschhoek. Reginald had an art gallery in Wynberg Village and lived in a commodious house in Claremont, with his Anglo-Irish wife Martha, whose family had farmed in Southern Rhodesia (now Zimbabwe).

Gys van de Bosch was one of those Anglicised Afrikaners one meets increasingly. He had attended Bishops, the fashionable and very English public school which is, in fact, the brother school of Herschel. He was certainly conscious of his cultural transformation and somewhat embarrassed about it. The Afrikaner community—close to 14% of the South African population, greatly benefit from Nelson Mandela's 'no retribution' policy. It was at the heart of his concept of a 'Rainbow Nation', where the myriad collection of races which constitutes the South African population would live together in harmony. There is less bitterness than there well might be within the Bantu African majority over their protracted disenfranchisement and the nefarious policies of apartheid. Some Afrikaners silently regret the dominance of their National Party, considering that under its rule, the nation developed dramatically; others would rather forget that period.

However pure the original concept of separate development might have been, it was simplistic in the extreme and its enforcement caused widespread misery. In Afrikaner circles, there is a remaining sense of community and a common effort to ensure their language survives. Gys, who was entirely bi-lingual, would have been distressed to think his social mingling with the English and his friendship with Reginald, was taken to indicate disloyalty to his race. He was proud of his Afrikaner heritage and particularly valued his collection of early colonial furniture handed down over generations. He also considered his relationship with his African workers entirely appropriate and in the best tradition of his forebears, but he recognised that his paternalistic respect for them was criticised as patronising by the more politically correct. Tall and robust, with a shock of very blonde hair, Gys was a thoughtful man and his habit of pausing before answering in conversation was considered by some to be a sign of intellectual deficiency. His friend Reginald knew this to be entirely false.

Reginald had thought long and hard himself, before deciding against a medical career and his father had applied no pressure whatsoever in this regard. On the contrary, he had often observed that a life dominated by treating people had robbed him of the opportunity of savouring the extraordinary beauty of the Western Cape. Reginald had developed a love of his country, its topography, its flora and fauna, its cosmopolitan population, its history and culture—in fact, everything about the Western Cape.

This had begun early in life. When Gys had invited him to his own, and grandparents' house in Stellenbosch, Reginald had been overwhelmed by the purity of proportion of the Cape Dutch architecture and had caressed the marvellous examples of stink and yellow wood furniture which graced the simple but elegant interiors. He had then thought of training as a cabinet maker but had soon realised he would have only been able to make imitations. This seemed almost sacrilegious; he would be better off as an antique dealer specialising in and therefore perhaps saving, the dwindling stock of the beautiful pieces the early Afrikaner settlers had made from the local hardwoods. In any case, the native hardwoods—even the common yellow wood, had been over-cut and other furniture-making woods of a bygone era—like pink ivory and panga, were now very rare. So, Reginald used his modest paternal inheritance to set up as an antique dealer. He was dark, small and wiry and his speed had recommended him to the rugby football coaches. Unlike his friend Gys, Reginald was extremely quick in motion and speech, and he reacted quickly to every situation he encountered. This had supported his ball handling on the rugby pitch but often provoked unwise decisions in later life.

The two friends had taken to lunching at the same restaurant—known as Simon's on the Groot Constantia estate. It was convenient to both, and its familiarity and warm welcome allowed maximum concentration on their conversation. By now, they had a regular table and no need to consult the menu. Naturally, they drank Boschenkraal merlot or sauvignon blanc, one of Gys's wines. Like all restaurants in the Western Cape, the staff at Simon's was largely Zimbabwean and one of these, a very good-looking Mashona girl called Reinika, had become their regular waitress—and a friend. Even when she was occasionally assigned to other tables, she would go over to greet them when they arrived.

A large Zimbabwean emigration south had followed the virtual collapse of their country under the corrupt regime of Mugabe. There were thought to be as many as a million and half Zimbabweans working in South Africa. They were sought after by the hospitality industry in the tourism-dominated Western Cape as they spoke better English than the resident Xhosa (themselves emigrants from the Eastern Cape) and had a strong work ethic.

The Rhodesia's, as British self-governing colonies, had provided superior education for the indigenous population than their neighbours in the south. Reinika had been easily identified as Zimbabwean by the two friends and her story held particular interest as Martha Carter had been born there to a pioneer family. Together with almost all the white commercial farmers, her family had been dispossessed. The two principal African tribes in Zimbabwe are the Shona in the north around Harare, formerly Salisbury and the Ndebele—a Zulu offshoot, from the south around Bulawayo. The prefix 'ma' is used to indicate 'peoples from', so Reinka would be called Mashona.

Gys had one or two bright Zimbabwean lads working for him at Boschenkraal—also Shona. One was apprenticed to the head plumber, a coloured man whose skills were invaluable in the winery, The large community of Zimbabweans in South Africa caused tensions, however—as the local South African citizens considered they took jobs from them.

Soon the friendship with Reinika was discussed at the van der Bosch/Carter weekly bridge game.

"We thought you chaps were talking rugby at your men's lunches. Now it seems you are flirting with nubile Mashona maidens!" said Elspeth van der Bosch with a smile.

"That poor girl!" said Martha. "You know they all send their modest earnings back to their folks in Zim. Half the country is living on remittances from family working here. What a disgrace it all is! When you think what that country once was."

"And on top of it all, there were riots in Jo'burg because the locals claim their jobs are being taken away by the Zimbabweans," said Elspeth.

"And they are—that's true," said Reginald, "because they are better educated, speak better English and work harder."

"Reggie, I can see your Reinika has seduced you!" said Elspeth in jest.

"And me!" chimed in Gys, after his habitual pause. "She's a bright and lovely lass. We're lucky to have those people here—but of course, it's causing some bitterness."

Reinika made no attempt to exploit her friendship with these two white customers and they had no expectation of such. Their interchanges were always brief; busy waitresses have little time for idle chat. Naturally, the sorry state of her home country was alluded to and Reinika told them her family were living in what used to be known as the Tribal Trust areas—but were now designated as Resettlement areas, following several land reform initiatives.

Over time, the pattern of her life emerged in fits and starts. She shared a shack in Khayelitsha, one of the shanty towns in the plain near the airport, with two other Zimbabwean girls. One was also a waitress, but the other worked as a cleaner and nurses' aid in an old peoples' home.

One day, after a week of downpours during the rainy season, Reginald addressed Reinika, as she poured his glass of wine.

"I hope you and your housemates are staying dry?"

"Not very, Sir," replied Reinika. "We have some leaks from the tin roof."

"Oh, I can send one of my estate workers to fix that," said Gys.

"Thank you, Sir—but I'm not sure we can afford that at the moment."

"Nonsense! Reinika, you won't have to pay anything! Some of my chaps don't have enough to do at home."

They could both see, Reinika was embarrassed, but she was bound to think of the comfort of her friends. They might josh her about accepting favours from white "bosses," but they would still be grateful. A visit was arranged. Of course, it was Gys's black carpenter and an apprentice—a white visitor in one of the townships is greeted with suspicion. Reinika's shack was quickly made watertight.

The incident was discussed at a weekly bridge game.

"Well, well! This relationship is becoming intimate—free services are being provided. I hope Reinika's virtue is not at risk in reciprocity," quipped Martha.

"Don't be silly!" said Reginald.

"I'm joking, my sweet! But it makes me think—how lucky we were back on the farm. There was always someone in the compound who could fix whatever went wrong in the house."

"And it makes me think, Martha, that you should know I can have anything you like fixed by people here (they were playing their weekly game at the van der Bosch residence). I'm surprised Reggie has never asked."

"Not much has gone wrong at home—and I would not want to impose," said Reginald.

"As I told Reinika," responded Gys, "some of our men are idle half the time—but with the unemployment in this country, letting anyone go is out of the question."

Martha Carter still had a relative living in Harare, and she followed events in her old country with interest. One day she said, "I would like to meet your Reinika to get her to take on what's happening in Zim. What say the four of us have lunch there on Sunday?"

"Good idea," said Gys. "I'll give the manager a call and tell him we'd like to detain Reinika for a few moments. He knows us well and won't suspect we are trying to pinch his staff."

As they settled in at their table, Martha began to elucidate on her cousin in Zimbabwe, "Actually, he's a second cousin once removed, and I am ashamed of him. He's a *skellum*, really—made a lot of money through connections in ZANU-PF, the corrupt ruling party. He's one of several oligarchs who have been making millions and funding the party while the people starve."

"But we'll still accept his hospitality if we go there," said Reginald, wryly.

"Why not?—and I'm keen to go as I want to check on a couple of our people from the farm," said Martha.

Reinika now arrived and bobbed a slight courtesy as she was introduced to the ladies. She handed them menus. Of course, the men knew them by heart, and she knew what they invariably ordered. Martha began to ask Reinika about her family and their whereabouts. They traded scraps of news and impressions about their country, and it was clear that they saw themselves as fellow citizens.

Finally, Martha announced, "My husband and I are planning a brief visit to Zim, Reinika—as there are some people who used to work for us that I'm concerned about. So, we would be happy to visit your family and take them something from you. We have a driver there who knows his way around."

"Oh, thank you, Madame—that would be very nice. Can I bring a small package when you come next?" And Reinika looked at the two men.

"Thursday suit you, Gys?" said Reginald.

"Absolutely—Thursday. Reinika? We'll be here at the usual time."

"Thank you, Sir. I'll be here."

It was not long before the planned visit was put in motion. A four-hour flight took the Carters to Harare airport, now very inactive, as most of the major airlines no longer stopped there due to re-fuelling and maintenance problems. The driver who met them with a brand new, upscale Mercedes model, was a former tractor driver from Martha's family farm and happy reunion greetings were exchanged.

Martha's cousin, removed genealogically as well as in her regard, was a large, bluff man in his early fifties named Robert MacPherson. He greeted them on the veranda of an imposing mansion in a suburb dominated by similar luxurious residences—mostly occupied by moguls from the ruling party.

Dinner, served by two red fez-hatted footmen, might well have been a dull affair. MacPherson was not known for his charm. But he was not short of bluster. And the cousins were soon engaged in a bitter argument.

"OK!" spluttered MacPherson, wolfing his food. "So, the country's flat on its back, there's no cash in circulation, the roads are full of potholes, if we didn't have a generator, we'd be in blackout most of the time—but there's still racing at Borrowdale, some chaps are still playing polo and social life goes on."

"Yes! For you and your chums, while half the African population starves," began Martha.

"Oh, come off it, Martha—you were living the life of Riley on the farm."

"But the people were not starving. Your friends at ZANU-PF have robbed the country blind and driven millions into exile."

"Oh, I can understand you are bitter. But if you commercial farmers had kept your traps shut and not gone against Mugabe, it might have been different."

"And if Sally Mugabe had not died prematurely, it might have been different," chimed in Reginald. "I'm sure Mugabe had a mental condition and that savvy Ghanaian wife kept him on lithium or something. He was probably schizophrenic."

"I agree, but in Africa, you only survive if you cooperate with whoever is in power, even if you don't like their politics. Mugabe began by saying he wanted the white commercial farmers to stay. And what did they do? At the first opportunity, they went into opposition and even told their farm worker to vote against him. He considered he'd been stabbed in the back and took his revenge."

"So that's how you justify your alliance with ZANU-PF is it?" asked Martha.

"I don't know what you mean by alliance—the top businessmen in South Africa keep close to the ANC—they are the ruling party and probably will always be."

"I think Bob is suggesting the CFU should have remained entirely neutral like the CBI does in the UK. Trade associations must live with whoever is in power so they shouldn't take sides." Reginald was trying to cool the conversation a bit.

"That's right, Reggie—that's what I mean. The CFU was I and a bit arrogant. They thought we're a democracy so we're free to vote for whatever party we like. But that's European democracy. This is Africa—one man, one vote, once. Once they are in, the African considers he's in for life—like a tribal chief."

"Well, I still think you are in cahoots with a bunch of *skellums*, Bob," said Martha, "and I am embarrassed for you."

"Don't be, my dear cousin—I'm realistic! You can't survive in this country without ZANU-PF, but my prosperity is for the common good; I employ lots of people, I contribute to food banks and local charities." MacPherson waved his arm to encompass his mansion. "All of this provided a lot of work and business for the construction industry and its suppliers."

"I suppose it's all relative," said Reginald. "Of course, the ANC had its serious bout of corruption with Zuma and the State Capture scandal. But you have to admit Mugabe and ZANU-PF top the league of African political corruption and have basically destroyed the nation."

"As you say, Reggie, it's all relative—and things might still come back here. Shall we have coffee on the veranda?"

Later, in their spacious bedroom suite, Martha exploded, "Smug, arrogant bastard!"

"Live and let live," said Reginald.

Zuzi the driver took them out to the Resettlement zone to visit Reinika's family. It was a good two-hours' drive from town and the snake which is nostalgia wound its way around Martha's soul as she viewed the countryside. The red earth and rolling hills sped by, dotted with the rundavels of the African settlements and compounds—round, stuccoed dwellings with thatched roofs, with *umfazis* sitting outside, surrounded by pot-bellied *piccanins*.

'*How strange*,' Martha thought; '*these terms have become offensive and yet they are simply familiar names of married women and children in a bastardised lingo whites and blacks exchange in Southern Africa.*' She saw little flocks of guinea fowl and the occasional red-winged partridge running through the veld and the crops of mealies and, of course, *mombes,* the Shona word for cows.

Rolling down her car window, Martha took in the sounds and smells that are so typical of the working day. Her mind rolled back to the days on the farm; the *shalili* summoning the men to roll call, the smell of the horse dung and straw burning in a slow fire at the stables, to ward off the horse sickness; her pre-breakfast ride to the far paddock, across the stream by the sheep dip, the leisurely days and soft nights, the paper chases on made up courses, the polo—yes, it was the "life of Riley," as her errant second cousin said.

But still, what had the 'independence' negotiated at Lancaster House, by a Colonial Office anxious to shed its charges as quickly as possible, done for the people of Zimbabwe? Driven then into the hands of tyrants and reduced southern Africa's richest country to near starvation.

The Carters found Reinika's family in a sort of double rondavel with the usual adjoining stand of mealy stalks. Martha immediately wondered where seed maize was now available as farms specialising in that special and critical crop had been expropriated. Soon a small crown gathered around curious about the visitors, and it was impossible to determine which were family and which were neighbours.

Reinika's father spoke good English as he had been in domestic service in Harare for some years. His wife—or at least Reinika's mother, was silent but rocking back and forth with joy, Martha gave her the packet from Reinika to the mother and Reginald handed a present to the father, who held out both hands—as is traditional. It was a quarter gold Kruger rand coin in a little plastic holder. This would keep the family for some time.

"Keep it somewhere safe as a reserve," said Reginald.

"I will give it to my brother who works in an office—he will keep it as the family fortune," said the old man.

The little crowd gazed at it in awe as the father held it up. Reinika's mother was uncertain as to whether she should open the packet immediately in front of everyone. But the consensus was clear, and the group's curiosity was overwhelming. The *umfazi* undid the string slowly, to wind it and keep it. Inside was a multi-coloured scarf, a long letter, photographs of the three girls in their township shack plus two of Reinka as a waitress in the restaurant and finally a sealed envelope probably containing bank notes, which the mother handed to the father.

Martha had a simple talk with the woman in the mix of Shona and 'kitchen kaffir', which the white farmers used in talking to their staff. Only a few in the local colonial service, having to deal with the native public at large, had trouble to learn the Shona language thoroughly. Reginald asked the father questions about the food situation. He seemed a bit reluctant to speak at length about it.

Clearly, Reinika had warned her family about the visit. Her mother went into the rondavel and brought out a parcel, presumably containing something she had made and handed it to Martha to take to her daughter. This was a signal to three other members of the little crowd to press addressed envelopes on the Carters for transmission to relatives in South Africa.

"I knew this would happen," said Martha, "we all know how hopeless our post is."

The ceremonies of departure took almost as long as the visit itself, with much triple African handshaking and tears on feminine cheeks. The visit had been certainly very welcome—but, nevertheless, slightly awkward. The younger people had been taught that whites were their oppressors, but the inherent respect for their elders, who showed little signs of disaffection, repressed any resentment they might have displayed had they been on their own.

Zuzi had been busy during the visit protecting his motor car from the intense examination it was receiving from a large group of youngsters. But he nevertheless offered the comment, "Them's nice people. Baas," as he drove away.

As she looked at the back of Zuzi's head, with a baseball cap on backwards, Martha thought of how the world worshipped American fashions rather than its traditional idols. The youngster's fascination with a western motor car seemed to overcome any embedded bitterness against the whites that had colonised their land. Just what was the true degree of inter-racial and inter-ethnic feeling in southern Africa, in the light of its tragic history of internecine warfare, ruthless exploitation and patronising impositions of western values and customs on the indigenous population?

Martha could not help speculating on this vast question as the minutiae of daily African life in the veld sped past her car window. How is it possible that the industrialisation and agricultural development of two centuries can sponge the blood and contain the resentment of such an historical context? How can the peoples of Africa come to love each other?

Martha smiled as they overtook a bedraggled 'bucky' (the local term for a pickup truck) with a white driver and numerous local, black workers hanging on in the back. Was this to be the future—the whites driving the blacks to work? No, that was too simplistic—a false symbol. Martha decided that what must bind all together was an abiding and deep-seated love of Africa—the mother country of us all, as the anthropologists keep telling us.

Back on the MacPherson veranda, they were subjected again to a rather pompous discourse from their host.

"The tragedy of the Shona," he exclaimed, "is that they are docile, long-suffering and easily exploited. Plenty of other African tribes would have risen and strung Mugabe and his cronies up on the trees—assuming there are any left."

MacPherson paused and, turning his head slightly over his shoulder, shouted, "Solomon!" He then turned back to Martha and said, "See how I've been retrained? In the old days, we shouted 'Boy!'"

Martha nodded, Solomon appeared, and MacPherson made a circular wave with his glass to indicate re-fills for all. He then continued-

"For example, if the Ndebele, who are originally Zulus, had been in the majority, they would not have stood for this. That's one reason Mugabe has ethnically cleansed them. The other is pure, belated revenge. The Ndebele used to hunt the Shona men like dogs and carry off their women and children. There was a season for it—like for grouse and pheasants. It was we Brits who put a stop to that and that's why we were considered their liberators."

"You are oversimplifying, dear cousin," said Martha.

"All history is an oversimplification," said Reginald.

On the return of the Carters to Cape Town, their visit to Zim (as the exiled whites dubbed it) was much discussed at the weekly bridge session—always followed by lunch and a healthy exchange of views. Gys was inclined to agree with the views of Bob MacPherson, while not condoning his support of ZANU-PF.

"We watched in dismay the farm grab in Zim," he said, "and of course, our black political class wouldn't think of criticising Mugabe. There's been a land re-distribution movement here for as long as I can remember. But it's far more problematic here. The government is the biggest landowner and after that the tribal chiefs. Who is going to take their land away?

"And then the Africans—particularly the young, are not interested in farming. They want to live in towns. If I asked my workers if they would like me to hand the place over to some of their people, they would laugh at me. 'Who will pay our salaries?' they would ask. The youngsters work for me so they can go to town and spend the money."

"We never expected you would come to our aid," said Martha. "We understood the situation here very well. The then President Mbeki was a particular chum of Mugabe."

"And your wine industry has greater economic value, even than the tobacco had for Rhodesia," Reginald pointed out. "That's some protection against a land grab."

"When it comes to African politics, economics don't count for much—even though so many leaders went to the London School of Economics. Anti-colonial feeling trumps everything else," Elspeth said.

At their regular lunch, the Reginald delivered the things to Reinika and gave an account of the visit. Gys's PA was struggling to find some of the other addressees whose families had sought to bypass the post office by charging the Carters with items for their relatives in the Cape. Reinika never showed a great deal of emotion, but she was clearly delighted with the account and the package.

As is so often the case, when the sea of life seems relatively calm, a storm is brewing not far away. Now it burst into the world with a particular relevance to South Africa and Reinika. It was a pandemic associated with a novel strain of flu known as Covid-19 and it originated in China. The global reaction was one of panic and political opportunism and travel restrictions imposed everywhere affected tourism to South Africa causing havoc in the hospitality industry. Many small businesses struggled to survive. The larger and stronger reduced staff. Together with thousands of other restaurant workers, Reinika lost her job.

Of course, she was assured she would be re-employed when normalcy was restored—but remittances home would have to cease if she could find no other work.

"We must find her some paid work," chorused the four around the bridge table, as the urgency of the matter was discussed.

Gys said, "I can use her on the estate. We have lots of casual workers coming daily."

"I can use her in the house," said Elspeth.

"Or in the staff canteen," said Gys.

"As you all know, I'm expecting," said Martha, "I wasn't planning to engage a nursery maid for a while, but she can certainly come now—there's plenty to do."

"I suppose she knows how to iron shirts," said Reginald.

A consensus emerged. Reinika would be asked which job she preferred, and the salary would be the same in both cases. There were standard rates for housework.

It was Reinika's last day at Simons restaurant, when the men saw her again and she decided, with no hesitation, that she would be happy to work at Boschenkraal. Reginald expressed surprise when he was home that evening.

"I must say I'm a bit taken aback," he said to Martha. "After all we have done for her, I would have expected her to come to us."

"Not at all, my love," said Martha, "It's perfectly natural—she will be employed with her own kind. For Reinika, Boschenkraal is a farm in Africa, owned by an African—yes Gys is more African than we are, with Africans working on it. And there are even a couple of her compatriots there, so it's far more familiar territory than a large house in Claremont. As it happens it's about the same distance from Khayelitsha."

"I bow to your opinion on all matters African," said Reginald.

All went according to plan. The two men missed their friendly waitress at their regular lunches. Reinika settled into her job in the canteen at Boschenkraal. Her commute was roughly the same as for Simon's restaurant. She had a walk from the gates of the estate, but there was usually a vehicle for other workers coming from outside.

But underneath the first-world veneer of the Western Cape, there is an underlay of poverty and its inescapable companion: organised crime. A mafia controls the drug trade, smuggling and protection rackets. But it also has more than a hand in the continuing territorial battles of the main taxi associations.

The non-car-owning, working population relies for transport on what are termed 'taxis' but are minibuses, rigged to accommodate up to 15 people. These stop on demand but have regular routes. They are driven recklessly and are a permanent traffic hazard as a result. But worse is the warfare between the two largest associations, which involves pitched battles between armed protagonists.

The sound of shooting in certain areas is not uncommon. Our heroine Reinika, with so many of her neighbours in Khayelitsha fortunate enough to have jobs in the prosperous Constantia valley—the southern suburbs, would board a taxi for a major terminal at Wynberg rail station and then change for another plying a route along the valley, where she could drop off at the gates of the Boschenkraal estate.

On one rainy day, her taxi encountered a pitched battle on the outskirts of the Wynberg terminal. Shots were fired as the passengers sought to disembark. The woman in front of Reinika was shot dead and Reinika herself received two bullets, one in the shoulder and one in the stomach. The targeted driver had jumped out of his door and escaped. The incident received immediate publicity on the radio and TV. The Western Cape Transport Minister himself rushed to the scene, now surrounded by SAPS (South African Police Service) cars and ambulances.

When Reinika did not turn up for work, the foreman at Boschenkraal went to Gys and said:

"Reinika's mobile phone doesn't answer, and she always sends an SMS if she can't come and Baas, that taxi with the victims of the shooting was from Khayelitsha. I think I had better go and check. My friend at the Wynberg SAPS Station may have some info."

Indeed, the foreman was told that a wounded woman had been rushed to the emergency department at Victoria Hospital, quite close by. In his estate land rover, he went quickly to the hospital and learned that the wounded woman was Reinika. Reporting back, he picked up Elspeth van der Bosch and her African maid and drove back to the hospital where they waited until Reinika came out of emergency surgery. Quite soon, a white doctor emerged and looked around for some person who might be connected to his patient. Elspeth rushed to him and heard his report.

"The shoulder's not a big problem. It stopped the bullet which I got easily. No permanent damage, time will fix it," he paused and looked at Elspeth, to judge her reaction.

"But the stomach wound is a bit tricky," he continued. "Bullet went straight through, but there's some collateral damage. I'll have to go back in when her condition settles a bit. I take it you are her employer. Are you in touch with her family? She's from Zimbabwe, I guess, although she had no ID on her when she got here."

Elspeth explained the situation in some detail and said a friend would know how to contact her family. The next day Elspeth and Martha were back at the hospital. Martha had contacted Zuzi through her cousin Bob MacPherson and he had immediately set out to find Reinika's family in the resettlement area. The two ladies were able to gain access to the intensive care ward where they saw Reinika surrounded and plugged into the usual paraphernalia.

She gave them a wan smile. Martha told her how her parents were being contacted and Elspeth said the estate carpenter had gone to her shack in Khayelitsha to tell her mates. One was going to come and see her after work that afternoon. Her cell phone and bag were still with the police as the taxi where they had been left was a crime scene. But they would be fetched tomorrow and brought back to her. Tears rolled down Reinika's cheeks and she held out the hand that had nothing plugged in.

The incident received considerable publicity the dead woman's family was interviewed. She was a mother of two and worked as a domestic at a house in Bishops Court. The press was quick to point out the wounded woman was Zimbabwean, but that there was no inter-ethnic tension involved. A remark considered by some to be unfortunate and conducive of more inter-ethnic prejudice.

The Minister issued the usual statement to the effect that the conflict between the taxi associations was entirely unacceptable and the strongest penal sanctions would be applied to those found responsible by the SAPS investigation which was continuing.

Reinika had a further surgical intervention which was deemed successful. A long period of recuperation would be required and Gys had her moved to a private ward at the Medi Centre in Claremont. The two ladies visited her frequently. One day Martha said, "Your job is safe, Reinika and my husband is ensuring the remittance to your family—just as you have been doing. But it will be a while before you can go back to work. Mrs van der Bosch and I think you might be more comfortable at our house in Claremont. The room that is going to be the nursery is still fitted out with a nice bed and everything and its own bathroom. You can stay there until you are fit to go back to work at Boschenkraal."

"But can I do anything?" asked Reinika.

"Can you sew?"

"Yes, Madame."

"Then you can sew—there are some baby things to do."

And so Reinika stayed and sewed, and her shack mates visited her with some degree of envy. And Martha paid her a bit more than pocket money. After two months, she was ready to go back to work.

"I'm sorry I won't see the baby, Madame," she said.

"Oh, you will!" replied Martha—"I'll bring him to Boschenkraal, and you can mind him while we play bridge—if they let you off from the canteen."

The following year, Reinika married the apprenticed Zimbabwean plumber. Gys had her father flown down to give her away and both families—including Reginald junior, were in attendance. It was one of those typical days with sun and showers together.

Driving back home after the wedding, Martha said, "Look at that lovely rainbow against the mountainside—it seems hardly curved. It must be huge—I wonder where it starts!"

Reginald glanced away from the road for a moment to look.

"Beautiful colours!—and notice they are together, but they don't blend."

"That's why it's a rainbow," said Martha.

FINIS

A Stenographic Marriage

It didn't take me long, as I was growing up, to realise that human nature is full of inexplicable inconsistencies. It's no good saying that these defy logic, as it's more than likely that there is no logic in human nature. My daughter-in-law is a prison visitor because, equipped with several degrees in the new social sciences, she works for a firm that helps secure employment for ex-convicts. She tells me that she meets inmates who appear to be nature's gentlemen in every respect yet are incarcerated for heinous crimes. When these quirks in behaviour appear in close friends, one is too easily tempted to believe one can use one's influence to correct the anomaly. But this is a false hope. And disappointment having failed, is bitter.

Adrian Wentworth and I were childhood friends. That condition is usually the result of either coincidence or parental arrangement. In our case, it was the former; we were at grade school together. Living in a privileged residential area on the east coast of America, we were nevertheless of somewhat different backgrounds. Still, we became fast friends in that exclusive private school which launched us both into a mutually familiar world. The Wentworth's were an old family of wealth and distinction, and Adrian was an only son. He was orphaned at a young age and brought up by an uncle and aunt—plus a succession of governesses.

My grandfather, named Miller, had been a jobbing gardener of Quaker descent, who through the good offices of an employer, had sent his son to a private school in Philadelphia, where the sporting activities favoured rowing on the Delaware River. That same employer, a member of one of the several boating clubs there, had noticed the young man's prowess sculling and as an oar in the school's eight man plus cox racing shell. There followed a scholarship to Princeton and a career on Lake Carnegie. Yale and Harvard were both beaten by lengths with Johnny Miller at a stroke. My father went on to take a master's degree at Corpus Christie, Cambridge in England, It had become the policy of

44

both Oxford and Cambridge to import American rowing stars and in two successive University boat races, the Light Blues, stroked by Johnny Miller, left the Dark Blues in their wake.

My father returned home something of a hero, found work in Wall Street as a Specialist on the floor of the Exchange—but hardly prospered. Angina—a frequent problem for ex-rowers, necessitated an early retirement. He had married the daughter of an impecunious but socially prominent Episcopalian clergyman from Boston. And so, the Jonathan Millers, now listed in the Social Register, were able to settle in a modest house surrounded by the Georgian mansions and estates of the wealthy denizens of 'old money'. I was named Jonathan Miller II ('Johnny Two'—as I was quickly dubbed) and grew up in a contented and stable family environment—unlike my friend Adrian Wentworth, whose parents 'outsourced' his upbringing.

We differed in other ways as well—and in childhood, one considers this entirely normal. Adrian developed a big and bluff personality. He was physically strong and knew it. He could be raucous in society with a barely suppressed desire to dominate. Many found him overpowering.

Certainly, he had charm. It might have been described as a fatal charm. And there was a clue to its superficiality. The ladies and people in general, I suppose, would fall for Adrian immediately—without troubling to search for his true personality. I happened to be slight and wiry, and I seemed somewhat timid and retiring in comparison with my close friend. More than one girl I courted would say it took a long time to know me. I was inward whereas my friend was outward. I rather cherished a remark I overheard from a teacher at school: "Adrian has the brawn and Jimmy has the brains."

This was false as Adrian's scholastic record was rather better than mine.

We both did well in secondary education—at different prep schools—mine being the less expensive and came together again at Princeton, where I had been awarded a scholarship due to my father's sporting fame. We shared rooms and were both elected to the Ivy, Princeton's oldest and most exclusive eating club. I suspected I had succeeded socially on Adrian Wentworth's coattails. He was certainly popular, meeting the triple test of success at these institutions: scholastic achievement, sporting prowess and social grace.

But a curious aspect of his personality began to emerge. Of course, we were increasingly interested in the fairer sex. That awkward social intercourse of youth known as 'dating' was a preoccupation—not only for one's own account but as an observer of the success or failure of those in our peer group. And Adrian always seemed to be focused on the wrong sort. His girlfriends were either too pushy or too shy, too cloying or too cold, too common or too snobbish. One could only describe them as unsuitable. It was not so much that there seemed no clear-cut match between them—no common interests or even different but compensating tastes. It was as though he had settled for one, as opposed to another, for the wrong reasons.

But an even greater oddity was noticeable as I witnessed a succession of Adrian's love affairs. Soon after a relationship was established, he would become critical, even deprecating, and almost insulting to the lady in question—in her presence as well as behind her back. In the former case, he adopted a humorous tone—as though his barbs were in jest. Of course, these taunts and remarks in bad taste received varying reactions. Some girls took it as affectionate banter; others were offended and, at the very least, confused. I could not fathom it all.

Although uninitiated in psychiatry, I reasoned that perhaps he was subconsciously aware of the inadequacy of his original choice (I called this the 'wrong girl syndrome') and was atoning for it through this adverse behaviour. I also speculated that his odd deportment with the girls he favoured might have some connection with the string of governesses he had been reared by. Naturally, I would remonstrate when I was myself fond of one of the girls in question. Adrian would scoff and accuse me of simple jealousy.

Away from these romantic concerns, Adrian and I spent time discussing career choices. Although taking different paths of reasoning, we arrived at the same destination. We decided on the Law. Wentworth influence played a part in our joint admission to Yale Law School. Our friendship had been duplicated by Adrian's aunt and uncle with my parents. They were close neighbours. Adrian's scholastic record was certainly more impressive than mine, yet both applications to the graduate school were successful and we ultimately gained an equal qualification in the New York State bar examinations.

Adrian's love life continued along the same lines; eccentric or downright unsuitable choices produced a string of girlfriends who tolerated his abusive manner with varying degrees of equanimity. I met a beautiful French girl with auburn hair and laughing eyes. She was on an exchange programme, and we became engaged with the intention of marrying as soon I was settled in a job. There could not have been a greater contrast with Adrian's stormy love life.

Adrian was against accepting the job offers we both received from a handful of well-known Wall Street Law firms—many with Wentworth family connections.

"We'll get lost in the shuffle!" he explained. "We'll be stuck in the boiler room for years—you don't get to interface with a client until some senior partner drops dead."

I had not actually agreed to follow Adrian's lead in joining the same firm. But somehow it became mutually assumed. Nor was I in such a hurry to advance my legal career, considering a learning phase in a prominent firm had greater long-term value. But Adrian had an intriguing idea.

"Have you ever heard of Baker & Wentworth?"

I had not—and I had researched virtually every New York practice.

"Well, they're small; they're uptown; they're specialised in medical malpractice and—here's the thing, the two partners are past retirement age and they have neglected to bring any youngsters on!"

Again, the intervention of Adrian's uncle put us in touch with the venerable but almost defunct firm of Baker & Wentworth, the eponymous partner being a distant cousin. They were delighted to suspend their search for a buyer and agreed to take the two of us in as partners whilst they withdrew into semi-retirement as limited partners.

To be fresh out of law school and already partners in a New York-based law firm was truly astonishing to me. Adrian took it as a matter of course. I will not test the non-legal reader's patience by describing the rise of our small firm. Suffice it to say we prospered by avoiding litigation on behalf of our clients and seeking alternative dispute resolution and other common-sense ways of solving problems. It is my friend and partner's stormy marital career which I hope to chronicle fairly.

Nevertheless, it is worth noting in advance, that Adrian was a human resource officer's dream. He was a patient and caring boss, being particularly solicitous to those in the lower ranks. He was both popular and inspiring. The quirk in his personality seemed to be reserved for the women he became close to. The launch of his new career had not paused his amorous instincts. I presumed he was looking for a wife.

We had no sooner settled into new offices than his search began. Adrian had taken to 'helping out' his aunt's charitable attendance at the Rehearsal Club, which offered reasonably priced meals and a peaceful haven for the many struggling young actresses in New York, whose ambitions greatly exceeded the capacity of the theatre to absorb them. There he met, courted and married a long-legged beauty from Kansas called Ruth. The lady's career opportunity, if it existed, was certainly rather more in musical comedy than in Shakespeare and Ibsen. She was a dumb blonde from central casting—to use a theatrical expression. My wife took pity on her almost immediately, sensing Adrian was going to mock her mental deficiencies while failing to appreciate her very generous heart. Sure enough, Adrian began collecting and relating 'dumb blond' jokes to the embarrassment of his audience—made even more acute by the fact poor Ruth did not immediately appreciate that she was the but of her husband's misplaced humour.

My wife, who was called Jeanette, took what I considered an excessive interest in Adrian's love life. Perhaps she thought our very conventional and harmonious marriage lacked dramatic flavour. She had certainly succumbed easily to Adrian's charm. At first, she was not sure where to place her well-meaning interventions. Should she deal with the abused or the abuser? Of course, I am not talking about physical abuse. Adrian would have been incapable of descending to that level. But mockery, repeated and intensified over time is a form of mental abuse. As Jeanette knew Adrian best, she began with him.

"*Mon cher Adrien*!" my wife often began in French and then switched to a rapidly improving English. "Think of poor Ruth! You are hurting her with your jokes. They are—how shall I say—*en mauvais gout*! Can you not see she is offended? Perhaps the poor child does not show it, but she is deeply hurt, I am certain."

"Oh! Come off it, Froggy, my love!" Adrian could not resist applying slightly offensive nicknames to his friends. "Ruth doesn't even get it half the time. She knows I love her, and she knows I'm a bit of a joker. Where's the harm?"

"Have you asked Ruth—talked to her about it?" insisted Jeanette.

"Who talks to Ruth? Look—you see that picture on the wall? It's beautiful, isn't it? But do we talk to it?"

"Your friend and partner is a brute!" said my exasperated wife to me a while later. But she still did not drop Adrian in any way. Instead, she went to Ruth, to sympathise—but to stiffen her backbone and persuade her to remonstrate with her cruel mate.

"Oh, Jeannette! I can't understand him. I know he loves me. In fact, it's almost too much. I mean, you know, he won't leave me alone. I guess those silly jokes are just his way."

Ruth said this in an embarrassed way, according to my increasingly concerned wife. She felt she could not press Ruth any further. Things deteriorated further. Ruth went into a serious decline—almost a depression. Adrian was insensitive.

"Maybe I should get her a gig in a chorus line," was his reaction, when concern was expressed by several friends. Finally, Ruth went home to mother in Kansas.

"Well, that's that," said Jeanette.

"Until the next time," I replied.

The whole business with Ruth and the abrupt divorce gave me cause for concern. Not for Adrian himself. I had long ago become accustomed to his strange romantic life. But our practice was in a critical stage of development, and I feared any distraction which could divert Adrian from his acknowledged leadership of the revived firm of Baker & Wentworth. He had suggested we rename the firm Miller & Wentworth, but I had strongly demurred, considering it lacking in respect for our newly retired, but still limited partner and grossly overstating the role I could play as a virtual novice. In fact, I was somewhat pessimistic. Despite the digression represented by his divorce, Adrian threw himself with gusto into the business of shoring up our existing clientele and developing a new one. Relationship management was his great strength. It was clearly an extension of his skill in dealing with the staff.

Using medical terminology, Adrian had an outstanding bedside manner. He had a way of putting the client immediately at ease, no matter how alarming the circumstances which had brought him or her, to seek legal advice. The Wentworth charm was on display. Often, I would be summoned to a meeting with a new client when it came to documenting a course of action. I would find the client entirely committed to the advice just received as though a relationship had existed for years.

Paperwork was not Adrian's forte; his briefs were sloppy, his legal terminology often flawed, his style unnecessarily repetitive. Almost everything he drafted needed to be re-drafted—a task which often fell to me. This format for our partnership suited me entirely and I dare say was one of the factors behind our success. I had nothing like the confidence Adrian exhibited in advising

49

clients and he was hopeless when it came to executing the course of action his own counsel had determined.

Soon, however, the distaff came back to haunt us again. Adrian had first engaged in brief and rather superficial relationships with ladies Jeanette (who followed all this more closely than I did) considered eminently suitable. But these hopeful cases petered out and, with much noise and considerable *éclat, a* Mexican widow appeared on the scene. Flamboyant and loud, Carmen dressed on the far side of fashion, almost like a circus performer and sashayed, rather than walked, into Adrian's life.

Immediately the nicknames began. Adrian insisted on referring to her as 'Miranda', even though the famous singer was Brazilian rather than Mexican; then it was 'my Mexican bombshell' and soon 'the wetback from south of the border'—a derogatory term applied to illegal immigrants that cross the Rio Grande River. The lady soon became Carmen Wentworth, and I don't recall Adrian ever referring to her as simply Carmen.

It became clear that the Mexican widow, who had inherited a fortune from an industrialist husband, was out for social, rather than pecuniary, gain. She began to solicit membership of fashionable charitable committees and Jeanette and I were enjoined to attend endless charitable balls where Carmen could mix with New York society. We would not have minded so much—we both enjoyed the dance music of Lester Lanin and Meyer Davis but sitting at the table with the Wentworth's, we were subjected to Adrian's tasteless sense of humour, often in front of third parties who could not readily understand why their host was amusing himself by insulting his wife.

At first, Carmen took it in good heart; Jeanette had hurried to brief her when the whirlwind romance was heading for the altar. "He just has this strange sense of humour," she had explained, "but I know he loves you."

But gradually it began to wear. We were witnessing a replay of Adrian's marriage with Ruth—even though Carmen was far more sophisticated and thick-skinned than the poor lass from Kansas. Jeanette made her usual effort to mediate and console Carmen. I stayed well away from the whole thing for fear of prejudicing my basic friendship with Adrian but also our professional relationship.

Our business did not suffer at all from Adrian's increasingly stormy marriage. He persisted in thinking that Carmen was just suffering from a temporary loss of sense of humour. Jeanette knew better and tried to persuade me to warn Adrian that he had better control his behaviour or risk losing his wife. But I hesitated to do so.

Finally, it all resolved itself in a predictable way. We were at a grand social occasion—the annual *Bal Blanc* of the White Russian émigré community. Adrian had managed to land a Russian Imperial Princess to join our table, He was in full flight on his range of Mexican jokes, not noticing the Princesses somewhat confused expression—when suddenly Carmen spoke up, "Excuse me, Your Highness, but I must make a telephone call," and she left the table. After an unusually long interval, she had not returned, and Jeanette went off to look for her. The attendant in the Ladies' said, "Are you looking for Mrs Wentworth? She has left a note for Mr Wentworth—can you take it please?"

Jeanette, full of premonition, returned and gave the note to Adrian. His face fell as he read it and he handed it to me.

It said, "Have your lawyer call mine. *Viva Zapata!* Carmen. "

The reference was, of course, to the famous Mexican revolutionary. Carmen had finally revolted. It transpired that on leaving the table, she had phoned her Mexican maid, a sweet girl we all adored—and told her to pack a bag with night and day things, take a taxi to the Carlyle Hotel, where Carmen was well known and book a suite. They would send for all her things the following day.

And indeed, the next day, Jeanette was called by Carmen and went to the Carlyle to pick up the maid. Together they packed up Carmen's things. Adrian went to the office as usual. All he said to me was, "I guess I should use Bill Brake again—he did a good job with Ruth, don't you think?"

Brake was a Yale Law school contemporary and friend who now specialised in divorce. I reckoned this divorce would cost Adrian little in monetary terms given Carmen's own fortune—but would it teach him a lesson? This second divorce prompted me to attempt another heart-to-heart discussion with my friend. Why did he persist in what the divorce courts referred to as "cruel and unreasonable behaviour?"

"You should ask—why do these ladies have no sense of humour," was Adrian's dismissive response.

But another lady was to play a key part in this strange charade—and she was already present. The former full-time partners of Baker & Wentworth had engaged a very bright girl called Rachel Feinstein as a secretary and had strongly advised Adrian and me to keep her, as she was already making a contribution beyond her basic role as stenographer. They considered she had the potential to become a paralegal and they were quite right. Highly motivated and interested in the detail of our legal work, she certainly stood out from the usual ranks of secretaries handling daily correspondence and other typical duties. Of course, Adrian would not spare her the indignity of one of his nicknames. Whilst highly appreciative of her work, he generally referred to her as the 'little Jewish girl from the Bronx'. In fact, her father was a successful accountant in New Canaan, Connecticut and she commuted daily from her home there. But Adrian's nicknames always contained some element of inaccuracy. This was on purpose to add some sting to the expression which was not designed to be complimentary.

Rachel's potential was rapidly being realised. We were soon called on to increase her compensation and she enlarged her workload voluntarily. No one benefited more than Adrian. His paperwork was always deficient and now it was Rachel who made the necessary corrections and even began to suggest certain improvements in the legal points being documented.

"Don't you think we should include some expression of derogation in para three? As it is, it could be taken to mean we intend the third party to undertake an obligation."—Rachel would suggest, and she would be correct. Not only was she assuming a legal role; she began to re-organise our small practice, introducing simple but significant administrative improvements.

Our productivity improved, our small staff became more efficient and prouder of their work. Our clients noticed it and began to say: "Perhaps Rachel could deal with this little issue?" Or, "Is Rachel around? There's an important errand I wonder if she could do for us." And Rachel began to provide odd client services which served to cement and broaden relationships. She took wives shopping, she picked up school children, she recommended dentists, she consoled widows—and she still maintained a hectic office role extending to all aspects of our practice. Adrian was impressed.

"I must say the little Jewish girl from the Bronx is damned useful!" he remarked more than once.

Jeanette, ever attentive to Adrian's romantic inclinations, began to suspect something. Certainly, Rachel seemed called upon to assist Adrian in an increasing number of situations—legal or administrative. To her face, she continued to be Miss Feinstein, a relief to us all. But subtle change became noticeable in the relationship between Adrian and Rachel. A slight variation in the contrasting pattern of his usual female relationships.

He became solicitous on the one hand—almost protective. But he also seemed to resent the considerable enhancement of her status in the practice, which her performance and utility had brought about. He would constantly refer to her 'Rachel the Steno' or order someone, "Find Miss Feinstein and tell her to bring her pad."

It was as though he was determined to keep her in her place—as he would have put it. But, at the same time, he displayed a strangely paternalistic attitude towards her. Ever observant, Jeanette, who was in the office from time to time, came to me with a frown.

"He's taking her out to dinner!" she announced as though reporting a negative turn in a war.

"So what?" I foolishly replied. How often do we react to portentous bad news in such a manner?

"But can't you see? Adrian is falling in love with Rachel. They are talking about it in your office."

"Water cooler gossip!" I retorted.

But it wasn't. Soon my wife told me: *"Prepare toi pour un choc!"* Jeanette often lapsed into French when she had bad news to report. I nodded and left for the office, Adrian called me in and said, "Gather everyone in the board room. You have an announcement to make."

"Why me?" I said, knowing full well. "You're the senior partner."

"Conflict of interest, old man! Conflict of interest. I want you to announce that the little Jewish girl from the Bronx and I are engaged to be married—so there!"

"It won't be a surprise to anyone—and Jeanette as much as told me this morning."

"How come that frog wife of yours is always so well-informed? I hope she is going to approve this time. And by the way, Rachel wants to carry on working—she's not the *hausfrau* type."

"She will approve if you are kind to Rachel."

"Why shouldn't I be?"

"Tell you what," I said—avoiding an answer. "Let's make her a partner—she is more than deserving."

"I like it!" exclaimed Adrian. "You can announce that as well—I know our limited partners will approve. They hired the little Jewish girl from the Bronx in the first place."

"I strongly suggest you drop that appellation." Of course, I had suggested that many times before.

My announcement to the staff was greeted by a round of applause and shy smiles from Rachel Feinstein. As many rose to shake her hand, Adrian was on his feet, as I suspected he would be. He enjoyed addressing the staff enormously. Rather reluctantly, all sat down again.

"I want to thank you all for your reaction to this great news. I'll bet few of you know what a morganatic marriage is," Adrian began and paused. Silence. "It's when a royal marries a non-royal—and thus drops out of the line of succession. (I wondered where Adrian had picked up that bit of trivial knowledge.) Well, I have just invented a stenographic marriage! That's when the boss marries his secretary. But there is no succession issue because I'm already the king! Ha ha!" A few titters.

I had a nasty feeling my partner was going to make a fool of himself, as he often did when his conversation became personal. He carried on.

"They say that when the boss marries his secretary, he loses a good secretary and gains an indifferent wife. Well, Rachel is losing an indifferent boss and gaining a great husband!" This brought another round of applause. I decided to cut in.

"I would like to add my very special congratulations to the happy couple. As many of you know a good number of large legal practices and also investment banks, have a policy against engaging or maintaining married couples—or even siblings, on the staff. Fortunately, we don't have such a policy—but that doesn't mean you should all start marrying each other! What say we all get back to work?"

I received the last round of applause.

That same afternoon, Rachel came to see me.

"I want to thank you, Johnny, for the partnership, It's been my dream."

"But we both think it's well deserved," I replied.

"I'm sure," said Rachel, "but I know Adrian would not have suggested it himself for a hundred years."

"He's not usually lavish with praise."

"Is that a lawyer's understatement?" Our new partner smiled. "I haven't come to love Adrian without knowing him well—and especially his main fault. Don't worry. I know all about Ruth and Carmen. She may not have told you, but I have had lots of girl talk with your lovely Jeanette. I think there's an insecurity in Adrian that few realise. That's why he seems to be down on people he's close to. He sees them as competition in a curious way. Ruth was loved by everyone because she was beautiful and amazingly kind. She was becoming more popular than her husband. Carmen was threatening Adrian's social position. She was the hostess with the 'mostess'—as the song goes. Just wait and see. I have no illusions. Adrian will use me as his legal partner, but he will act as though he doesn't regard me as such."

"That won't bother you?"

"No—because I can read him like a book—and I can take it. It's perhaps understandable that everyone picks on Adrian's glaring fault when it comes to his women—particularly the ones who get close to him. Because it's so odd! But what makes it odd is that underneath he is an angel. Ask anyone who works here. He is generous and caring and his interest in people is genuine—not just a good boss thing. You know that as well as I do—because you are his oldest friend."

I was impressed not only by Rachel's prescience but her wisdom. Of course, I thought I knew Adrian was no bully despite his manner—and I also thought I could understand what was underneath that strange, selective exterior. I had become convinced his upbringing was responsible to a great degree. The duty performed by uncle and aunt is no substitute for parental love, even augmented by the occasional benign governess. I had no sufficient knowledge of psychiatry to explain it all. It was just a common-sense suspicion on my part. Even the exceptions seemed to confirm the theory. He certainly loved my wife, Jeanette.

In fact, one day he said to me, "I lust after your wife, old man, but you needn't worry because I've told you—so I won't do anything about it." This was typical of Adrian. There was no threat to anyone in this situation. With the others he loved, it seemed there was one; but I could never understand what it was. Perhaps Rachel was right. But, on the other hand, I suspected she was hoping to reform him. There—she was quite wrong.

Rachel took her New York State bar exams and passed with ease. She was now a fully practising lawyer. An inverse relationship developed between Rachel's contribution to the partnership and Adrian's acknowledgement. The more she did the more he belittled it, but Rachel rose majestically above it.

As a firm, we made great progress and began to take our place amongst the leading legal lights of Wall Street, whilst retaining our modest uptown presence and manageable size. The importance of our clients grew rather than their number. Cases that were traditionally the preserve of major firms, were now brought to our practice. And Rachel began to be spoken of in legal circles in her own right. One case was sufficiently notable to earn a full article in a major law magazine.

"Rachel Feinstein is the wife of senior partner Adrian Wentworth of the eponymous firm, but practices under her maiden name. Feinstein has set an interesting precedent in the class action suit against Consolidated Mines and there is speculation Delaware corporate law will need an amendment to deal with the issues raised. Her analysis of the jurisdictional inadequacy of the litigants demonstrates how a smart lawyer can make a nonsense of a principle previously taken for granted."

When Adrian slapped the article on my desk, he could only comment, "You had better deal with the swollen head of our Jew partner, Jimmy. I'll have to get a bigger pillow for our bed at home."

On another occasion, we were celebrating the completion of a difficult case with a late evening drink in the office.

I remarked, "I haven't seen as satisfied a client in a good while."

"That client was satisfied as soon as Rachel flashed her big brown eyes at him," barked Adrian.

"It was a team effort," said Rachel.

"Come on, Delilah—he was eating out of your hand, and you had the scissors ready."

When he could not think of any way of running down his wife, Adrian liked to characterise her as a man-eating seductress. In the office, everyone had long appreciated the eccentricity which seem to exist in the personal relationship between the married partners. To the growing annoyance of Adrian, respect for Rachel grew by leaps and bounds.

Naturally, Adrian had long since taken a new PA—a personal assistant, as secretaries now preferred to be titled. She was a competent girl named Gwendolyn and hailed from an old money family down at the heel—but old friends and even cousins of the Wentworth's. Rachel lost no time in briefing her.

"He'll insult you and make a pass at you at the same time. Take no notice of either action. It's just his way and entirely harmless," she had advised. And Gwendolyn coped knowing she had her boss's wife at her back. But Adrian's permanently roving eye produced inevitable consequences.

Again, Rachel took these comfortably in her stride producing the interesting twist whereby the erring spouse becomes jealous of the tolerance exhibited by the wronged party. One affair of Adrian's threatened to have a nasty ending, with a strong aroma of blackmail overpowering the heady scent of illicit romance. Rachel stepped in at a crucial moment and dispatched the paramour and her threats with a skill and aplomb which left my wife (always my source of such tales) breathless with admiration. But Adrian was bitter rather than relieved and thankful.

"I don't want this firm slipping into marriage counselling and ending up as low-life divorce hacks—that's as degrading as ambulance chasing. You might tell your frog wife to pass that on to our esteemed partner from the Bronx."

Adrian liked to use my wife as a messenger whenever an issue mixing professional and marital concerns came up. As Rachel's influence in the firm grew, Adrian's declined, and he resented it. He was particularly sensitive to the growing external image of the firm within the profession and in business circles in general. I thought I would have trouble containing his rage at a client meeting followed by a lunch at which Rachel was not present.

"It seems to me," said the client, incautiously, "that you've got a name change issue. You should be Baker, Wentworth & Wentworth—or maybe Miller, Wentworth & Wentworth—but Rachel uses her maiden name, doesn't she?—so what about Miller, Feinstein & Wentworth?"

Adrian choked on his dry martini, struggled to regain some composure and assumed as pompous a tone as he could muster.

"First of all, Jimmy refused to put his name on the shingle years ago. Secondly, we do not, as a rule, make stenographers partners, even when they marry their bosses and we certainly don't add their names and finally, we are a WASP firm. Does that meet your concern?"

I could not tell directly how the marriage was proceeding on the purely domestic front. We saw each other socially; we were near neighbours, belonged to the same country club and moved in the same circles. Rachel was always calm and demure in the face of Adrian's frequent quips at social gatherings when he considered his curious brand of humour would be accepted as just that. Friends and acquaintances had given up trying to identify some reaction from Rachel indicating pain or humiliation. There was none.

On the contrary, Rachel proved adept at clever repartee, parrying her husband's barbs and often turning the table on him.

For example, once Adrian said, "Careful what you say—Rachel will put it down in shorthand as soon as we're home."

"But you needn't worry about my husband taking notes—he only just does joined-up writing,"—was Rachel's response. The general laughter was strained in Adrian's case. He also enjoyed reminding everyone of Rachel's humble career origins.

"I had to remind Rachel to bring her handbag—she automatically picks up her pad."

"I use it as a coaster for the drinks he usually spills."

Neither Ruth nor Carmen had been able—or had dared defend themselves in this way. Adrian became confused, rather than angered by this evolution in the relationship. Not only was the increase in Rachel's share of the business activity troubling to him, but she was far more solicitous of his personal comfort and well-being than he had imagined possible. When he had any health issue she was at his side, nursing, securing expert assistance and monitoring his recovery.

Whereas both Ruth and Carmen—perhaps in different ways, had shown caution and reserve in their physical contact with Adrian in public, one now observed Rachel straightening his tie, smoothing his hair and holding his hand. Whilst in public together. Adrian would forebear this more intimate attitude, with some sheepish embarrassment. In her absence, he redoubled his efforts to demean her and to belittle her contribution, referring to her as 'uppity' or 'pushy' or even as a 'counter jumper', suggesting she should remember she was just a "jumped up secretary who struck lucky on a deal or two."

But all the while, Adrian's professional dependence on his wife was growing and it was becoming clear that he was losing his own touch. Clients were asking to be looked after by Rachel—or even myself, where I had not been the engagement partner. The quality of Adrian's advice, which had been so pristine, now seemed impaired. On a growing number of occasions, Rachel had to gainsay him tactfully and quietly—always beginning with a phrase such as, "Oh! Adrian, there's a detail I forgot to brief you on so I'm sure you'll agree that it should be—"

As time went on the problem became more noticeable. Competing firms referred to it—always politely, in the context of general admiration for our firm—but just hinting that maybe the senior partner was not as he was once. This hurt Adrian more than anything else and while suggesting in the office that his wife was not doing enough to protect the firm's good name—"but after all typists are not trained in PR," he would say. But that night he would be crying on Rachel's shoulder.

This dichotomy between Adrian's attitude towards his wife publicly and most notably in the office and privately in the sanctity of the home, was noticed and analysed by Jeanette. My wife seemed to have an almost unhealthy interest in the trials and tribulations of this couple—and an uncanny ability to seize on the subtle signs of marital discord and re-accord. Adrian was often perturbed by this.

"Your froggy wife seems to spend a lot of time with my not-so-better half. What do you suppose they are up to?" Adrian asked me one day.

"Nothing—they're just good friends."

"You don't suppose—I mean, you've never noticed any Sapphic inclinations in Jeanette? They say a lot of frogs swing both ways."

"Good grief! Don't be ridiculous, Adrian. Haven't you noticed that because you are hard on your wives, mine likes to console them?"

Jeanette was highly amused when I reported this. She told me Adrian had once asked her if she minded being called Froggy.

"I said to him, would he mind if I called him '*rosbif*'—that's what we call the English. All Adrian could say was 'but I'm American!' You see, there is not quite a normal sense of humour there." Jeanette sometimes almost had the answer to Adrian's inner self—but never entirely.

Then—quite suddenly Adrian became quite seriously ill. This produced a significant pause in the work of our firm because Rachel devoted herself almost entirely to caring for her husband—and so not only our senior partner was inactive. My workload increased exponentially, and I met every evening at the Wentworth house to consult on firm business with Rachel, but also to check on Adrian.

Jeanette stepped in to free up Rachel from time to time. We began to operate on a rota basis. Adrian was almost more disturbed by the onset of almost total dependence on Rachel, than by the illness itself. His condition was of the sort that defies precise and incontrovertible diagnoses and a succession of specialists, convoked by Rachel, began to intervene.

As a degree of hopelessness began to creep in, with no improvement and no agreed diagnosis, a change in Adrian's attitude towards Rachel began to be perceived by Jeanette—and eventually by me. The blustery confidence which was Adrian's hallmark was almost eliminated by his disease. But it was replaced, not by an emergence of admiration and gratitude for Rachel's support, but by a wistful and almost playful continuation of his persistent demeaning of his wife.

It was as though the whole saga of the 'little Jewish girl from the Bronx' was now a revered family joke, a loving tradition binding rather than separating the protagonists. Soon, Adrian had to be hospitalised and with what seemed almost indecent haste, he had to be moved towards a semi-hospice unit. There his condition became one of quiet resignation; he joked with the nurses, exhorting them to marry the doctor—"raises you in the world like my secretary," he would say.

He asked hourly when Rachel would be coming and held her hand throughout when she was there. She often asked me to join her—she felt it eased the angst which now possessed us all. We were encouraged but also horrified by his smile. It signalled a total acceptance. He spoke less and less but seemed very attentive to our chat designed to lighten the leaden atmosphere. Then one day the doctor told us to 'stand by'—as he put it. "I'm afraid it's any moment now—no point in increasing the morphine—if you'd like to be in at the end."

Rachel and I stood by Adrian's bed and watched him, still connected to all the life-supporting gadgetry which now robs hospital death of dignity. He opened his eyes and a smile appeared. With a slight nod, he beckoned Rachel to come closer. She took his hand. He was straining to speak. In an almost inaudible croak he said, "Take a letter, Miss Feinstein," and his smile just broadened a touch.

Rachel leaned over him, kissed his forehead, and said, "I quit! Mr Wentworth."

As she turned, the monitoring machine gave out a steady tone and I saw the green line which had been oscillating was now steady. Rachel almost collided with the resuscitation team that rushed in. I stood there for a few moments as they went through their mandatory but hopeless business. My friend and partner was gone.

Outside, Rachel was sitting, staring straight ahead—tears streaming down her face.

"I loved that man," she said.

Jeanette had been waiting outside.

"I saw the rush of the medical team to his room, so I knew it was over," she said.

"Yes, they have to go through the resuscitation process even when it's hopeless." I took her arm to leave.

"Should we wait for poor Rachel?"

"No, she can cope; she always has. But I was just thinking."

"What?"

"The resuscitation process on Adrian should have started a long time ago."

FINIS

A Winding Path

A ramble in the manner of Marcel Proust

I walk each day along a winding path that skirts the mountain range overlooking the Constantia valley here in the Cape and may form a boundary for what was the Alphen estate—the property of Lord Charles Henry Somerset, a younger son of the Duke of Beaufort and a Governor of Cape Colony in its early days. Lord Charles gave his name to the large town of Somerset West, which sits at the foot of the Hottentot-Holland mountains, on the Lourens River, from which the traveller is launched onto Sir Lowry's Pass to cross the imposing mountain range, that feature named after another governor of Cape Colony—Sir Galbraith Lowry Cole, soldier son of an Irish peer, whose place in South African history derives not from his own distinction but from the philanthropic activities of his wife, born Frances Harris, daughter of the 1st Earl of Malmsbury, who, in the early 19th-century, as the Governor's lady, championed the cause of the coloured population, ensuring their children learned useful trades.

The feminist reader will justifiably ask why the pass is not named Lady Cole's and will not be satisfied to learn that the South African town of Malmesbury, is indirectly named for Frances—her father, the Earl, never having set foot in the Cape. Neither of these two governors was popular during their tenures, Lord Charles having managed to engender almost immediate dissatisfaction, despite his commendable initiative in drafting in some of his father's Beaufort hounds to form the Cape Hunt which, in traditional English attire, hunted fox and jackal on the Cape Flats and whose offspring, crossed with further drafts from the North Cotswold, hunt drag to this day.

Yet, Lord Charles has even another Somerset named after him in the Eastern Cape, requiring 'West' to be added to his original named site and Sir Lowry enjoys proxy fame for the good works of his wife unless you believe his own Governorship was sufficiently marked by accomplishment to have the town of Colesburg in the Cape named after him. Still, nomenclature justice may be served by the fact that his name has been mangled in the dedication of the pass, for Lowry is a middle name, taken from his mother, who was born Anne Lowry—Corry, brother of Galbraith Lowry-Corry, from an Anglo-Irish clan. It should be Sir Galbraith's Pass.

Lord Charles's Alphen Estate, on which I now walk, passed to the Cloete family whose forebear Jacob, a native of Cologne, landed at the Cape in 1652 with the famous van Riebeck and prospered—with his progeny intermarrying with all the most prominent Afrikaner families, thus enabling the acquisition of historic properties, including at one time Groot Constantia itself, the original Cape wine estate, where the first, clumsy attempts to make wine from the easily grown vines was such as to prompt the Dutch East Indies Company to recruit French Huguenots, languishing in Holland after Louis XIV's revocation of the Edict of Nantes, to come and teach them the finer art of viniculture.

Now as I begin my walk, I pass behind the Cape Dutch-style mansions which first graced the estate and ensure the continuity of an aura of colonial elegance, only gently dulled by the practicalities of modernity—as the estate is now a hotel complex. These ruminations on the sweep of history relieve my mind temporarily of the dust of nostalgia—now to be replaced by the dust of the path on my shoes and force me to concentrate on the uniqueness of my walk's environment, which holds the winding path in an embrace of verdure, under a canopy of blue sky help up by the mountain tops.

The way, which meanders for several kilometres before being interrupted by clusters of luxury residences, celebrates the primacy of the Western Cape as the home of the world's largest collection of arboreal species and various flora and the variety of trees on either side, combining the great number imported from various regions by the early colonists with a degree of indigenous self-propagation, would be a distraction to an expert, but serves the exercise walker and the *flaneur* both with refreshment for tired eyes and landmarks for the *habitué*.

As I set out, I believe I am first encountering the remnants of what might have been a grand *allée* to the Manor house as there are properly spaced Lime trees on either side of me, which seem to match another group, set at right angle on the other side of a recently built wall. On my right is that which is so unfortunately termed a 'babbling brook'—perhaps the most hackney expression of all those in wide use to describe an aquatic feature, and this will continue to trace its watery path during the entire length of my promenade, with the occasional weir and a number of crossing facilities, ranging from the log of a fallen tree to wooden bridges and even simply a series of stepping stones.

Soon I am on the most shaded section of the path, with the giant English oaks reaching heights undreamed of in their cold and wet natural habitat in the north Atlantic and other celebrated imports such as Norfolk Island pines, the many varieties of eucalyptus gums, imported from Australia for their water absorption properties—useful for draining land, the plane trees and the pepper tree, from South America, but distinctive for having been spared the degrading title of 'invasive' which is applied to the large number of trees which were imported for various useful reasons in the 18th and 19th centuries, largely by the squires and burghers anxious to improve their domains and—let it be said, to ape their colonial masters in England and Holland.

As I enjoy the shade offered by the green canopy of my winding path, I visualise the seedlings of trees destined for the Cape swaying in ship's cargo holds as they progress on their storm-tossed voyages from points north, east and west and consider especially those imported by the English timber merchant Charles Henry Arderne, who began, in the 1840s, to commission the various ship's captains who were calling in at the Cape during their global navigations, to bring him examples of tree species native to many locales in Australasia, Japan and the Americas, establishing an arboretum bearing his name and containing a unique selection of trees of the world.

At one point, my path truly begins to wind gently, and the way broadens to include patches of open ground, allowing the dogs, permitted off lead, to chase each other with abandon and the occasional equestrians to have a canter on their sleek horses, clearly displaying signs of loving care by numerous African grooms. The conifer-studded face of the mountain range is now clearly visible, its peaks sometimes decorated with the softly shaped mist the local's name 'tablecloths' from its frequent presence on Table Mountain.

As I raise my gaze from my feet, skipping over the odd protruding tree root and take in the new perspective, I experience a sudden moment of Proustian, nostalgic sensation—a visual equivalent of the taste of the great, wordy author's childhood *Madelaine* biscuit, which had conjured up his memory of the missed mother's good night kiss and prompted a description spanning some twenty pages of the angst associated with this moment of maternal deprivation, written exhaustingly in later life in Proust's cork-lined room, causing many a reader to pause, put down the book and turn to the evening newspaper.

In my case, no childhood frustration is triggered, no sadness from a memory of parental neglect, no deep-seated psychosis planted by infantile depression emerges in the dusky end of day which envelopes my walk. No—I am simply reminded with pleasurable mental freshness of the *papier peint* which covered a wall in my parent's apartment in the Rue Octave Feuillet, off the Avenue Henri Martin and in easy walking distance to the Bois de Boulogne in the Paris of the 1930s.

It can be noted here that the street is named after a 19th century novelist and dramatist, who hailed from Normandy, was a lifelong, hypersensitive semi-invalid, very popular during the 2nd Empire and whose novel *The Story of a Poor Young Man* was made into a film no less than seven times. Sadly, at the age of nought to four, when I resided in the Rue Octave Feuillet, I was not able to savour the literary output of M. Feuillet or even to ruminate over the peaks and valleys of his literary career and delicate state of mind.

Papier peint, decorative wallpaper, so dubbed to distinguish it from the ordinary, repeating pattern paper you buy in rolls, came into being in the 17th century as an economical substitute for tapestries which adorned the walls of the financially fortunate and became a decorative art form of note, depicting panoramic scenes, ranging from simple landscapes to historic battles and other subjects worthy of reproduction, much in use in public buildings to commemorate historic occasions.

So popular did wallpapering become in England that a tax was imposed on the material in the reign of Queen Anne and remained in force until the 1830s. The example that adorned the walls of the dining room at the rue Octave Feuillet was in four panels, each framed above the chair rail and depicted a bucolic scene, coloured in soft greys, composed of hillocks and groups of trees of various sizes and shapes and, central to the landscape, a winding path leading towards a mountain range in the distance, but disappearing mysteriously at the crest of a rise in the ground.

It was that culmination of the winding path that intrigued me when I studied it in its later locations—for the *papier peint* could be removed and rolled up and went first to London and then to New York. I would imagine myself standing on that hill crest and now looking down on the further meanderings of that winding path, as it progressed to the foot of the mountain range. What would I see? Might there not finally be a house, some sign of human habitation or was the scene one of uninterrupted rural splendour, free even from noisome agriculture or sporting action—the only sign of human endeavour being the winding path itself?

But now I pause in my daily peregrination in the far-off Cape and savour the memory-inducing, observable equivalent of the *Madelaine,* for the scene before me is almost an exact reproduction of that conceived by the artist responsible for the *papier peint* in my parents' various residences—the winding path, the escorting groups of trees, the hillocks, gentle slopes and grassy spaces, the ultimate mountain range as the finish of the visual banquet, that version lacking only the bright sun and multifarious colours of the Western Cape—for is not grey the shade of the northern hemisphere where the work was no doubt executed and, in any case, do I not sometimes dream in black and white, so that my juxtaposition of the two visions remains moving, despite the difference in text and time that separates them?

The lapse in time is the rhythm of its remembrance, a passion in which the human mind indulges in its desire to boast of its conscious existence and I now consider the adventures of the *papier peint* as it crossed the Channel to Norfolk Crescent, between Oxford and Cambridge Squares, the place of our London house in 1939 and then the dangerous trip across an Atlantic patrolled by enemy submarines, the lengthy sojourn in dusty storage, its re-emergence in an apartment at 116 East 63rd Street in Manhattan and then what? Like the winding path that disappears over the hill, leaving one frustrated but still keen to exercise one's imagination in the creation of a further fairy tale, full of the dragons, castles, gnomes and maidens of one's childish dreams, the known history of this decorative wall covering, now pricking my nostalgic consciousness, ends in the roar of Madison Avenue traffic, audible from 63rd Street, with all its trebles and bass notes of New York City's cacophony.

Marcel Proust's taste of that little, shell-shaped cake, experienced in later life, threw up an exhaustive—and exhausting, panoply of images from his sharply remembered childhood, which he transformed into a prose which greatly exceeded the verbosity of past and present writers of his time; but remained, nevertheless, confined in its environment to the imaginary town of Cambray— identified by some of his biographers as at least partially inspired by, if not entirely modelled, on the town of Senlis, where the cathedral spire seems identical to the one described by Proust as being in Cambray, is easily viewed from most points in the surrounding forests of Ermenonville, d'Halat and Chantilly and is a credible choice for me, being the town where my parents had

66

restored an *Hôtel Particulier,* of double antiquity—16th and 18th century, devoid of the famous *papier peint* of uncertain fate.

But the nostalgic images prompted by the winding path on the Alphen walk, travel with the *papier peint* on its journey from city to city and wall to wall, where I would stare at its scenic perfection and mystery—always excluding the rue Octave Feuillet where the broad, starched white collar of my Swiss nurse would have been my main scenic delight—and my ruminations would have matched my mood and condition, influenced by the world outside the room and contemporary experiences.

And so now time runs backwards, as Hawking suggests is possible, and I experience an irresistible urge to briefly review that world I would see should I glance from the windows of the room where the *papier pient* was holding nature static on the wall and re-live, as in a dream composed of quick takes, my life outside. I begin with my inspiration's final destination—the 'glittering crowds and shimmering clouds in canyons of steel' of Vernon Duke's *Autumn in New York* and I sensate that concatenation of events that filled my incipient social life; my first steps in the route to becoming that frivolous and useless being—the 'deb's delight', the cotillions, the coming out parties, the post ball visits to La Rue, the Stork and El Morocco, the white tied and ball gowned patronage at three in the morning, together with the odd taxi driver, of Hamburger Heaven on Madison Avenue, the leisurely lunches at the Westbury's Polo Bar, the culinary adventures at Henri Soulé's Le Pavillon, the early dawn walk home in evening dress on the deserted pavements, spewing steam from the man hole covers, the shopping for Christmas toys at FAO Schwartz, useless gadgets at Abercrombie & Fitch and button down shirts at Brooks Brothers, the real tennis games at the Racquet Club and, finally, the dreary repair to Penn Station to take the LIRR home.

The clock now turned back, less fulsome, due to my tender years at the time, is my montage of London life surrounding the *papier peint* in Norfolk Crescent, but remembered actions of my parents are interposed to enrich my imagination of a capital briefly in morning for George V, which perhaps silenced the nightingale in Berkeley Square, but hardly altered the pre-war elegance of the gentlemen in bowler hats and tightly furled umbrellas, the ladies in hats, gloves and frocks to the mid-calf; Nanny in white with a grey cardigan and a pork pie hat; my sister in a frock with puffed sleeves and a white bow in her hair; and myself in a white silk shirt buttoned to my grey flannel shorts, white socks and buttoned patent leather pumps.

Smith, the butler, is tall enough to lift our tricycles over the black iron fence that surrounds the crescent garden; tea with Nanny in the nursery is what our evening meal is called and our parents are giving a dinner party which will necessitate our brief presence in the drawing room in pyjamas and flannel dressing gowns to be introduced to the guests—my sister Ariane to curtsey and I to bend over the ladies hands and then, with very slight pressure on the back from Nanny's hand, to return to the nursery, the compliments and laughter of the grown-ups still ringing in our ears as we climb the stairs.

And I look forward to playing with my toy London Bobby, which comes apart, having contained a secret supply of sweets, quietly—so Nanny will not hear and Ariane will whisper her impressions of a beautifully gowned lady, who turns out to be Nancy Mitford, who, when the men have been left in the dining room to their port, will stand on her head for the ladies, her skirt decorously held with one hand—to illustrate a latest health giving exercise.

I recall no moments of sadness in the nursery and mother's good night kiss, whether always regular or not, was a source of wonder and pride for us as the parents were often on their way out in evening dress—father in white tie and tails and mother in an evening gown by Jean Dessès, the Alexandria born, Paris couturier.

These brief and happy days in London, even as the war clouds gathered, ended with a fateful return to France—on holiday to Vichy and I still have the faintest recollection of having wondered whether we might be visiting my first home in the Rue Octave Feuillet, having perhaps not understood that we had moved permanently. But I had left my London Bobby behind, which gave me comfort as we journeyed to the spa town, with our mother's maid only, as for reasons unclear, Nanny had been left in London, perhaps, I only now speculate, because of an aversion to French cuisine, which traditional English nannies were said to share, but in any case to our ultimate disadvantage, because my father was unable to secure a visa for her when war's outbreak forced us to board at Cherbourg the French Line *Normandie* en route to New York.

But still, I can give the clock one further turn back in time, as I continue along the Alphen walk—my progress accelerated by these Proustian remembrances, even though I am not conscious of walking faster, but only of the freedom from daily cares which indulgences in the pernicious vice of nostalgia will bring as a heady draught of liquor will momentarily quell an inward sadness and I can drain my cup of flashing images of the past by thinking of the Paris of the '30s with its *après moi le déluge* round of parties and entertainments.

The costume balls of Bestigui, the Russian gypsy nightclubs, the *Ballet Russe* of Diagelief, the dance sensation of the dusky Josephine Baker, the surreal photos of Man Ray, the elegant theatrics of the Murphy's, the Cole Porters and Elsa Maxwell, the films of Jean Renoir—all the cosmopolitan culture of Paris celebrating as war clouds gathered and extreme political parties clashed and rioted, the Franc declined, and the politicians cheated.

For myself, I can admit to only one true memory, barring those several we all assume to be genuine when they are in fact garnered from perusing in later life the albums of snapshots our parents have so carefully assembled, and we so rejoice in whilst pretending to recall the circumstances in which the photos were taken. It is an ominous recollection—as I am sitting on my grandfather's knees, not far from the *papier peint* which can be seen through the double doors leading to the dining room and he is turning the pages of my favourite book—which I ask for on each of his visits, is entitled simply *1914* and is filled with photographs of the famous statesmen in frock coats and elegant cravats, monarchs in full uniform, be-medalled generals—all the players in the macabre political dance which brought us the war to end all wars.

Why, in 1938, should a small boy, born in the most gratuitous circumstances, be attracted to such an account of the greatest geopolitical disaster of our times, on the very edge of the resulting and further precipice which was to engulf the Europe of my youth, is one of the mysteries which pepper our childhood recollections and is at this present moment, the culminating impression in the range of such which, prompted by my linkage of the winding path I tread with the *papier peint* of my parental residences, has been my mental companion.

For I have now reached the end of my winding path, which, unlike its imaginary, wall-covering counterpart, does not disappear over the crest of a hill, but simply terminates at an ordinary tarred road, on which are parked motor cars belonging to walkers that begin their exercise from the end opposite to mine— possibly due to a preference for the setting sun at their backs at our universally popular walking and jogging time, in this most felicitous of Southern Hemisphere summer climates, when the November to March days are hot in the sun and cool in shade and night.

I turn and begin the remaining half hour's walk back to my car, observing the variety of canine companions to equally various walkers and joggers, incorporating the great cross-section of our ethnic population and the generation span from white-haired, slow strollers to infants circulating like satellites as they cavort around their parents. Two young, pretty, and well-accoutred girls, mounted on matching horses walk by at a stately pace—they are so alike they could, at first sight, be twins—but one is white and the other is black, as the Scottish terriers who advertise a whiskey.

As I reach my end of the winding path, I realise that one feature is entirely lacking from the *papier peint* that has so occupied my thoughts for the last hour or so and that is the tritely termed babbling brook. But I view that disparity as significant, as it separates the fantasy of the decorative arts from the natural beauty of reality, as it is moving and, moreover, is moving in a forward direction, as opposed to the gentle breezes that rock the treetops back and forth, so that in this way it tells us that the remembrance of times past may be a comfort in troubled times, but the forward course of the stream represents hope—for it does not just 'babble', it actually recites from Alfred, Lord Tennyson's poem *The Brook:*

For men may come and men may go
But I go on forever.

FINIS

Down Under

Tom Gardiner was sitting in the bar of the Imperial Hotel in Tokyo with a cablegram in his hand. He was shaking his head back and forth, having read it more than once.

Tom. Congrats on Kyoto deal. While you're out there pop down to Australia to see what's cooking.
Uncle Bill

"While you're out there?" '*He must be kidding!*'—thought his nephew. Had his uncle fallen asleep in geography class? Wasn't there a globe somewhere in the office? If he had been in London, would his uncle have suggested he pop down to Cape Town? He was tempted to reply to his uncle—and business partner, in New York, suggesting he 'pop down to Buenos Aires'.

Tom was junior partner in the family firm of Gardiner Brothers, insurance brokers in New York and London. In fact, his father had died some years ago and so the current partners were uncle and nephew. The firm specialised in placing the most difficult risks—usually in connection with large projects, where a so-called 'act of God' exemption limited the extent of a claim.

Gardiner Brothers would find takers of 'top up' insurance, happy to cover damage from natural catastrophes such as earthquakes, hurricanes, and other environmental effects. Often there were certain Lloyds syndicates prepared to take high risks for a proportionally high premium. And since the Gardiners' fee was based on the premium, the firm had prospered.

Now Tom, a well-set-up young man of 31 years, brooded over his uncle's unreasonable suggestion that he travel to Australia from Japan simply because he was 'out there'—that is to say, in the Pacific region. Having just completed a highly remunerative transaction, he was looking forward to a few days in the

London office and some sporting activity in the English countryside. He ordered another drink and sighed.

Nevertheless, business was business, and his uncle was his uncle—so he must comply. To his surprise and increased annoyance, he found that there was no regular passenger air service from Tokyo to any Australian city. With great difficulty, he managed to find accommodation on a cargo flight which also took half a dozen passengers but stopped in Singapore and other intermediate locations to discharge and take on cargo. His trip was going to take 36 hours. Many passengers got off at Singapore and Tom had more room, the crew kindly arranged for him to sleep on some cargo which was stored in the heated portion of the cabin.

Tom did have two Australian contacts in his address book. One was a long-established firm of insurance brokers in Melbourne—correspondents of Gardiner Brothers. But the other was a Mrs Smythe in Sydney, where his flight was to terminate. This contact was courtesy of an old London friend Billy Featherstonehaugh—pronounced Fanshaw—to general relief among friends and acquaintances. His description had been brief, but intriguing.

"It rhymes with alive, don't forget," had explained Billy, who knew about such things, "and I can tell you she is alive and lively! Sorry about the pun, old chap! She's well known in Sydney society, good-looking, filthy rich, owns an art gallery as a hobby and if you are ever out there—she'll make your stay great fun—which is more than you can say about the Aussies in general."

Tom decided he would certainly take up this introduction and would no doubt stay in Sydney a day or two before going on to Melbourne. The concierge at the Imperial in Tokyo had booked him into the Fullerton, which had celebrated views over Sydney harbour. Having arrived at six in the morning, he thought he might just sleep through the day after an arduous journey. But he didn't feel tired enough to be sure of sleep—and what would he do in the evening? And so, he looked in his book again and called Mrs Smythe.

"Hello to you!" she began. "And how is old Billy? Has he finally hitched up with that nice filly—what was her name?"

"Carol—they were married last June," Tom replied.

"Oh yes, Carol—I must say he took his time about it. He's lucky she waited—she was very attractive."

They exchanged a few more banalities until Mrs Smythe said, "Are you feeling up to lunch? Meet me on top of the Tower. The restaurant is called 'Infinity'—1 o'clock?"

Tom was amused she had not waited for a reply as to his potentially jet-lagged condition. But he acquiesced in good grace, asked the switchboard to call him at 12:30 and took a cat nap.

He had little difficulty finding the tower. These were springing up in major cities—including London and they all had rotating restaurants on top of distinctly varying quality. As he was being shown to a table near the windows, where a lady and gentleman were sitting, he could see the view of the city was certainly panoramic.

As Tom greeted her, Mrs Smythe held on to his hand as she introduced him to an elegant, elderly gentleman who he understood was called 'Wally' Jordan—presumably for Wallace and who rose to shake his hand. Mrs Smythe turned out to be more than a comely lady; Tom reckoned she was in her well-preserved mid-thirties. She had luxurious auburn hair and striking eyes of the same colour. Her face just missed having perfectly arranged features, which added to its attractiveness.

If her face just missed perfection—her figure did not, and she clearly dressed to show off its perfect proportions. But her eyes were the most striking features at first sight; they seemed to carry an expression unique to themselves and oblivious to whatever sentiment the rest of her face was signalling. They were laughing eyes and there was just the slightest hint of mockery within the humour they conveyed. They even survived a slight, questioning frown.

Tom caught himself staring at Mrs Smythe and he quickly realised that Wally Jordan had noted this with amusement. After an exchange of London news and orders placed, the three turned to the view, with a semi-compulsory motion. One felt the restaurant insisted on it.

Sydney was in the throes of a massive construction boom, as the city was assuming its relatively new place as the prime business and financial centre, leaving Melbourne to enjoy its Victorian elegance in some peace. The rotating view on which the three were casting their dutiful gaze included a forest of tall construction cranes. Particularly noticeable was the fact that half were painted bright red and the other half bright blue, and they seemed clustered so as to mark the colour contrast.

Mrs Smythe spoke up. "You see all the blue cranes? Those are my husband's!"

"I'm glad he chose blue," said Wally Jordan.

"Oh, it's all blue with him," said Mrs Smythe.

"Not his mood, I hope," said Tom.

"Oh no! Not with his business—talk about booming!"

The talk turned to business and Wally Jordan suggested the economy was overheating. Tom listened politely, asking suitable questions, and trying to avoid staring at Mrs Smythe. But she made that more difficult by putting her hand on his arm every time she had something to say. Her conversation was certainly intelligent and informed; she had only the slightest Australian accent and Wally Jordan had none. She had an intriguing habit of introducing slang expressions in an otherwise almost literary exploitation of the English language.

After more pleasant conversations and several turns of the revolving restaurant. Tom left the luncheon party with a visiting card from Mrs Smythe, whose forename he noted was Adelaide, showing her residence in Darling Bay and on the reverse, her art gallery. Wally Jordan also gave him a business card on which was written *Investments* under his name: Wallace B Jordan, Jr. But Tom left with something else. A distinct feeling that his friend Billy had undervalued the introduction; and this was accompanied by a keen desire to see Mrs Smythe again. In fact, he felt like someone who has tasted a dish and distracted from its immediate enjoyment, suddenly yearns for it again sometime later.

The next day, Tom, refreshed by a good night's sleep, was able to indulge that yearning. At the previous day's luncheon, Mrs Smythe had exhorted—almost ordered, him to visit her art gallery. On his way, he found the streets of central Sydney rather clogged with deliveries of construction equipment. The gallery, under a gilt sign: SMYTHE, Australian and Oriental Art, was housed on the ground floor of a two-story office building. In the window were several pen and ink drawings by Joy Hester.

As he entered, Tom immediately spotted two large Ned Kelley paintings by Sydney Nolan. He understood such works now commanded very high prices. A very pretty secretary sitting at a desk seemed to expect him.

"Mrs Smythe will see you—through that door on the left," she chirped.

The gallery owner was delighted to see him and gave him a peck on the cheek. Tom was a bit taken aback at such familiarity after such a short acquaintance but took it to be Australian custom. Mrs Smythe took him on a tour of the gallery, and he got the impression she viewed the pictures as personal possessions stored in a gallery for convenience's sake. There was no sign of customers during his visit and the little receptionist seemed to be there only to smile at him.

The tour over, Mrs Smythe said, "If you are not doing anything on Saturday come to lunch at my house in Queenscliff. There's a regatta on we can watch. I'll send my car to fetch you at noon. You're at the Fullerton?"

Once again, here was an invitation which seemed more like an order— preceded by a peremptory query as to his availability, which was, in fact, taken for granted. Of course, Tom was free; how could he be otherwise having not expected to be in Sydney in the first place? A rather classic Rolls Royce, still with the single headlamps and a uniformed chauffeur took him to the Northern Beach area—a coastline dotted with resort villages.

The Smythe beach house was on a rise and seemed to be mostly veranda looking out to the ocean, now dotted with small crafts. Wally Jordan was there and another lady, whose name Tom strained to catch. She was very blonde from the bottle and was certainly not Mrs Jordan. As they stood on the veranda looking out to sea, it was clear a race was on, and most boats were already on a downwind tack—with spinnakers set or being set.

"It's the Royal Sydney Yacht Squadron against the Middle Harbour Yacht Club," explained Mrs Smythe. "Do you see that big sloop with the blue spinnaker? That's my husband."

"Naturally," said Wally Jordan.

"It looks like he's in the lead," said the nameless blonde.

"Oh! The Royal Squadron always beats the Middle Harbour—I don't know why they bother," said Mrs Smythe.

When they heard the gun from the committee boat signalling the finish, they sat down to lunch which featured some outstanding shrimp. The conversation was mostly Sydney gossip and Tom's hostess would again put her hand on Tom's arm, sitting on her right—as she interposed little explanatory asides such as 'she just lost her husband' or 'they were divorced a while ago' and 'he's big in oil' and even more uselessly 'she's now engaged to Jack'.

This laudable attempt to aid Tom in trying to follow a conversation about people he had never heard of—was mostly a failure. But Tom certainly enjoyed the hand on his arm and the confidential whispers of Mrs Smythe, who he guessed was wearing Guerlain's *Shalimar*, his aunt's favourite scent. He also enjoyed watching her eyes change expression whilst the rest of her face seemed off duty in displaying an emotion. In fact, he now began to entertain generous thoughts about both his uncle Bill and his friend Billy Fanshaw, who, between them, had sent him to Mrs Smythe. After lunch and coffee, Mrs Smythe took Tom to see the rest of the house, which contained a good deal of wicker furniture, some well-framed nautical prints, more of Joy Hester's pen and ink abstracts and a collection of seashells.

Turning a dark corner, just before re-entering the veranda, Mrs Smythe suddenly grabbed Tom by the shoulders and kissed him on the mouth. They were on the veranda with the others before he could react in any manner, but a glance from the blonde lady made him suspect she had seen or was somehow aware of the incident. Mrs Smythe behaved as though nothing had happened and rather concentrated on Wally Jordan, continuing some 'people talk'—before finally saying, "Poor Tom—I'm afraid we are boring him with all this gossip about people he doesn't know."

"I suppose it would be indiscreet to ask him which of the people we've been mentioning he'd like to know," remarked Wally Jordan.

"Oh, all of them of course," said Tom tactfully, "they all sound interesting."

"Now you're fibbing!" said the blonde lady.

"No, Wally's right—it is indiscreet," said Mrs Smythe.

"But I thought he handled it rather well," said Wally.

"You Poms sure stick together," said the blonde lady, putting on an exaggerated Australian twang.

At last, there was a general move to go, and Tom began saying, "I can't thank you enough—Mrs Smythe," when he was interrupted.

"Good grief! It's Adelaide! I always forget how formal you Brits still are. Anyway, Tom, yes Tom!—it was a joy to see you. You're giving Gretchen a lift to town—Wally's going to visit a sick horse further along the coast—or so he says."

Tom received a peck on the cheek again; its lack of ardour was in sharp contrast to the secret embrace he had enjoyed only a short while ago. He had forgotten to remind the party he was American, not British.

In the Rolls, Tom was relieved he finally knew his companion was called Gretchen—but the surname had escaped him completely.

"What's Mr Smythe like? Very busy I suppose?" he asked.

Gretchen had just lit a cigarette.

"You don't mind I hope?" And she rolled down her window halfway. Tom shook his head.

"He's like any husband, I guess," she continued.

"You sound a bit cynical."

"I've already had two."

"Oh, I'm sorry."

"Don't be!—but what I mean is—there's nothing very special about Jack Smythe."

Tom considered that he had best not press his enquiry.

"I take it you've known Adelaide for some time?"

"Years."

"And Wally is a close friend?"

"Very."

Tom was beginning to struggle. Gretchen put out her cigarette, closed the window and turned to him.

"Don't think you have to make conversation, Tom," she said, with a sweet smile. "Adelaide has already hung a 'reserved' sign on you."

Tom was speechless. Gretchen continued, "I'm giving a dinner party on Tuesday. You're about to see where I live. It's not far from the Fullerton and Adelaide is a close neighbour. She'll be there. Seven thirty for eight. It's not black tie."

"That's a relief, I didn't bring one," said Tom—also relieved he didn't have to respond to Gretchen's remark about being 'reserved'.

On arrival at a nice town house, Gretchen said, "Don't get out," and shook his hand.

Tom said, "See you Tuesday."

On Sunday, Tom did something he never expected to. He took a tourist bus tour of the city. He was rather pleased with himself for doing so. Despite his relative youth, Tom had travelled through much of the world on business for his family firm. But his schedule had never provided time for tourism. It was always there and back—business accomplished or not, as the case might be. Now he enjoyed the tour and even the drone of the guide with the microphone and a strong Australian accent.

Tom was not very partial to the recently completed and already iconic opera house—where the tour started from. He admired the engineering, but not the architectural concept. Otherwise, there were pleasant sights to see, including the inevitable square and statue dedicated to Queen Victoria, the town houses with the typically colonial double verandas, the market areas much populated by hippies and the fast-growing population of skyscrapers.

Tom could not avoid the conclusion that Sydney was striving to be an Asian Manhattan. It could certainly boast of a superior harbour and coastline as its watery contribution to the metropolis. But build as they might, it would still turn out to be a secondary New York.

On Monday, Tom decided he should do a bit of work to satisfy his responsibility to Uncle Bill—but also to take his mind off Mrs Smythe. He put a call through to Joseph O'Rourke—the Melbourne-based insurance broker with whom Gardiner Brothers had a long-standing professional relationship and friendship. Joe had been a good friend of his father and known Tom since he was a lad.

"Good morning, Mr O'Rourke—it's Tom from Gardiner Brothers."

"Tom! Good lord—where are you calling from?"

"Sydney."

"And what are you doing there? I've had no word from your Uncle Bill—but it's lovely to hear you." Joe would have expected to be forewarned of his arrival and Tom felt his uncle had been remiss.

"I hadn't expected to be here, Mr O'Rourke. I was closing out a contract in Tokyo when Uncle Bill cabled me and said 'since you're out there'—yes—that's what he said—can you believe it? 'Pop down to Australia'. I had a hell of a time getting here—there's no direct passenger service."

"Yes, there's a diplomatic problem—we must fly to Singapore to get to Japan. But when can I see you—are you coming to Melbourne?"

"Certainly—in next few days. I will let you know." Tom was beginning to hate himself for thinking of Mrs Smythe all the time.

"Wait, Tom—now I think of it, there's a lead you might follow up in Sydney. Have you heard of the Alusuisse alumina project in Gove Bay?"

"Yes, I heard about it in Japan. They are going to be the main buyer of the product. But isn't it covered already?"

"In the main yes, but I just heard the other day there's an environmental risk exclusion clause for the dams where they stick the red mud from the bauxite extraction."

"That does sound interesting, do I need to get all the way up to Gove Bay?"

"No, a top man from Alusuisse is in Sydney, He's from the Ticino and is called Ventimiglia—no, that's the name of a town on the French border. It's something like that. I can find out and get back to you. Where are you staying?"

Tom told him—his business acquisition instinct was well and truly aroused. Mainstream insurers were increasingly avoiding environmental risks as individuals and communities were being encouraged by lawyers to take class actions against companies whose activities could theoretically be polluting. And juries, now highly sensitised on environmental issues, were awarding huge damages. Mining projects had to accept that claims arising from environmental damage would be excluded from all the general risks covered in their insurance—or they had to pay a much higher premium for a separate policy covering such claims. And finding insurers to write such policies was the business of Gardiner Brothers.

That afternoon, Tom had a call back from Joe O'Rourke giving him the name of Alessandro Trentafiglio, an executive director of Alusuisse, an office address and telephone number. Tom called and Mr Trentafiglio's secretary hardly hesitated to put him through.

"Mr Gardiner!" spoke her boss. "This is extraordinary! I was about to ask Zurich to contact your company. You are here in Sydney? But this is marvellous! You are staying at the Fullerton? But we are not far at all. When can you come to see me?"

The man from Alusuisse had a musical voice, accented as though from the German-speaking part of his country rather than the Italian. Tom was received warmly in one of the rather cold new skyscraper office buildings. He was first given a video presentation of the Gove Bay project in the board room, then, in Alessandro Trentafiglio's office, a fat file was produced, and he was shown a series of Environmental Impact Assessments, most focussing on the red mud issue.

It was agreed that head office in Zurich, which had all the copies, would send these to William Gardiner, Senior Partner of Gardiner Brothers in New York, and the Chief Financial Officer of Alusuisse would arrange to meet with Tom's Uncle Bill. Trentafiglio explained that the Australian representative of Swiss Re-insurance was a friend of his—and he had recommended Gardiner Brothers as brokers specialised in placing this kind of supplementary insurance.

"0 che coincidenza!" almost shouted Trentafiglio, bringing his secretary to the door—who was clearing anxious to go home. It was now 6 o'clock in the

evening and his new friend insisted he would take Tom to dinner at the best Italian restaurant in Sydney—Buon Ricardo in Paddington.

"I will pick you up at the Fullerton at quarter to eight," said Alessandro to Tom—and then to his secretary, who was still waiting, "Cheryl—book a table for two at Ricardo before you go, will you? Thanks."

Over a dinner featuring *vittello milanese,* Alessandro spent a good deal of time explaining why the Swiss from the Italian part—the *Ticino,* were considerably more civilised than their compatriots from the German-speaking side ("that terrible dialect—like a disease of the throat!")—and as for the French-speaking side; "a bunch of snobs—bitter at not being in France." This rather brutal diatribe on his native country exhausted, Alessandro passed on to his hobby: new world wines.

"Speaking Italian, I have been able to ferret out some obscure vintages of very high quality—all in the hands of Italian family owners. They produce small quantities, not suitable for export—known only to the cognoscenti." Alessandro pointed to Tom's glass and said:

"You're drinking one."

He reached to a small side table behind to take the bottle and show him the label. It was *Sangiovese Castagno* and Tom was happy to admit it was outstanding. After a further exposition of Alessandro's knowledge of this unique aspect of one of Australia's important viniculture, he was gratified to receive an invitation.

"I'm giving a little wine-tasting dinner party on Wednesday; said his new friend and I would be delighted if you could come—eight o'clock and informal. Have you a wife with you?"

"I'm unmarried," said Tom.

"Well, mine is in Lugano for a month. Have you a lady friend here you could bring? I'm short of ladies."

"Well, yes—possibly, can I call you tomorrow to confirm?"

Again, Tom noticed Alessandro had assumed he would be free. This must be a curious Australian social habit.

Of course, Tom would be seeing Adelaide that Tuesday evening, but he needed to confirm her availability to Alessandro sooner. He had her number at the gallery and could easily call her. But, with a gnawing feeling of guilt, he decided to visit instead. The little girl at reception showed no sign of surprise—as though he was a regular visitor.

She just gave him a big smile and nodded her head towards the inner office. Mrs Smythe gave him a big Spanish-style *embraço*. Tom wondered how many varying indications of affection she usually practised. He had already experienced the prolonged handshake, the grip on the forearm the peck on the cheek and the kiss on the mouth. Next might be the hand on the knee and thigh and then?

At this point in the story of Tom Gardiner in Australia, it might be useful to describe him in greater detail. "A well set up young man of 31" hardly suffices, particularly as it was finally dawning on him the Mrs Smythe was physically attracted to him. Almost exactly six feet tall, of an appropriate but not ungainly slimness, he had straw coloured hair with a slight, natural wave. His face was distinguished but not entirely evenly featured, his nose having a slight bump in the middle due to a youthful fracture. His eyes were a very deep blue and his eyebrows, somewhat darker than his hair, were set well apart. He had a mouth that was more naturally mirthful than determined. Certainly, the fairer sex would consider him very good-looking, but not with a smarmy, film star sort of male beauty. His movements were graceful and, it might be said, a bit too languid to signal determination. He was more likely to be identified as connected with the arts, rather than City business. Only his fondness for pin-striped suits would make one opt for the City.

Now, he explained the invitation to the wine-tasting dinner and its history.

"I'd be absolutely chuffed to come! How intriguing! Alessandro Trentafiglio—what a lovely name! Does he really have thirty sons?" Adelaide gushed.

"I see you know Italian," said Tom.

"And French and German—but Tom, I'm so impressed you are already doing business here." And her hand was back on his arm.

"It is the reason I'm here, after all."

"I'm so happy to give you another reason!" and Adelaide—giving his arm an extra squeeze.

On the way out, Adelaide held his arm with both hands. He stopped by an amusing, small pen and ink drawing of a camel, by Joy Hester.

"Do you like it?" asked Adelaide.

"Yes, it's charming—I knew about the feral camels here," said Tom, sensing danger.

"It's yours as a present."

"Oh, no—I couldn't possibly!"

"You couldn't possibly not. It will be nicely packed up and delivered to your hotel."

Once again, a friendly gesture turned into an order.

At the door, Adelaide said, "I'm seeing you tonight! My cup runeth over." and gave him a peck on the cheek. The smiling receptionist was still smiling.

Walking back to his hotel, Tom's mind was busy. What was behind all this? A married lady, probably somewhat older than him, after the shortest of acquaintances, making such an overt pass at him? She had not even enquired whether he was married—or romantically engaged elsewhere. He understood her husband was frequently absent. Were they separated perhaps? Or estranged?

He might expect to meet the mysterious Mr Smythe, of the blue cranes and blue spinnaker, this evening. But Gretchen had mentioned Adelaide would be there; surely, she should have referred to the Smythes or 'they' rather than just 'she'. Now Tom was not sure whether he hoped the husband would or would not be there. Certainly, he would blush on meeting him and how would Adelaide behave?

Troubled in mind and yet flattered, Tom lunched at the nice, old-fashioned dining room in his hotel and then—not unaccountably, had a nap in his room. Jet lag catches up late. He asked the switchboard to call him at six thirty. The operator told him a small package had arrived for him.

He was careful to reach Gretchen's house at 7:45, as he always did when the invitation was seven thirty for 8 o'clock. But he found most of the dinner guests already assembled and chatting. Gretchen came up to him and said, "Usually around here, the lazy hostess says, 'I expect you know everyone.' I'm not going to do that with you!"

There were at least a dozen people in the room. In colonial fashion, the men and the ladies were grouped separately. Tom tried hard to remember the names as Gretchen led him around. He was hoping, or was he?—that one of the men was Mr Smythe. In fact, none answered to that name. Adelaide smiled sweetly as she took his hand and kissed him on the cheek, after Gretchen had said, rather loudly, "Of course, you do know Adelaide."

Tom found himself seated on Gretchen's left, next to Adelaide on the other side. On the other side was an elderly gentleman who quickly engaged Tom in conversation, across the front of Gretchen, who seemed complacent.

"You from England, Sir?" he barked.

"Tom," interposed Gretchen.

"America—but I spend half my working life in London."

"Keen on racing, Tom?"

"As a matter of fact, I am."

"Fancy anything for the Derby, Tom?"

"Well, that filly of Sheik Mohammed's that came second in the Oaks has a chance."

"Robinson, who was up, held her back a furlong too much."

"Have you horses in training here, Sir."

"Charlie!—a few."

Finally, the hostess decided enough of this racing talk was enough.

"Sir Charles is our biggest and most successful owner—now talk to Adelaide, please."

Gretchen was apparently a social sergeant major when it came to drilling dinner party guests.

"Did you get the picture?" said Adelaide and, sure enough, he felt her hand on his thigh under the table.

"Yes, thank you but really you shouldn't—"

"Nonsense, my darling—it's nothing. I have a lot of Hesters," interrupted Adelaide. "She didn't do many animals. She died young. I knew her well and was a good friend."

"She must have," said Tom, still recovering from the 'darling'.

"Must have what?"

"Died young, if you knew her."

"Why?"

"Well, I mean—"

Adelaide laughed—with her whole face—not just her eyes, "You're in a muddle, my sweet—are you trying to find out my age?"

"No, I just thought—" Tom felt a playful squeeze on his leg.

"I'm thirty-five—so there! Satisfied?"

The rest of the evening passed in a similar fashion. Tom talked with Gretchen who filled him in on Sir Charles Young, who was now talking racing to his neighbour. Finally, Tom summoned up his courage, assisted by several glasses of some great Australian vintage. He was again turned to Adelaide, who had released his leg to eat her dinner.

"I was hoping to meet Mr Smythe," he said quietly.

"Jack? He's in Brisbane," and now Adelaide's eyes carried a mischievous and slightly mocking, glint.

Now, Sir Charles caught his eye again.

"Do you know Sheik Mohammed, Tom?" he asked in a slightly accusatory tone.

"Not at all, Charlie," replied Tom, boldly. "I did know his trainer Noel Murless, but he was sacked a while ago."

"He sacks them every other week. Thank God, he doesn't race here. We're not going to let those bloody Arabs take us over as they have the Brits. Are they doing the same in the States?"

"Not really, they don't race much there—but they keep a great many brood mares in Kentucky and fly in the sires in private jets. My firm dabbled in thoroughbred stud insurance at one point—but we quit. As the prices of the stallions went through the roof, we couldn't place the risks."

"You are insurance brokers?"

"Yes—very specialised. We try and find cover for risks most mainstream underwriters won't touch."

"So, you don't cover mares being covered anymore?" and Sir Charles burst into raucous laughter and came close to slapping Gertrude on the back. It was clear he was going to savour his joke for the rest of the evening and beyond.

"You are naughty! Dearest—you set him up for that, like a comic's straight man," said Adelaide—joining in their laughter which was becoming general at their end of the table.

"No! I didn't knowingly—in any case, it's a pun quite common in our business."

"Don't be a stuffy bear, my darling." Adelaide's hand was back on his knee.

Tom returned to his hotel more disturbed than ever. Adelaide's extensive repertoire of terms of endearment left him feeling as one does having eaten too many chocolates. He was to see her again the next evening at Alessandro's wine-tasting dinner. He wondered if he should plan an escape. And yet, he was intrigued and felt some oncoming arousal in thinking of her physical beauty.

In one way she was next to impossible, but in a way that touched him with some annoyance—she was intensely desirable. How was he to cope with further intimacy? As he took his key from the concierge, he was handed the expertly wrapped picture from the SMYTHE Gallery. He decided to leave it wrapped to be packed in his suitcase which was not overfull.

The next evening. Tom went in a cab to pick up Adelaide, who, he was able to confirm, was almost next door to Gretchen. She leaned against him in the back of the taxicab chatting happily about Gretchen's dinner party and Sir Charles stupid pun—or so it had now become after everyone had laughed. But Tom had a sudden thought as they were arriving at Alessandro's apartment block. He had not explained to his host that Mrs Smythe was a married lady, whose husband happened to be away.

Last evening, her flirtatious behaviour seemed to have raised no eyebrows— perhaps because everyone knew her nature. But this evening the other guests will probably regard her as 'his woman' and Tom knew Adelaide's behaviour was unlikely to mitigate that impression. Alessandro opened the door to them himself and, in the warmth of the exchange of greetings, Tom was unable to slip in his clarification of his escort's status.

The flat was very large and spacious duplex with views of the harbour. Its décor was an agreeable mixture of European traditional with various Australian artefacts. On the walls were Swiss landscapes. The fellow guests were also a mix, a wine critic who wrote for various periodicals, a lady decorator who seemed to be with him but was not his wife, a couple from the Swiss Consulate— French-speaking, a Norwegian mining engineer, an Italian in the wine trade and Italian academic with an Australian wife.

Adelaide immediately began to circulate freely—to Tom's relief. He thought she might hang on his arm. Now she spoke French to the consular couple, Italian to the Italian professor, but fortunately had no Norwegian. Alessandro took Tom aside for a moment to say, "I had no idea your lady friend spoke such good Italian!"

"I've only just met her," said Tom and as he was about to continue, his host smiled and moved away to join another guest.

Finally, all sat down to *melone con figura* and *osso bucco;* the conversation became general and entirely devoted to wine. Alessandro introduced the vintages with anecdotes of their discovery, followed by technical terms and phrases associated with viniculture to describe their characteristics. There were the usual references to every conceivable fruit and flower said to be ensconced in the flavour and aroma of each. It all went over everyone's head except the wine critic's, who nodded wisely throughout.

But, the enjoyment of the tasting, in the half a dozen glasses placed before each guest, was positively bacchanalian. Adelaide was having a whale of a time and Tom was enjoying the relief from her amorous advances, tinged with some jealousy. As he got up from the table, he found himself in need of the *expresso* coffee about to be offered to the guests. In a visit to Alessandro's downstairs cloak room, he stared at a display of framed wine labels on the wall—and they seemed to be slightly blurred.

Nevertheless, when it was time to go, he felt himself again and he found Adelaide very gay—but not drunk. Outside, the guests all had taxis or cars with drivers, waiting—for understandable reasons. Adelaide put two fingers in her mouth and whistled like a Welsh sheep herder calling his collie and a taxicab appeared as though out of nowhere.

On the way to the Smythe residence, Tom began mentally kicking himself, in a determination to refuse the invitation for a night cap which he fervently hoped Adelaide would issue. If ever the flesh was going to be weak, he greatly feared it would be now. Alessandro's vintages had done nothing to shore up his powers of resistance.

"You're coming in for a while and I'm going to give you a marvellous antidote to vineyard whoopee," instructed Adelaide as the cab pulled up. "It's called *Fernet—Branca and* it's good for absolutely everything you can think of."

Tom felt himself obeying like a recruit in front of the Sergeant Major. Adelaide's house was somewhat over decorated. The theme was English country house with lots of chintz and cushions and an explosion of colour. She sat him down, bade him remove his jacket and went to a cabinet which opened on a glass-lined bar. Handing him a small glass of yellow liquid she said, "Bottoms up! I'm just going to splash some cold water on my face."

Tom waited for her to say, "and slip into something more comfortable"—but she didn't. Nevertheless, in what seemed the shortest of intervals, Adelaide reappeared clad in a negligée of astonishing cut. It had short, puffed sleeves on the shoulders from which descended a V-shaped opening to her navel, revealing half her breasts and indicating an absence of night dress—or anything underneath, as the skirt was split, showing a leg as she walked to the drinks cabinet.

There she poured herself a *Fernet—Branca,* which she downed in one gulp. Floating over to Tom she took his hand to raise him to his feet and said, "Come, I want to show you my prize Joy Hester."

In her bedroom, which featured an Emperor sized four-poster bed, there was a large painting of a naked lady, lying on her side, with her head resting on one arm. As Tom was gazing at it, he felt Adelaide's hands unbuttoning his collar and shirt. Then he heard a slight swish as the negligée fell to the floor and a naked body pressed against him—hands now at his trouser belt.

"But your husband?" he said.

"Brisbane," she whispered and put her tongue in his mouth.

When Tom awoke, with sun streaming into the room, the first thing he thought of was the concierge and the maid at the Fullerton, who would wonder at the key uncollected and the bed not slept in. They would hardly consider he had skipped without paying his bill, as his effects were all still there. But this trivial thought was interrupted by movement from the naked body next to his, signalling an intention to repeat last night's amorous exercise.

This was accomplished with perhaps even greater fervour, Tom finally escaped to the bathroom containing a huge shower, with shower heads on both sides. One tap turned on and temperature adjusted, he closed his eyes to savour the memory of what had just occurred when suddenly he felt small hands soaping him all over.

Adelaide said, in a throaty voice, "It's special lavender soap you can taste like a sweet," and she dropped to her knees.

An hour later, over orange juice, toast and coffee, Tom was lost for words. He had dressed in a small bedroom which showed little sign of occupation but was certainly masculine in style. Was it Mr Smythe's?—he couldn't ask. Adelaide chatted in an entirely mundane fashion, making no reference to the previous night, explaining the local weather patterns, and trying to remember the names of the vintages they had sampled extensively. They might have been an old married couple at a habitual breakfast together. Adelaide mentioned casually, "We're going to the Opera tonight—it's *Rigoletto*. I'll pick you up at 5:30."

At the door, she gave him a quick, wifely peck on the cheek.

At his hotel, the concierge handed Tom his key with not the slightest sign of a smirk. There was also a note asking him to lunch with Wallace Jordan, Jr. at the Australian Club in Marquerie Street. He first composed a long cablegram to his uncle, outlining all he had learned about the Gove Bay project. He then asked directions at the front desk and walked to the club, which bore a startling resemblance to every men's club he knew in New York and London. Wally offered him a dry martini and they ordered *goujons* of sole.

"You've been seeing a good deal of Adelaide?" Wally began.

"You can say so! She's been most kind and welcoming."

"She certainly is that."

"But I'm so happy to have this opportunity. I've seen no sign of Mr Smythe—he seems to be away a lot. I thought perhaps you could tell me something about him."

Wally Jordan didn't just pause. He stopped dead and looked out the window at the harbour view. Then he slowly sipped his glass of white wine. Tom waited—perplexed.

"This is going to come as a shock I fear," he started and this time just paused, "I can't tell you much about him because he doesn't exist."

"You mean he's dead?" exclaimed Tom.

"No, he never existed—he's an invention of Adelaide's. There is no Jack Smythe. That's Adelaide's maiden name."

"But why on earth—" Tom was searching for words.

"Why invent a husband? Well—there are lots of reasons. You must know that Adelaide Smythe is looking for a husband—desperately."

"Good grief! But I would have thought candidates would be queueing—she's rich and beautiful!"

"And fussy and 35 and has left it too late, turned down too many and built a reputation as bossy."

"But why does she think inventing a non-existent husband will help her find a real one?"

"You'd have to be Freud and Jung rolled into one to figure that out. But I have one idea—she believes that men will wonder why she is unmarried at 35— with all her advantages. There must be some fatal flaw, they might think. I suppose that's not unreasonable. It might be true for someone from overseas and I think she favours a Brit or a Yank."

Tom felt himself going cold all over, He wondered if Wally would notice he was shaking.

"So, she's looking for a home breaker!" Tom covered his unease by adopting a moral stance.

"Not really. Once the fish is on the hook she explains, she and Jack are virtually estranged—it hasn't worked out—it's going to be an amicable divorce and so on and so forth."

"But surely there will be a documentary trail of some sort—"

"With Adelaide's money that's easy to fix. By the way, the gallery, the yacht, the construction company—it's all hers and professionally managed."

"But don't people here know the story?"

"Gretchen does and maybe some suspect—but she's been clever."

Tom was aghast—but tried not to show too much emotion.

Wally continued, "Of course, she'll bag her game—but it will have to be someone who accepts that Adelaide wears the trousers. You may have noticed she's a very take-charge lady."

Wally was now looking at him in a very intense manner.

"Yes, rather—I do see that," said Tom quietly.

"She has certainly taken a liking to you." And Wally looked even more intense.

Tom laughed, as naturally as he could. "Oh! No—I'm not in the market—no way!"

"Well, I should be careful if I were you. Watch out for the hook."

Tom managed to move the conversation away from Adelaide Smythe. He thanked Wally warmly for the lunch. On returning to his hotel, he asked for his bill and the next flight he might catch to Melbourne. There was one at 16:00 hours. He booked a seat. He wrote a note to Adelaide, explaining he was called to Melbourne on urgent business and asked it to be delivered by hand. After two nervous days with Joe O'Rourke in Melbourne, he was back in London and a week later in New York. It was hardly a story he could tell his uncle.

Some two years passed, leaving Tom's adventure 'down under' a multi-coloured memory. There was the red of passion, the blue of shame, the yellow of luck and not a great deal of white. In England for a while, he went racing during Ascot week. Perusing his racing form, he suddenly caught sight of some familiar auburn hair under one of those silly hats where the amount material used is in inverse proportion to the price. At least they hardly hide the lady's face.

It was unmistakeably Adelaide Smythe, nor could there be any doubt that she was just as attractive as when he had last known her. She was standing with a gentleman who had a familiar look about him. Tom stopped and considered. Why not? What could he lose now? He was safe and her escort would block any recriminations. He sauntered over, doffed his top hat and said, "Hello, Adelaide, remember me?"

"Tom Gardiner!" she exclaimed. "Of course, I do—how wonderful!" and then to the gentleman, "Darling! This my lovely friend Tom Gardiner!" She then gave Tom a peck on the cheek and carried on, "I can't believe it!" The man put out his hand which Tom shook with a smile.

"Tom—meet my husband," said Adelaide, recovering from her initial gushing. "Wallace Jordan, the third!"

"I know your father," said Tom.

"I know you do," said Wallace Jordan III.

"Listen, don't move you two!" said Adelaide, looking away. "I've just seen Carol Fanshaw over there by the rails. I must go and thank her for the dinner before I forget." And she was off.

"I expect they call you Wally as well?" Tom had put his top hat back on.

"You are right, and I am delighted to meet you."

"This may seem a bit sudden to you, Wally—but I'm off back to New York on Monday, I don't suppose you'd be willing to lunch with me at Boodles on Friday? I have reciprocal privileges there from the Knickerbocker."

"I would love to, Tom. We don't race on Friday. But it's my club, so it will be on me; 1 o'clock?"

They met in the bar at Boodle's and then proceeded to a corner table. Both ordered potted shrimps and lamb cutlets. Business came first—not technically permitted in London clubs. Wally explained his firm was called Jordan & Sons and acted as investment advisors, helping institutional trustees choose investment managers by tracking performance and doing 'due diligence' trustees were too lazy to do. Tom recounted the story of Gardiner Brothers placing environment damage claims insurance for the Gove Bay bauxite processing. Finally, Wally 'cut to the chase'.

"I suppose you wondered why my father told you that cock and bull story about Adelaide?"

"Was it a cock and bull story?"

"From start to finish."

"Why?"

Wally, the third, put in a pause—he must have learned how from his father.

"I must take you back to the beginning. Adelaide de Terrier and I grew up together—we were in the same primary school outside Sidney. My father was in love with her mother and carried a torch for her until her death—even though she was married to his best friend. My mother died when I was three and I was brought up by Nanny, who was a New Zealander and hated Australians, I suppose that is bye the bye.

"Although she approved of my playing with Addy because of her Norman name. Nanny was a terrible snob. In any case, Addy and I played innocent house

90

together so often that when we were about nine, we decided we were engaged. It became my father's main ambition in life that we should be married. But he also wanted me to be educated in England. So, I was sent to Cheltenham and eventually to Kings College, Cambridge.

"Of course, I was home at least twice a year and Addy and I just assumed we would eventually be married. But coming down from Cambridge, I made a foolish marriage. My father was furious and would not even meet the poor girl. He refused to speak to me for over a year. In the meantime, Addy was sent to finishing school in Lausanne and eventually to the Sorbonne.

"When she came back to Sydney, she started a very 'artsy' phase, joined up with the Angry Penguins and the Heide Society. She wasn't an artist herself, but she was very good at promoting contemporary artists. In fact, she became President of the Contemporary Arts Society. She also became a great chum of Joy Hester.

"After an unhappy love affair with someone from that crowd (I never knew who). She married Jack Smythe on the rebound. They were chalk and cheese. He had no interest in art—I don't think he ever put a foot in the gallery. He's a great sailor (yes—he's still very much alive) and mounted an America's Cup challenge boat. He had already made a fortune in construction when he married Addy."

Now, Wally took a well-earned pause and drank some wine—a nice Meursault.

"All right—my father had not worried so much about Addy's marriage. He seemed to know it wouldn't work. In fact, they were soon living virtually separately. Of course, everyone had written me off—I was in England. supposedly happily married. But in fact, I wasn't. Poor Caroline never got over her rejection by my father. She had lost her own early and I think she was looking for a substitute.

"And then it turned out that she—well, we won't go into that. But my father's hope for his pet scheme—it had become an obsession, took an uptick when he learned that my marriage was in trouble. But then suitors began to turn up—like bees to the honey pot. My father began telling outrageous lies about Addy to put them off. I tell you; my father could sell fridges to Eskimos; he is so convincing. Then you turn up—a stranger, introduced by Billy Fanshaw, a casual friend who had no idea. You are unfamiliar with Sydney society."

"You can say that again!" interrupted Tom.

"OK—you are unfamiliar with Sydney society; Addy takes a sudden liking to you and you to her—my father notices it immediately. He dreams up this story about an invented husband. You are not likely to go about checking it out. You take French leave—and the coast is clear. The Smythe's are divorced two months later, I was divorced early last year. We were married in December."

It was Tom's turn to pause, while Wally finished his cheese.

"What did Adelaide know about all this?" he asked, his throat very tight.

"Everything—eventually."

"What a fool I made of myself!"

"Not at all—Addy says you behaved like the perfect gentleman you are."

"But—" Tom stammered.

"No buts about it. Look here, Tom, Addy and I understand each other perfectly and have since we were five years old. There is something very special about affection between two children which matures slowly into adult love—true love. We have it."

"Well, Wally, I can tell you I was never more confused in my life. I didn't know whether I was coming or going."

"Ah! Well, you know what they always say: everything in Australia is upside down. Shall we go down for coffee and a glass of port?"

FINIS

Fraud in the Fjord

I

Tom Pettifer was very satisfied with himself—perhaps with some caveat. He had enjoyed some important help. But still, as a mere associate in the venerable, Wall Street firm of Foster, Forbes & Co., he had secured a mandate under the very noses of Lambro's Bank of the City of London. It was an international bond issue to finance the great hydroelectric project of Opplandskraft in Lillehammer, Norway. And he had scored a 'double'!

He now had in his pocket, so to speak, a mandate to do the same for the hydro project at Sira Kvina, which would supply energy for Norskhydro, the aluminium smelters. Now Lambro's Bank basically owns Norway in a banking sense. School textbooks mention them as a typical international bank. The State Treasury official, Mr Grinck, had expressed great surprise that this business should go to other that Lambro's.

Two critical items had boosted Tom's chances. Foster, Forbes were the principal market makers in outstanding Norwegian foreign bonds—from its Zurich office. And then it so happened that the great Norwegian statesman Trygve Lie had become a Foster, Forbes client whilst the first Secretary General of the United Nations at Lake Success in New York State.

Tom's father, the Foster, Forbes partner in charge of international, had given him a letter of introduction to Trygve Lie. He had met Mr Lie in the lobby of the Grand Hotel in Oslo. The whole of Oslo had seen them sitting together as they passed to the bar—which opened only at cocktail hour. "You won't need any other introductions now," Mr Lie had said to Tom. "Anybody who's anybody in this town will now know you are my friend." And so it was.

Now Tom was waiting in that very same bar in the Grand Hotel for the son of another of his father's friends—the ship owner IB Trauken. He had inherited his vast fleet of Panama registered tankers from his father, who was also known as IB—no one seemed to know or question what the initials stood for. But the current Trauken was always called IB Jurgen, meaning the 'younger'. The Norwegian shipping world is a very exclusive club and IB Jurgen Trauken was not its most popular member.

Norwegians are a very conservative people in general. They distrust anything 'showy'. One has only to know Ibsen's plays to realise they are somewhat dour, very reformed Protestants, living rather simple lives. IB drove around Oslo in a Rolls Royce, was estranged from his wife, kept a pleasure sloop in St Tropez harbour, shot and hunted in England and might be found at the Four Hundred in London or El Morocco in New York.

Night clubbing was frowned on by the Norwegian establishment and there was certainly no such establishment in Oslo. Now IB arrived, greeted one or two acquaintances, and sat down next to Tom on a banquette.

"I must say, Tom, your pinching that business from Lambro's is the best story I've heard in a while—and I need the light relief. How's your dear Papa?"

"He's fine, IB—he sends warmest regards and wonders when your sloop is free to charter later this summer," said Tom.

"Tell him any time it suits him. I'm not sure when and if I can get down." IB frowned.

"Problems?" Tom signalled a waiter.

"Yes!" IB ordered a whiskey and soda.

"I'm so sorry."

"Well—it's something I would want to discuss with your father, but you are here, and he isn't. And you are his son so I will trust you as I trust him. Come to the office tomorrow."

II

The offices of IB Trauken resembled the interior of a ship. There was ship style deck planking on the floor, port holes looking out to a balcony with a view onto Oslo fjord and a large ship's wheel and compass on a stand under a series of framed charts with red flag pins indicating last known port locations of the fleet.

IB Jurgen Trauken sat behind a big desk.

"Tom, I'm being blackmailed! It's as simple and devastating as that." IB leaned back in his office chair as if to let the shock sink in.

"I take it going to the police is out of the question."

"Totally!" barked IB and he tossed a single sheet of paper to Tom's side of the desk.

It was not in the classical format—with individual letters cut out of some publication and then pasted and strung together to make the text. It was printed rather than typewritten and the printer had used letters of different sizes and type fonts to compose it.

Its message was straightforward: unless IB would pay two million Swiss francs in a manner and location to be arranged 1) the bank and account number he maintains in Zurich would be disclosed to the Norwegian Treasury, Fiscal Authority and Central Bank 2) the name and address of the lady he maintains in Monte Carlo would be disclosed to his wife Fru. Trauken, Hedda at her residence near Stavanger.

"That second threat is nonsense. Hedda and I are separated—she knows I have a girlfriend." IB waited as Tom read the letter a second time before putting it down on the desk.

"How did you get this?" he asked.

"A messenger—a young man brought it to reception."

"They didn't ask his name, of course."

"Trudy thought he seemed American—but every young man in Oslo seems American—they all want to be Elvis Presley."

"But the thing about the lady is significant in terms of trying to identify the blackmailer," said Tom thoughtfully.

"Yes, I see that. But the problem is the first threat. I'm sure you know we have exchange control here in Norway. There are all sorts of concessions allowing ship owners to hold foreign currency. But they are accounts that must be declared and must be in corporate names. Undeclared personal accounts are strictly forbidden." IB picked up the letter again and stared at it.

"Obviously, he's had to trust a professional printer," said Tom pensively.

"Of course, the bank will refuse to confirm anything," said IB. "It's a crime under Swiss law to disclose client information. But the accusation is fatal to my reputation here—even if it can't be proved—and I would have to lie under oath."

"The fact that he knows of a lady in Monte Carlo must narrow it down." Tom was nervous about pressing this point.

"Look, Tom, I'll be totally open with you. Of course, I have a lady friend in Monaco—as I said, I'm sure Hedda knows it. Although maybe not who and where. But I will have to pay this money. I simply cannot take the risk. Already, I risk the blackmailer will collect and still talk. That's why it would not be helpful to try and identify him. He might panic. All this must be handled in the most discreet manner."

"Will you allow me to visit the lady in Monte Carlo?" suggested Tom.

"Yes. Of course, I don't imagine she has anything to do with this—but, as you say, the fact this villain knows of her existence is important—and maybe, a lead of some sort. But remember—I intend to pay up."

"Leave it to me," said Tom.

"Discretion! Discretion above all!"

"Leave it to me."

III

The apartment of Madame Solange Beranger was in one of the earliest apartment buildings in Monte Carlo, which was very *belle époch* in style. Her very commodious flat was decorated with a tasteful mix of 19th century copies of Louis XV and *fin de siècle art nouveau.* Solange herself was a raven-haired beauty, rather like the profile of a goddess on a Roman coin. Her naturally curled black hair, olive skin and aquiline nose were the hallmarks of the typical Mediterranean look. She might have been over 30 but certainly appeared younger.

Now, she was lounging in a satin dressing gown on a *chaise longue.* Opposite her sat a small, middle-aged man, dressed in a tight Italian suit of buff shot silk, snakeskin shoes and wearing an Old Etonian tie which he was certainly not eligible to do. He had wavy pepper and salt hair and a small black moustache—probably died.

"My dear Solo, I still worry Olga might rat on us," he said.

"My dear Luca, how many times do I have to tell you, she is entirely safe," replied Solange—apparently happy to be addressed as Solo.

"But how can you be so sure?"

"Look, she was pregnant. I paid to fix that. I gave her a little extra. She knows I could tell her father at any time."

"But being pregnant and having an abortion is not a crime."

"Tu blague! It is to her father, a Serbian refugee taken in by a rich Swiss lady, a Madame Mercier. He took her name. She arranged to bring the girl from

Yugoslavia, sent her to school and got her a job in the bank. He would throw her into the street if he found out."

"Well, all I can say, Solo, is having sold some account information once, she might do it again."

"That is not our affair, Ludo."

"Apparently her boyfriend is English."

"That is also not our affair."

"But also, why don't we just split the cash, rather than working through the accounts?"

"Because you can't swan around here with large amounts of cash. Olga has explained that. That's why you got that form from the casino, which we have filled out appropriately—and make sure you slip that stamp back! If you show the bank evidence of winnings, no questions are asked. This is for your own protection. With your record, suspicions are easily raised."

"I suppose you are right—but can I trust you, my sweet Solo?"

"My dear Ludo, you have enough on me to put me away."

"And you are sure, IB has the original note?"

"Yes."

"But you won't tell me how?"

"No—I've explained all this, Ludo—the less you know about the original demand, the safer you and I will be."

"All right—but don't forget, it was my idea and I found Olga in the first place."

"You hooked her, but I landed her. But let's not argue. Let's go over the plan. You are going to tell Marius in St Tropez that he must contact IB in Oslo and tell him something needs to be done about the boat. And give him the envelope to keep for his boss. I'm sure IB is planning to charter again to his American friend. He'll be down quick enough. Marius hands him a sealed envelope. For the tip he's getting—he will invent some maintenance problem.

"In the envelope is the instruction: 'place bag in left luggage Geneva Airport and post ticket to *Case Postale* 205 Montreux 1815' Even if Marius opens the envelope, he won't know what it means. He likes his job. I will leave for Montreux next week. I remember the man who opened the *case postale* account. I gave him a phony address here in Monaco. But they don't reveal the identity of an account holder to anyone else. I come back when I have collected the bag in Geneva, go to Banque Monegasque, deposit the money with the casino receipt and transfer one million to your account. I do it at the counter—I don't have to give any explanation. You must take it out slowly. Are we clear?"

"Can I watch you do it?" asked Ludo, by way of reply.

"Certainly not—idiot! They'll suspect you are blackmailing me! You'll know soon enough if it hasn't worked. But don't try and leave the country—you know about the Interpol warrant."

"All right, yes I know, but how will you know it's been paid?"

"Well, I might have to hang around Montreux for a few days—but I'll call you when I have the ticket."

"What if they keep watch at the Montreux post office?"

"You don't think I can spot that and avoid a watcher?"

"Oh, all right—I trust you, Solo. Have you got the note ready?"

"Tomorrow. I have three school children lined up. Each is going to write part of the note. It's on English paper."

"There is a lot that could go wrong," said Ludo.

"That, my dear Ludo, is true of everything in life. But relax. Don't forget, it will take a while for IB to draw the cash."

"Won't they be suspicious?"

"No. IB is always moving money around."

"So are we, it seems," said Ludo—to himself.

IV

A week after Ludo had departed with the note to St Tropez, Solange had a card brought to her by her maid.

Thomas L. Pettifer

Associate

Foster, Forbes & Company

40 Wall Street, New York 1005, N.Y.

On it was written by hand 'at the suggestion of IB Jurgen Trauken'.

Solange stared at the card. This was a surprise. She hadn't expected IB to take this man into his confidence—although she knew Mr Pettifer, Senior had been a friend of IB's father, He often chartered the sloop in St Tropez. Still—these Pettifers were in finance. Perhaps he was helping arrange the money.

"Show him in," said Solange.

"Thank you for seeing me, Madame Berenger," said Tom. "IB has an awkward problem and has asked me to help resolve it discreetly. He has most specifically suggested I call on you for assistance."

"He knows I am at his disposal to help anyway I can, Monsieur Pettifer," said Solange, looking again at his card and signalling him to a chair.

Tom explained the situation as briefly and succinctly as he could. But he ended by saying, "You will understand Madame Beranger, that IB is determined to pay. He wants to make no attempt to apprehend the blackmailer for fear the whole thing might be made public."

"This is most shocking, Monsieur Pettifer—poor IB! And what does this say about Swiss bank security? How terrible! But you say reference is made to me as part of the threat?"

"Yes."

"Well then, the villain cannot be from Oslo! Everyone knows Hedda and IB have an amicable separation. So that is no threat. Here in Monte Carlo, we are often seen together, of course. We make no secret we are—ah, friends." Solange smiled discreetly. "I could ask the concierge at the Hotel de Paris if anyone has been asking questions about IB."

"Please don't, Madame—IB insists on maximum discretion. There must be no sign that anything is amiss."

"Well then, how can I help?"

"We have received a further communication instructing the payment—in a very strange way. Marius, IB's captain of his sloop in St Tropez, was given a letter for IB. He was to ask his boss to come down and collect it. IB was suspicious as Marius gave him some cock and bull story about a maintenance problem—so he told Marius to send him the envelope."

"Did Marius ask who the person was who gave him the envelope?"

"No, he just said the man seemed Italian."

"I wonder if Marius can tell the difference between an Italian and a Monegasque," said Solange.

"I doubt it—but here is the note."

Solange examined it with keen interest. "It looks as though it was written by children!"

"That's just what we thought."

"How very curious—but how can I help, Monsieur Pettifer? I take it he will not want the police to try and identify the owner of the *case postale*?"

"No! Certainly not—he does not want the Swiss or any police involved."

"They would investigate the bank."

"Exactly—he wants to avoid that as well. He often draws out large amounts of cash—they have raised no question."

"He already has the two million in cash?" Solange was quite genuinely surprised, but also somewhat concerned at this departure from plan.

"Yes, I have it in a bag in my hotel. I've just come from Piraeus. IB had the bank in Zurich arrange for the money in his office there—less suspicious, you see, with his shipping business. But I wanted to see you first. He has asked if you would be willing to take it to Geneva, put it in left luggage and post the ticket as instructed." Tom looked at Solange rather anxiously.

"I go!" Solange was truly shocked.

"I think it is a great imposition and I told IB just that. But he argues that the blackmailer may have you under observation—and if he sees you following the instructions, he will believe IB is acting in good faith. You see, IB is afraid this man might just be vindictive and contact the Norwegian authorities. Particularly if he thinks we are on to him. Of course, I offered to go to Geneva. But IB says I look too much like a detective! I think it's silly."

Solange remained silent for a few minutes.

"Can I not give you something to drink," she said. "I must think for a moment on this."

"I'd love a glass of white wine," said Tom.

Solange went into the pantry. Tom heard a fridge door being opened and closed. He looked around at the flat '*What a little love nest!*' he thought to himself.

Solange was back with a bottle and two glasses.

"Of course, Madame Beranger," said Tom, rising from his chair, "IB would pay all your expenses—first-class flight from Nice to Geneva and so on."

"Certainly not!" said Solange, pouring out two glasses. "IB has been extremely generous to me for some time. This will be my little gesture—which can hardly repay him."

"So, you will do it?"

"Yes."

Tom raised his glass, and they drank a silent toast.

V

Hedda Trauken poured a second cup of coffee for Jake Barnes. They were sitting in a breakfast nook of a farmhouse before a big picture window, overlooking Lysefjord, near Stavanger. Hedda was what is called a strawberry blonde and the nearness to full redhead was indicated by charming and childlike freckles that extended even to her nose.

Her face had no sharp features and was so youthful as to belie her 30-odd-years. It was almost a baby face and would probably remain wrinkle-free for some time. Her generous mouth and soft expression indicated an absence of any sternness. But her grey eyes suggested keen intelligence. She had a figure that was trim rather than voluptuous. She was wearing a taffeta dressing gown lined partially with rabbit fur.

Jake Barnes was a very fit American. Perhaps around 40, with blonde hair cut quite short and a very tanned face—except for a line across his forehead, as he habitually wore a Stetson hat, like any good Texan. Now he was dressed in blue jeans and a cream-coloured, turtleneck jersey. He was speaking, "I still say I hope your old man has got a terrific sense of humour. The whole thing is crazy to me. You know, he could probably bring an action against you—if he doesn't see the joke."

"I don't think he could actually, and he knows a joke when he sees one," said Hedda, as she put down the coffee pot and returned to her toast.

"Well, I told the guy at the printers in Houston it was a party joke and he said 'some joke! I hope the cops don't see it.'"

"But he did do the job," said Hedda.

"Fifty bucks for a few lines of crazy print—sure he did it."

"Tell me again what the girl at reception in my husband's office said?"

"She didn't say anything! As I told you, I said *God Morgen, dette er fur IB Jurgen Trauken* in my best Norwegian and the cute little thing smiled and took the envelope."

"I'm glad you didn't stay and chat—your accent is terrible," said Hedda.

"But what about that gal in Monte Carlo, what's to stop her from double-crossing you?" said Tom, draining his coffee cup.

"I know far too much about her," replied Hedda. "We've been in touch a good deal lately. We've become friendly. We understand each other. There's no problem there."

"Well, I'm sure glad someone understands someone around here. I sure as hell don't," exclaimed Jake, "Here's a couple who are apart but still love each other—didn't you tell me that? She's in touch with his girlfriend and is having a little marital holiday with me! Boy, you Norwegians are real swingers."

"My dear Jake, I've tried to explain it to you. Yes, we love each other. The problem is a temporary lifestyle conflict. When IB inherited one of the most successful shipping businesses in Norway, we all thought he would settle down. He was a complete playboy before and the bane of his father. But he didn't. He seemed to have an early mid-life crisis—he's only 35 for goodness' sake! I could no longer hold my head up in Oslo society. Some hated me for not getting my husband under control; some pitied me and, I suspect, some were jealous. I had to leave. It's that simple."

"Well, I ain't no marriage counsellor," said Jake, "and I'm hardly in a position to comment anyway."

"You've been very helpful and played your part beautifully in this little play of mine." And Hetta leaned over and kissed him. "When are you due back in Houston?"

"I'm leaving next week," replied Jake, "I gotta say, underwater seismic exploration work is a lot tougher here than in the Gulf of Mexico. But I'll tell you what—I'm going to quit diving myself! I have a new contract with Occidental and I will just supervise and train. I'll be back to work in the British sector, but I'll be popping over to Stavanger. By then, I hope to find you back with hubby. And before you know it, every diver working in the North Sea will have been trained by Jake Barnes!"

"I imagine you had a girl in Galveston when you were working offshore." Hedda smiled and ruffled his hair.

"I'll never have a gal like I had when I was working the North Sea!" said Jake.

VI

Solange Berenger sat and stared at the Louis Vuitton satchel that was lying at her feet. Could this be a trap? She did not like this variation in the plan. It had been expected that IB would draw the money from his bank in Zurich and leave it in the left luggage at Geneva airport—posting the ticket to the *case postale* in Montreux as the blackmailer had instructed. Of course, this change and the introduction of young Mr Pettifer made it all simpler—but perhaps to simple! Could IB suspect her?

No! That was too obvious. What she was witnessing was supreme caution by IB. Once he had decided to pay, it all had to be kept secret. Identifying and apprehending the blackmailer would make it public. This is what IB feared most. Even moving the money through Piraeus was super caution.

Solange decided to wait a few days before carrying out the final phase of the plan. She became a bit nervous with the satchel and stayed at home. Two days later, Solange entered the Banque Monegasque de Credit carrying the Louis Vuitton satchel. She asked for her friend, Assistant Manager Franco Fragiotti, who came immediately and showed her into a private room. Solange produced the slip from the cashiers' cage at the Casino, indicating that their *jetons,* won on their tables by Madame Solange Beranger had been converted into so many Swiss Francs and indicating the exchange rate.

"I have the odd change in my purse," said Solange with a smile.

"*Felicitations!*" said Monsieur Frangiotti, as he counted the notes and began to fill out a deposit slip.

"I have some transfer instructions to make," said Solange.

"I will get the forms," said Monsieur Frangiotti.

Solange looked lovingly at the Swiss Franc notes lying on the table in neat little piles. Frangiotti came back with forms and a canvas bag into which he began to place the notes.

Solange began to fill out a transfer form, Sw. Fr, 1,500,000 (one million five hundred thousand Swiss francs) to Den Norske Krediet Bank, Oslo, Norway for the account of Fru Trauken, Hedda, account number 026 674 5588—reference 'reunion'.

She then signed the deposit slip and the transfer form. Monsieur Frangiotti showed her to the door and bowed over her hand. Solange walked back to her apartment to fetch a suitcase she had already packed. The pre-ordered taxi was at the door, and it drove her to Nice Airport where she boarded a flight to London Heathrow.

Two days later, she sent a telegram to Ludo, 'envelope in *case postale* contained note: I won't pay—no ticket. Something did go wrong, Solo.'

She then posted an anonymous note to *Service Sécurité, Société des Bains de Mer de Monaco:* 'suggest you investigate Ludovico Capone re theft of form and stamp from cashiers cage casino.'

Solange then flew to Marseille and on to her mother's house in St Remy. "*Me voici, Maman—pour de bon,*" she said.

VII

Tom Pettifer was leaving IB's office, after giving him a 'mission accomplished' report when he ran into a lady entering the lobby. She was an attractive strawberry blonde wearing a tartan skirt and a Norwegian knitwear jersey.

"Mr Pettifer!" she cried. "I'd know you anywhere! You are the spitting image of your father. I'm Hedda Trauken. Your father and my father-in-law were great chums. I'm pleased to see you are a friend of IB Jurgen."

"I'm Tom," he said, somewhat dazed, as she shook his hand.

"How long are you in Oslo, Tom," said Hedda.

"I'm flying back to New York this evening."

"What a shame—but I hope we see more of you soon."

Trudy, at the reception desk, was witnessing this conversation, slack jawed.

"*Fru Trauken! God Morgen,*" she croaked.

"*God Morgen,* Trudy, Is he in?"

Trudy just nodded and Hedda swept through the door with not so much as a gentle knock.

IB was sitting at his desk and his expression began to resemble that of his receptionist outside.

"Hello, *min kjaere,* I've come back!" said Hedda and she slapped a bank statement on the desk, which IB looked at—stupefied.

"You see that big fat credit item in my account?" she continued, "that's the kroner equivalent of one and a half million Swiss francs—your Swiss francs. Solange thanks you warmly for your generous goodbye present of half a million!" and Hedda leaned across the desk and gave him a peck on the cheek. "That's from Solange and you can stop paying her rent in Monte Carlo as she has gone to live with her *maman* in St Remy.

"Now, you can have the balance of your two million transferred to your account at Andresen's Bank if you do one or two little things: you close your account in Zurich and bring the money back here where you know it belongs— not a whisper from me to the tax man; you sell your Rolls; you sell the sloop with Marius in St Tropez to the Pettifers, who have always wanted it—and the place is becoming vulgar—Brigitte Bardot! Can you imagine! Finally—there is a young girl called Olga Mercier working for the bank in Zurich. You give her a job in that nice little office you have in London next to the Baltic exchange. You do those few simple things and I am yours again, now, and forever. Oh!—you also get my sweet farmhouse at Lysefjord near Stavanger."

IB sat numb for several minutes. He looked again at the bank statement on his desk then he looked up at Hedda for some minutes. He slowly rose and walked around from his desk, enveloped Hedda in a close embrace, kissed her passionately on the mouth and then sobbed quietly on her shoulder—as she rocked him back and forth.

FINIS

Morisot

Seated at his favourite table at *Le Veau d'Or* restaurant in Manhattan, Morisot sipped his Pernod and reflected, for the hundredth time, on his good fortune. He had come to love New York City—its bustle, its sophistication, its variety. He thought at once of the *Vernon Duke* song:

Autumn in New York
Why does it seem so inviting?
Autumn in New York
It brings the thrill of 'first nighting'
Glittering crowds
And shimmering clouds
In canyons of steel
They're making me feel
I'm home!

Of course, Morisot was not home. He was one of thousands of Frenchmen who had sought refuge in America after the collapse of France under the *blitzkrieg* of the Nazi invasion in 1939—a collapse no one had expected. The surrender had been particularly shameful, and this had been exacerbated for many by the creation of a puppet state—Vichy France, under the leadership of the hero of WW1, Marshall Petain.

Within it were harboured the Nazi sympathisers of pre-war France and some hapless Jews soon to be rounded up and shipped East to camps. Like many, Morisot had fled first to Casablanca, nominally part of Vichy France and then via neutral Lisbon to the United States. But he had been prepared for this sudden exile and the guest he now expected to join him for lunch had been a central figure in that process.

Pierre Morisot was a short man, but his military carriage added to his height in the mind's eye. He was dapper in dress but not flashy. He favoured pin-striped, double-breasted suits and starched collars—although with a frequently worn bow tie, his collars were soft, and friends noticed that softness extended to his mood when he was bow tied. In his lapel, he had the ribbon of the *Medale Militaire;* he had been severely wounded in a heroic action in the Great War and a very slight limp and a small indent in his forehead attested to that incident.

In his mid-fifties, he wore his whitened hair *en brosse.* He sported a monocle on a thin black cord, which he used to read small print—but also as a modest affectation. His English was only slightly accented, as he had been raised by an English nanny in Cannes, where his affluent parents had resided permanently.

But his manner was unquestionably Parisian—that very civilised and charming attitude of the *bon viveur,* a condition that does not really translate well as 'good liver' or even 'playboy'. He certainly considered himself intensely cosmopolitan and counted many nationalities among his close friends.

"J'attends Monsieur Datskevich," Morisot had announced to the *Patron* on arrival. *Le Veau d'Or* was a favourite watering hole for the French colony in New York. It was a remarkably faithful copy of an up-market Paris Bistro, owned and operated by a French family from Normandy.

Over the bar was an evocative painting of a veal calf in bed with a gold-trimmed headboard and one foreleg resting on a lace coverlet. The house speciality was *cervelle au beur noir (*calf brains fried in slightly burnt butter)— no dish for those squeamish about offal. There was a great feeling of familiarity about the place and if one shut one's eyes, one was easily transported to the *Rive Gauche* of the Seine by the *soto voce* babble of French conversations from waiters and guests.

Morisot's guest was one Ivan Sergeievich Datskevich, a White Russian émigré and partner in the Wall Street house of Foster, Forbes & Co and, until recently, manager of its Paris branch. During his tenure throughout the 1930s, his office had done fabulous business, as hundreds of prosperous French, conscious of the gathering clouds of war—and shocked by the often-violent struggles between both left and right extremes which then poisoned French politics, had shifted their savings to the United States.

Morisot recalled seeing queues outside the offices of Foster, Forbes & Co. in the Champs-Elysées, as well-dressed *boulevardiers* waited to open US$ accounts. He had been one of the first clients. His savings were small by Wall

Street standards, but he had been well introduced by his socially prominent French bankers and Ivan Datskevich had been delighted to accept him. Now his nest egg was in safe hands, and he had become a great friend of Datskevich and his French wife and was frequently a weekend guest at their Long Island home.

Morisot had been a prominent portrait painter in Paris, having risen rapidly through the patronage of the fashionable. His was an easily transported occupation and he was already enjoying success with East Coast society figures in America. He was in all things a realist and well understood that his was less an artistic success than a social one. To be painted by Morisot had become a matter of prestige. As he liked to put it, his 'brand' was more important than his brush and palette.

Now, he could see Ivan Datskevich handing his Homburg hat and coat to the pert little girl in the cloakroom and heard the *patron* say, "*Bonjour M. le Comte.*" Datskevich was no such thing and belonged to the untitled nobility of Russia—by far the majority. But the owner of the restaurant preferred to assume that all White Russian émigrés were either princes, counts or barons. He was greeting a very tall gentleman, who liked to say that he was a typical younger son with a smaller older brother.

Although it was not an appropriate comparison, Datskevich would refer to Nicholas II, who was very short, whereas his first cousin Grand Duke Nicholas Nicholaevich, was 6ft 6 inches. The elder Datskevich was hardly 5ft 5 inches and had been killed fighting with Admiral Kolchak for the Whites in the Civil War. Ivan Sergeivich had the languid manner often associated with very tall men—as though signals from the brain to the limbs take longer.

He had the courtly style so typical of the Russian nobility in exile. He was very blonde, and his features could be described as Scandinavian, with only his slightly hooded eyes indicating a Slavic element in his make-up. This was a common characteristic of the Northern Russian elite which claimed descent from the Viking warriors who had assumed leadership at the invitation of the Slavic tribes indigenous to the region in the 9th century. One could not help but wonder if their very obviously western European cultural bias had not been a cause of resentment within the Russian peasantry and more still the slavophile intelligentsia, which had been crucial to the revolution.

Now, Datskevich had adapted to the Wall Street circles which had ensured him a career when many of his exiled compatriot had found rich American wives to fund their imposed idleness.

Arrived at the table, Datskevich shook Morisot's hand warmly and said immediately, "This lunch is *pour mon compte*—you are a client for goodness' sake!"

The two mainly spoke French together, but as was invariably the case in their set, switched perhaps to freely from French to English and back again—a habit which Madame Datskevich deplored.

"But I protest!" countered Morisot. "I am in funds as I have just received a generous advance for a portrait I am painting of a lady in Lexington, Kentucky."

"I smell horses," said Datskevich.

"Yes, she is a celebrated breeder. Discretion prevents me from naming her— but you would know one of her successes if you followed racing."

"I don't particularly, *mon cher Pierre*—but you don't have an expense account and you are not painting me—so you cannot use a tax deduction. If you insist—let's go Dutch. But what takes you into the horsey world?"

Morisot looked surprised.

"Didn't you know? I started as a painter of horses."

"No!"

"When I came to Paris to study painting, I had a little weekend cottage in Chantilly. I started sketching those four-legged treasures and mingled with trainers and jockeys. I went to London to study the works of Stubbs, who used to dissect dead horses to examine their muscular structure. I met a Lady Fitzwilliam, whose family have the largest collection of Stubbs. I recently did her portrait, by the way.

"I had no horse corpses to dissect but I developed another method. I would first photograph the horse from every angle and then paste the prints on a big board while I attacked the portrait from the traditional angle, which is always the side view. Well, I began to do quite well. My commissions came first from the trainers, but my work was soon being viewed by owners at Chantilly. I even did a polo pony at Deauville."

"And so, when did you start on people?" asked Datskevich.

"A lady wanted to be painted next to her horse—with her arm resting on its neck. I did a sketch in the stable yard and then the lady in my studio. I have never looked back and painted my last horse. But my contacts in the racing world produced my first portrait commissions."

A waiter came to take their order and they both chose the *cervelle au beure noire.*

"So now you paint society ladies?" said Datskevich, culinary matters having been settled.

"Just as I did in Paris," replied Morisot, "but I am pleased to say they pay better here!"

"On a less pleasant subject," interposed Datskevich, having tasted the Bordeaux just produced by the wine waiter, "what do you think of Gaston Henry-Haye making the cover of *Time* magazine?"

"He's a pompous turncoat!" was Morisot's stern reply. "They are all traitors—that Vichy crowd. I remember him strutting around Paris society—he had made a lot of money in some sort of contraband. When he voted to give Petain full powers, he lost most of his friends, except amongst the Nazi sympathisers—and there were more than a few of them in our circles."

"But, my dear Pierre, he is nevertheless the ambassador in Washington for the only French government the US recognises."

"That is the great mystery! Many of us Free French think it's simply because Roosevelt cannot stand de Gaulle. Of course, the General is not very sociable—apparently, he drives Churchill mad. But he has organised the Free French into a fighting force as Britain's main ally against Hitler."

"But surely that is the reason the US State department thinks that recognising de Gaulle and the Free French would compromise American neutrality."

"My dear Ivan!" Morisot put his hand on Datskevich's arm, "Don't you think American neutrality is already compromised by the assistance FDR is giving Churchill behind the back of Congress?"

Datskevich smiled. "Yes, apparently military equipment is almost blocking the roads into Canada. Amazing Congress pretends not to notice."

"Not so amazing. The country is against joining the war. There are still pro-German elements—especially in Chicago. When Antoine de St Exupery was here giving speeches for the Free French, he was booed in Chicago. That's where the German American Bund was based. But more importantly, Congress knows very well the country wants to remain neutral."

"I imagine it annoys you to have to use Vichy's consular services here. I hear that from my other French clients. I don't think we have a Vichy supporter on the books."

"I should hope not!" said Morisot. "Bye the bye, do you know an Auguste Lebrun?"

Datskevich paused, "I believe I have met him socially once or twice."

"What do you know about him?"

"He's a peasant from Normandy who made a fortune on the Bourse before the last war. He took his money to Casablanca. By the way, he's not a Foster Forbes client or I would not be telling you this. Here, I think he is regarded as a bit of a social climber."

"I must tell you I think there is something not right about him. I think he is a Vichy supporter." Morisot carefully applied some excellent brie cheese to a piece of baguette and looked meaningfully at his guest as he ate it.

"What makes you think that?" asked Datskevich, wondering to himself how *Le Veau d'Or* managed to get a hold of such a cheese—probably via Vichy. "He will hardly get far in our circles here if he is."

"That is true—but it's full of Vichy types here in New York. I saw him hob knobbing with some of them at the Alliance Française. They are shameless there, by the way. They claim they must be neutral between Petain and de Gaulle, for 'the sake of France'. What rubbish! How can one condone a virtual alliance with Hitler?"

"Maybe they are just separating culture from politics."

"Ha! Goering started filching works from the Louvre as soon as they occupied Paris. How's that for separating culture from politics?"

Datskevich did not reply. He was anxious to change the subject. Their lunch ended with stock market chat. But as he walked along Madison Avenue, Morisot continued to think about Auguste Lebrun, He was convinced he was a Vichy supporter adopting a pose. He wore the cross of Lorraine in his buttonhole. Morisot had overheard him praising de Gaulle at a crowded cocktail party.

But Datskevich was correct. Surely, Lebrun would not declare a Vichy bias, if he wanted to be accepted in the best East Coast aristocratic circles. On the other hand, official Washington was technically pro-Vichy reluctantly in some cases. It was not universally considered a social sin to be pro-Vichy. So why would Lebrun not be open about it?

One of the causes of Morisot's suspicions emanated from a commission he had received. But he had been reluctant to disclose all this to his friend. Of course, he trusted Datskevich in all matters, but this was so sensitive, so inherently confidential; in questions relating to Vichy France, the fate of nations was involved. Morisot stopped so suddenly on the pavement that another pedestrian ran into him from behind.

"*Mes excuses, Monsieur*—I'm so sorry!" he blurted, having temporarily forgotten where he was. A confused citizen walked on, looking back for a moment. Morisot had suddenly wondered whether he was not slipping into some foolish conspiratorial mode, having greatly exaggerated the significance of his suspicions. But one incident rankled particularly.

A while ago Morisot had received a commission from a lady in Darien, Connecticut—referred by a satisfied client. She wished to be painted in her garden. He had travelled to Darien to meet her and to explain he would be happy to start the portrait in situ but would need to finish it in his studio. This was a cardinal rule. She had received him in her drawing room in which was a grand piano laden with photographs.

He had immediately noticed one showing Auguste Lebrun with Charles Lindbergh. His subject had left the room briefly. He looked further and found several photos of the Lindbergh family. When the lady returned, Morisot said, "I see you know the celebrated aviator."

"Oh yes!" She replied, "The Lindbergh's are neighbours and very old friends. Why I grew up with Charles—our parents were friends."

"I couldn't help noticing the photograph with Auguste Lebrun."

"Of course! You must know him. Charles has so many French friends. He is such a hero there—the Legion and ever so many French honours. I imagine you see Auguste very often?"

"Not very—are he and Charles Lindbergh close friends?"

"Oh yes! They love to have long discussions about France."

Morisot had let the matter drop—perhaps somewhat abruptly, he now thought. But the implications were profound. Lindbergh was a well-known Nazi sympathiser, a follower of Spengler's theories about genetics and racial superiority. There could be no question that he would be pro-Vichy—and Auguste Lebrun was a close friend! This was the evidence that Morisot had hesitated to share with Datskevich. But now he wondered how many other people with an interest in the French question, in general, would also be aware of Lebrun's friendship with Charles Lindbergh?

The months went by, and Morisot's suspicions of Lebrun grew in him like a noxious worm working its way to the heart. He began to haunt occasions at which he knew Lebrun would be present. He was trying to draw some confirmation of his suspicion through Lebrun's associations. At one point—and to his shame, he began to follow his nemesis. One day he followed Lebrun to what seemed to be a *couturier* on 92nd Street. He thought '*seemed*' for why would a legitimate dress shop be so far uptown?

In the next days, he went to visit the shop himself. He was greeted by a stern, mannishly dressed lady with a braid curled around her head as her *coiffure*. He immediately realised the establishment designed gowns to order and had no ready-made stock. He quickly invented a story that his wife had sent him to investigate because she didn't believe a shop a friend told her about was so far uptown.

"And who is the friend of Madam," asked the manager in a severe tone.

"I have no idea," replied Morisot.

"We only accept new clients on referral."

Morisot excused himself and left, his suspicions greater still. But he returned quietly in the next days, posted himself in a coffee shop across the street and waited. Soon a car with consular plates drove up and a man got out and entered the shop. He noted the number. He was excited as he knew how to trace the number. The cop on the beat outside his studio on Lexington Avenue had become a friend. He had asked him in for a coffee on a cold day and the Irish cop had admired the equestrian prints Morisot had on his walls.

"Say, Officer Kelley, can you check a number plate for me?" Morisot asked when he next spotted his friend.

"Sure thing! Badly parked?"

"No—just curious—no rush."

"Leave it to me, Mr M."

Morisot waited, his serpent-free heart still starting to beat a bit faster. His policeman was not on duty for a few days but then returned and spotted Morisot.

"Hi there, Mr M," he said. "That plate number you wanted? It's the German Consulate on 34th and Park."

Morisot was almost too delighted to thank Officer Kelley properly.

Auguste Lebrun had a lady friend named Madame Labouchère as a frequent companion—perhaps even a *maitress atitrée*. They were so often paired that hostesses would invariably invite both and expect them to arrive together. Madame Labouchère was Belgian and presumed to be either divorced or a widow. But in this social world, new to Morisot, one didn't enquire too closely. He decided to consult his friend Ivan Datskevich.

"Ivan—you know that lady Labouchère who is so often on Lebrun's arm?" Morisot enquired one day.

"I know of her, I should say—I don't think I've exchanged two words with her. But she seems charming."

"Can you find out who she was married to and his fate? Is she divorced or widowed?"

Datskevich hesitated. "Just how would you expect me to do that, my good friend?"

"Surely, you check up on potential clients—particularly foreign ones these days."

"In the first place, Madame Labouchère is not a prospective client as far as I know and our methods are strictly confidential, my dear Pierre."

Ivan, this is very important to me, I can't tell you everything—but I increasingly believe Lebrun is not only a Vichy sympathiser but a Nazi agent as well.

"Then you must go to the FBI."

"I have not anything close to enough evidence."

"Look, I am violating my firm's policy here, but we do maintain a rather special relationship with an immigration official who does confidential enquiring for us. Otherwise, we would have to go through official channels which is time-consuming and potentially embarrassing. And let me say, *mon cher*, that your pursuit of the unattractive but potentially entirely innocent Lebrun could be embarrassing for you! And remember, America still maintains diplomatic relations with Germany. Still, what are friends for? I will use our contact to find out what you want."

Morisot waited for weeks, that worm of suspicion advancing ever closer to his heart. But doubts still stayed its wriggling progress. Was he perhaps just motivated by a dislike of the man? Was he just a snob? Did he really have conclusive evidence or was he acting on some sort of possibly distorted instinct? And in any case, was the fact that Lebrun was pro-Vichy going to be a vital factor in the outcome of the war for France? Of course not! Still—had he, not a duty to do everything he could to help the General even from his own comfortable outpost in neutral America?

Two weeks later, Datskevich invited Morisot to lunch at *Le Veau d'Or*. He found his friend already installed at a corner table, far from the bar and generally somewhat apart. It took Datskevich an age—or so Morisot thought, to get what he knew to be the point of the lunch.

"All right, my dear Pierre, Labouchère is the lady's maiden name which she resumed after the death of her husband in 1934. He was a German named Freiherr von Guttenberg. She lived in Antwerp (Anvers) in Belgium before applying for visa to come to America as a teacher of German literature. That's all I can give you. I don't know—nor does my source if she has ever worked as a teacher. As you know, Freiherr is a title of German nobility. A good many Baltic families were Frei Herren, and they were officially incorporated into the Russian nobility some time back. I don't think that's particularly relevant to your enquiry."

"My dear Ivan, I love hearing about old Russia from you. But now we know Madame Labouchère had connections, to say the least. I will try and find out about Freiherr von Guttenberg—he doesn't sound very Nazi, does he?" Morisot sounded almost disappointed.

"I don't think I can help you there—and I don't suggest you call the German Consulate," said Datskevich.

Morisot brooded over the apparently contradictory facts that were emerging. Leaving aside the mysterious background of Lebrun's lady friend, he could not help but notice that this presumed Vichyite was achieving a smooth penetration of the higher echelons of Long Island's society, having purchased a not inconsiderable estate in Oyster Bay. Many of Morisot's portrait commissions were secured in this crowd. His lady subjects like to chat as he struggled to make them keep their pose. Of course, as their artist was French, they tended to season their gossip with references to the French and, Auguste Lebrun, who was making his mark in society. One of them quoted Lebrun as saying de Gaulle was a great leader and it was a shame FDR did not like him. But this lady was a strong opponent of President Roosevelt and held to the theory that he had taxed the rich in revenge for failing to be elected to the Porcellian Club at Harvard.

Another lady remarked that Lebrun had called de Gaulle a ruthlessly ambitious man out for his own aggrandisement rather than for France. A third provided a more subtle insight into Lebrun's thinking. She had asked him what he thought of the war in Europe, and he had replied, "We are well out of it."

So, Morisot thought to himself—'*Lebrun was in favour of continued American neutrality.*' This was the position of Vichy France, whose masters the Nazis would do anything to keep the United States for throwing its military and industrial power on the side of Britain and its imperial allies.

Still, Morisot agonised. Was he right about Lebrun? In fact, was he right to be concerned in the first place? He was an artist—not a political analyst. But he was also a decorated French patriot, and the very existence of Vichy France was an outrage to him. At a dinner party in Locust Valley, he met a young man called John Warner who was serving in naval intelligence in Washington. After dinner, he had a chance to talk to him about the war.

"Of course, our eyes are on what's happening in the Pacific and Japan's aggressive follow-on after its invasion of China," remarked the young man, "but the European situation is linked. Everything is linked these days; I can tell you— as it's not formally classified, we have a source in Tokyo. He's a Soviet spy under cover as a Nazi German journalist and he's monitoring Japanese intentions against the Soviet Union, but also following the increasing chummy relations between Nazi Germany and the Japanese military. On the face of it, he is encouraging it as a German reporter. He thinks Germany might encourage Japan to attack British interests in the Pacific, to assist a Nazi victory over Britain. He tells us the main role of Vichy France's representatives in the US is to keep us neutral—out of the war in Europe. It's a dangerous game for everybody."

Morisot listened to this with fascination to young Warner. It was his first exposure to the geo-politics behind the war in Europe—which he thought of in narrow French interest.

Surely, if Lebrun was connected with any covert activity of Vichy to help the Nazis against Britain, America's oldest friend in Europe and the headquarters of the de Gaulle and the Free French, he Morisot as a Free French patriot must do something but—what? He had not forgotten Madame Labouchère and her presumed dead husband von Guttenberg and was reminded when a gossiping portrait subject asked him what he knew about the lady—a regular companion of Lebrun.

One day, during a discussion about his obsession with Datskevich, his friend suggested that a possible source of information about von Guttenberg might be one of the many German actors who had fled to Hollywood due to Jewish origins or some other anti-Nazi regime activity.

"That's an idea," said Morisot. "I don't know any German actors—I don't know many Germans in general. But I do know Jean Renoir who has arrived recently—and also Marcel Dalio who worked with him on *La Regle du Jeu.*"

It did not take long to reach Jean Renoir in Los Angeles.

"Bonjour Pierre—cher ami ! Alors ça marche—les portraits?" Renoir was affable. As the son of the great impressionist, he took an interest in artists.

"Von Guttenberg? Doesn't mean a thing to me. I take it you have good reason for not checking through the German consulate. I'll call Fritz Lang. He was very active in Berlin until he left in disgust. Did you know Goebbels offered him the top job in the German film industry? Yes! He called him to announce he was banning his latest film and then, cool as a cucumber, offered him a job. *Quel toupé!* You know, we stay away from politics now that we are in this blessed country—but Fritz may know if your man had anything to do with the regime."

Morisot waited, somewhat on tender hooks and wondering if his suspicions were gaining currency and might be talked about. But, once again he began a vigil in a coffee shop opposite the dress designer on 92nd Street. He soon noticed that the severe lady he had met seemed to have few customers. Another lady seemed to come and go. She might be a client having fittings.

But then, suddenly as Morisot was paying for his coffee and doughnut, a taxi drove up and Auguste Lebrun stepped out. But he did not go immediately to the door of the house. Morisot shrunk back out of sight and watched Lebrun walk to the end of the block and then back, before finally entering the house. Morisot did not wait but walked himself to Lexington Avenue where he hailed a cab.

Morisot was excited once again. He considered, very briefly, making another visit to the place on 92nd Street on some pretext but decided against it. He could not think of a credible excuse for a further visit and—if there was something irregular about these visits of Lebrun, he would not want to reveal his interest. But was there something false about that establishment? Even the German consul's wife might be a client after all.

It was months later when Morisot received a call from Fritz Lang.

"Monsieur Morisot? You speak English I hope—my French is terrible," said Lang.

"Of course," Morisot replied.

"Jean has been talking to me, but I have been on location which is why I am late getting back to you."

"It's no problem—I told Jean my enquiry was not urgent."

"In that case, I am in New York next week and invite you to lunch at the Algonquin on, say, Wednesday, when I can tell you all about Freiherr von Guttenberg."

"That's perfect—it will be my treat. Shall we say 1 o'clock?"

"Fine—I'll be wearing a red carnation and carrying a copy of *Variety*—I'm joking! I've been shooting a spy movie. Renoir tells me you are a portrait painter. You won't want to do me; I am very ugly."

"Ha ha! I only paint ladies! See you then."

The Algonquin had been host to the famous literary circle in the 1920s which included Dorothy Parker and Robert Benchley. But being quite close to Broadway, it remained popular with the 'showbiz' crowd. The head waiter pointed out Lang to Morisot, who certainly did not find him ugly. He wore a monocle in his left eye which immediately created a sort of bond between them.

"You remind me of Adolphe Menjou. Monsieur Morisot," remarked Lang.

"Please!—it's Pierre. I have met his wife Verree Teasdale, as I painted a friend of hers."

"She is great fun," said Lang.

They each had a dry martini and had just given their orders to the waiter when a very elegant lady came up to the table and greeted Lang. Both men rose.

"Kate! How lovely to see you. And congratulations! Metro must be over the moon," said Lang, as he kissed her on both cheeks. "This is Pierre Morisot, the portrait painter. Pierre meet Katherine Hepburn. What a subject she would make for you—eh?"

Miss Hepburn laughed as she extended a hand. "Oh, I have heard of Monsieur Morisot—I couldn't possibly afford his fee."

"That's a problem I have securing commissions—everyone thinks I am more expensive than I actually am," said Morisot.

"The studios think the same thing about me," said Hepburn, "but please, sit down, gentlemen—I must run. How long are you here for, Fritz?"

"I'm back on the Coast next week."

"So am I. We'll get together. Nice to meet you, Monsieur Morisot—happy painting!"

"A remarkable woman, *la* Hepburn," said Lang, as the star walked away with a mannish stride. "She hawked her *Philadelphia Story* project all over town before settling on Metro. I have to say, I suggested Jimmy Stewart to Cukor, and he was sceptical at first."

This movie talk was rather over Morisot's head, but to remain on the subject out of courtesy, he asked how his friend Marcel Dalio was doing in Hollywood.

"Oh, poor Marcel! He and Madelaine Lebeau had a terrible time getting into the States via Mexico. But he will do just fine. He has Renoir behind him, of course. Marcel will be handed character roles in profusion. I would love to find something to give him a lead. He is a truly fine actor."

No sooner were they about to begin on the main purpose of the lunch when Douglas Fairbanks, Jr walked over to their table.

"Fritz! I didn't know you were in town. Scouting for talent on Broadway?" he said. "And Morisot, we have met before with Jock Whitney at Belmont Park."

All shook hands. After various pleasantries were exchanged, Fairbanks left and Fritz Lang said, "Perhaps this wasn't the best idea for our lunch. There are too many people here I know—but perhaps we won't be disturbed again."

"Ah! You are a celebrity!" said Morisot, "you are probably accosted everywhere. But let me give you a bit more background than perhaps you had from my friend Jean Renoir. I am interested in von Guttenberg because he is believed to have been the husband of a Madame Labouchère and I am interested in that lady because she is the very permanent companion of a man called Auguste Lebrun. And my interest in that gentleman has to do with complicated French politics which I will not bore you with. I assume our talk is confidential?"

"Absolutely!" Lang assured him, "and you will be surprised at the coincidence which puts me, rather unusually, in a position to give you some information you might not get anywhere. But you could get this information out of the Almanac de Gotha. Karl Ludwig von Guttenberg married a Princess Schwarzenberg. He was never married to Yvonne Laouchère. She was his mistress. You won't find that in the Gotha! And not many knew it because Karl Ludwig was a staunch Catholic—and a monarchist politically and so it was all very discreet. Why do I know it? Because Yvonne Labouchère was a stage-struck lady keen to get into films and I auditioned her in Berlin sometime around 1935 or 36. She was Belgian but fluent in German—very beautiful and well-educated. She was writing a book on Goethe. I had people who ran checks on anyone who approached us. We had to. Goebbels kept a keen eye on our film industry. He was certain we could be used to spread his horrible propaganda. Do you know he tried to recruit me to run the film business as part of his department? And this was after he had banned my latest film! *Ausdruch Fick dich!* I told him. Actually, of course, I didn't; do you know German? That's something beginning with 'F'. But I thought it.

"Anyway, back to Karl Ludwig—they are a Bavarian family, by the way—from Franconia. He was chummy with Kurt von Schliechen. They had been war buddies. Von Schliechen was briefly the last Chancellor before Hitler took over.

He was a political acrobat, switching sides all the time. But he was mostly anti-Hitler and at one point he and von Guttenberg had a scheme to put Prince Ruprecht as a sort of benevolent dictator in Bavaria, to counter Hitler's growing political base there. Not as king, although Ruprecht was actually the Crown Prince—because the Socialists would not have accepted that. Still, Hitler considered it treacherous and when he had all the SA leaders assassinated in '34, he included a bunch of other enemies such as von Schliechen. Now von Guttenberg was arrested, but he was not killed like his friend and was released. Still, he turns up on lists of victims. I believe he is now serving in the Navy. If Yvonne claims she was married to him, it may have been to ease getting a visa for here—as Karl Ludwig is definitely anti-Nazi. I knew him slightly."

Morisot was dumbfounded. He was also overwhelmed with gratitude.

"What you have told me is of great importance. I will repeat it to know one—but I may ask you confirm it sometime in the future."

"Delighted to at any time," said Lang.

They parted with many assurances of some future meeting. Morisot took his time thinking about this extraordinary story. He wanted to relate it to Ivan Datskovich—but he had promised to tell no one. But it would certainly seem that Lebrun's relationship with Madame (who apparently should be Mademoiselle) Labouchère was no confirmation of any pro-Nazi leanings.

Still, Morisot could not shake off his suspicions. He had the impression that Lebrun's pro-Vichy stance was vaguely known by the Long Island society he now frequented, but no one seemed particularly fussed by it. After all many—French and non-French, held the view that Petain had saved at least part of France and its overseas empire, from German occupation. And the State Department must be happy that Vichy's obvious allegiance to Germany does not constitute a threat to American interests as the US still maintains diplomatic relations with Petain's regime.

Morisot discussed his doubts frequently with Datskevich—without disclosing all he now knew about Lebrun's lady friend.

"Allons enfants de la patrie," Datskevich, quietly sang the first line of the Marseillaise at lunch one day at *Le Veau d'Or.* "You French! You cannot decide which are the true children of the *patrie* and which are the traitors. I feel for you all. Of course, I am for the Free French and would fight with them if I was young and able to. But allow me to remind you that if Clemenceau had not been obsessed with revenge for the defeat of 1870, we might not have that mad,

trumped-up Austrian corporal at all! The reparations in the Treaty of Versailles, destroyed the German economy, humiliated the people, and laid the path for Hitler."

"I cannot disagree with you," said Morisot.

"But you know, cher ami, I blame von Bismarck for the whole thing," continued Datskevich.

"Bismarck?"

"Yes, Bismarck! When Germany was a collection of principalities, dukedoms, etc., at the heart of the Holy Roman Empire, it was a race of gentle, civilised people, perhaps the most important contributors to our Western civilisation—after the French, I know you will say. We had so many Baltic Germans in St Petersburg—everywhere in Russia. They were marvellous. But when those pesky Prussians took over the whole show—everything changed."

Morisot always enjoyed his lunches with Datskevich, even if he thought his historical perspectives were sometimes eccentric. But he also kept in touch with John Warner in Washington.

"We're anxious about the Vichy assets in North Africa, air and ground. The Brits have broken with Vichy after destroying the French fleet at Mers-el-Kebir," explained Warner.

"De Gaulle was not best pleased himself," commented Morisot.

"We know. Confidentially, we advised against it. But Churchill thought the risk the fleet would fall into German hands was just too great. North Africa is the main ball game for the Brits. Its Egypt and Suez, the route to India."

As the year of our Lord 1941 ran its fateful course, America remained calm and enjoying a strong economic rebound after the depression years. Morisot became very active, and his social circles widened as commissions poured in. He was certainly the portraitist of choice for the ladies in the Social Register and— under pressure from some lady subjects, he had also painted one or two husbands.

As to Auguste Lebrun, he saw him from time to time in large social gatherings, invariably with the Labouchère woman. He felt it was generally recognised that Lebrun was pro-Vichy and not an admirer of de Gaulle. Morisot also kept in touch with John Warner and was speaking to him in June, after Germany invaded the Soviet Union.

"We always knew the Molotov/von Ribbentrop pact was phony," explained Warner. "The Reds were gaining time to build up their military. But there were secret accords on dividing up Eastern Europe between them. But you will be interested in North Africa. So are we. It seems, some Vichy units there, are switching over to the Brits. Your friend de Gaulle and his people are busy there. In Syria, there are clashes between Vichy and Free French."

All of this was music to Morisot's ears. An entire symphony was soon to drown all before it. The weekend of December 6th and 7th saw Morisot staying with the Auchinclause's in Locust Valley. He had just delivered the portrait of his hostess. All were unaware of rumblings in Washington. Apparently, the Japanese Embassy had a document in preparation and had made an appointment with Secretary of State Cordell Hull. Morisot discovered later that his friend John Warner was one of the few in military and naval intelligence who knew about this—as they had microphones planted in the Japanese Embassy.

Early on the morning of Sunday, 7 December, Japanese carrier-based aircraft attacked Pearl Harbour in Hawaii and destroyed the bulk of the U.S. Navy fleet based there. Fortunately, the U.S. carriers were all at sea on training exercises. Roosevelt termed it 'a day of infamy' as he addressed Congress, who approved a declaration of war against the Japanese Empire. Germany, according to a treaty with Japan, declared war on the United States. Some weeks later, Morisot was talking to John Warner.

"Well, we've incarcerated all German citizens living here. Of course, most are entirely innocent but still must be investigated. But we've also grabbed what can only be described as a nest of spies in various places—the biggest in New York of course. And we've caught some Americans who were working with them."

"Have you arrested Auguste Lebrun?" asked Morisot—his heart in his throat.

"Auguste Lebrun? Certainly not!" said Warner.

"But why not?"

"Why not? Because he's one of us—he's been working for us all along and he has been crucial in identifying the biggest control group that were operating out of a house on 92nd Street. They were supposed to be supplying Berlin with info on American shipping. We started feeding them false information months ago."

"Auguste Lebrun is working for U.S. Intelligence?" Morisot was almost speechless.

"Yes, we recruited him in Casablanca. His mission was to pose as pro-Vichy and penetrate Nazi espionage circles here. He did a fabulous job and took in that lot on 92nd Street completely. Apparently, they awarded him an Iron Cross! Now I think de Gaulle is going to decorate him. We're arranging for him to be received at the White House."

In the New Year, Morisot lunched with Ivan Datskevich at *Le Veau d'Or*.

"Mon cher ami! Thank you for not saying 'I told you so,'" he said, as he attacked his *cervelle au beur noir.*

"But I didn't say I thought Lebrun was a secret American agent," countered his friend. "I just suggested you should not jump to conclusions."

"Well, I am certainly going to stick to painting portraits. How could I be so wrong about a compatriot!"

"I take it you are now friends?"

"Oh yes! We see each other often. He tells me the toughest thing was having to dance attendance on Gaston Henry-Heye, the Vichy Ambassador—without telling him what he was up to."

"And Madame Labouchère?"

"Yvonne? She is charming and beautiful! Auguste has commissioned a portrait of her. We are great friends. I have been careful not to mention Fritz Lang to her."

"Fritz Lang?" said Datskevich. "Why Fritz Lang?"

"Ah, *mon ami*—that is a matter I am not at liberty to disclose."

Morisot took a sip of his *Chateau Neuf du Pape*, glanced about the room, and tried to look as much like a secret agent as possible.

FINIS

The Fifth Commandment

It would seem that contentious relations between fathers and sons are more common than is the case with mothers and daughters. Certainly, this is borne out in literature and drama, but I cannot quote reliable statistics to prove it in general. Nor can I offer a credible explanation as to why this should be so. It may be yet another characteristic of the masculine personality—that much-abused theory about testosterone and its influence on behaviour. The cultural heritage of primogeniture benefiting the eldest male child—now much in disfavour, may be a factor. The father has higher expectations of the son than the mother might have of the daughter and is therefore more easily disappointed. But let's face it— perhaps it's just that men have a greater tendency to row than do the ladies.

A striking example of this phenomenon could be observed within the upper echelons of Boston society. Perhaps the circumstances were unusual, but it was clear relations between Nathaniel Whitmore Senior and his only son—also named Nathaniel, were strained even before the lad reached a conscious age. The wife and mother, named Adelaide, née Underwood, had died in childbirth—and this had not predisposed the father to regard his son with favour. His period of woeful mourning had buried this underlying sentiment, as the baby—Nathaniel Underwood Whitmore had been whisked away to be reared by Nanny and Aunt Sophie, Adelaide's only sister and sole sibling.

Nathaniel Senior had adored his wife to distraction. She had been the be all and end all, of his life. Hailing from one of Boston's ancient and premier families, there had been a distinct social divide between Adelaide and Nathaniel, whose whirlwind romance had culminated in elopement and the disapproval of the bride's family. Grandfather Whitmore had been a modest shipwright in Marblehead whose son had built a fortune with a fishing fleet and canneries. For the Underwoods—Adelaide's family, the Marblehead millionaire's son and heir, although Harvard-educated and member of a final club, still smelled of fish.

The couple had met at Cambridge, as Adelaide Underwood was a Radcliffe girl. Nathaniel's good looks and easy charm, plus Adelaide's beauty and poise had marked them out as a glamorous and fashionable couple in Boston society—whatever the Underwood clan might mutter in private. Many observed, with mixed feelings, that the intensity of their love affair had continued well after the nuptial celebrations, which had gathered Boston's 400. In that old and traditional city, the passion of gilded youth was supposed to be somewhat contained even in courtship, but for it to continue into young married life was thought generally to be—well, somewhat vulgar. But Nathaniel seemed heedless of this accepted discretion and lavished affectionate and sometimes almost lascivious, caresses on his wife in public. It was also noted that his considerable intake of celebratory libations, if justified at the wedding, hardly abated as the two settled into married life.

In fact, the Underwoods began suggesting to a widening circle of friends, that Nathaniel might well be alcoholic. One must know Boston society to appreciate the gravity of such an accusation—as the puritan traditions, still much in evidence in New England, are sadly punctuated by a good deal of alcoholism.

The Whitmore's remained childless for some years, and this was ascribed to various causes. Some thought Nathaniel's obsessive and possessive love for his wife kept him from accepting any possible dilution of her reciprocal affection. In other words, he wanted her all for himself alone. Others noted that his drinking, now more evident, made him violent at times—and this might even cause interruptions of normal marital relations. The curious are so often given to extreme conclusions in their observations.

Nevertheless, truth lurked behind the less generous thinking of friends and family. The marriage was under strain. Adelaide's sister Sophie—still unmarried and inclined to misandry, was quick to notice it.

"You must know there's something wrong, Ady," said Sophie, as they drove home from shopping. "Look at the way he behaved at the Wilson's the other night. He was already tight when we went into dinner and after—well! I thought he was going to strangle that silly girl."

"He was tired and that silly girl, as you rightly call her, was goading him," replied Adelaide.

"But he's 'tired' a good deal of the time—and that doesn't stop him from being violent."

"Alice Smith is a typical flirt. When she doesn't seem to be getting anywhere, she starts trying to pick a fight. That's what she was up to at the Wilson's. I saw her before dinner—all cosying up and lovey-dovey. When Nat wouldn't play, she turned on him."

"Well, I don't want to pry Ady, but I can't help being worried for you. I know we've talked about this before—but childish sounds from the nursery are the best marriage music."

"And I've explained before, Sophie—Nat says he doesn't feel ready to be a father. I can't tell you how often we've discussed this. I don't understand it—but there it is."

The two sisters continued to have similar exchanges for some while—and Nathaniel's behaviour continued to raise concerns. But then, quite suddenly, Adelaide announced she was pregnant, and Nathaniel's conduct turned from boisterous affection to gentle and solicitous tenderness. Sophie felt justified and pronounced the cautious opinion that Nathaniel might be a changed man. He had no settled occupation at this time and was under no financial pressure to find one. He played golf and polo at Myopia—the latter hobby having led to a first lapse in faithfulness with a girl groom.

In fact, he had received warnings from the committee and was now quite widely regarded as a 'bad actor'. But he seemed now a changed man and began frantic preparations for the coming event. He supervised a thorough makeover of some rooms in their house in Wellesley as a nursery suite and equipped them with every comfort and baby-friendly gadgetry.

As it was not yet possible in those days to determine an embryo's sex, Nathaniel went on a toy-buying spree in anticipation of either eventuality. Pink and blue cribs, rocking horses and dolls houses—no alternative plaything, game or decoration was spared. Adelaide could not help reflecting that all this confirmed her suspicion that Nathaniel was far more given to extremes in his comportment than she had noticed at first.

"I think it's almost *maladif!*" observed Sophie.

"It's better than chasing girl grooms at Myopia," countered Adelaide.

"Agreed—but, honestly Ady, don't you think it's 'over the top'? Has anyone suggested Nat might see a psychoanalyst?"

"Good grief! I wouldn't like to be in the same room when anyone suggested that to Nathaniel!"

Adelaide certainly had learned to treat her sister's concerns over her husband as essentially a reflection of a general aversion to men and their 'nasty habits'—as Sophie would often say. But she could not but feel, in her heart of hearts, that her husband was not what he had seemed to be as a lover/fiancé in those palmy days in Cambridge academia.

It might well be drink-related, but Nathaniel did show signs of both extreme and even violent behaviour. An unexpected circumstance never seemed to prompt even a moment's reflection, but, on the contrary, some unthinking and extreme reaction would result—confounding Adelaide's instinctive desire to help and accommodate. And friends found it difficult to sympathise when condolence would normally be due.

Although frequent examinations by Boston's most eminent gynaecologist had suggested no possible complications for the sound thirty-year-old that was Adelaide—tragedy struck. A healthy male child was delivered, but haemorrhaging could not be contained, and the mother was dead. Nathaniel's grief was extreme—as all expected it would be. But it was not witnessed for long, as the bereft father soon disappeared to an unknown destination.

Efforts to trace him by family and lawyers failed entirely. Sophie moved into the Whitmore homestead in Wellesley, with the nanny and two nursery maids which had already been engaged and formally assumed responsibility for the child's upbringing.

"You can't sacrifice your own life forever, Sophie," said Mrs Underwood to her surviving daughter.

"Nathaniel is bound to come back soon, Mama."

"Not if I know that brute—he does everything to extremes."

At this juncture, the senior family lawyer decided his intervention should become more active. Family honour was at stake. What were the implications of Sophie simply assuming domicile at the Whitmore homestead without the consent of her brother-in-law—now apparently unreachable? And how were the considerable financial assets of the grieving but absent father to be accessed?

Francis Bramwell, Esq, of the venerable firm of Bramwell, Bramwell & Brief regarded Sophie as a somewhat flighty, man hating spinster—hardly qualified to oversee the upbringing of young Nathaniel Underwood Whitmore. But he quickly ascertained that finance was not a problem as Grandfather Whitmore, he of the fishing fleet and canneries, had established a generation skipping trust fund. The only son was a trust fund baby.

"But, my dear Sophie, what will you say about the father when the young lad begins to enquire?" intoned Francis Bramwell, with a frown.

"My dear Francis, shall we take that hurdle when occasion requires? And that nasty man might be back by then." Sophie sniffed at the very mention of her favourite bugbear.

"The bankers are tight-lipped about how and where he is drawing funds. I have argued that circumstances override private bank confidentiality, but to no avail. We must also consider the contingency that Nathaniel Whitmore may never return."

"Good riddance to bad rubbish," exclaimed Sophie.

It could hardly be said that Sophie was over jealous in her role. On the contrary, it would be more accurate to state that she outsourced the upbringing of young Nathaniel to a succession of Irish nannies and nursery maids. Despite their efforts, the child was dour and taciturn. At early play school, proscribed by Sophie to avoid interfering with her social lunches and bridge parties, the lad did not mix easily with his peers.

At a prep school, prior to entering the sound Episcopalian halls of Groton, he was aloof and unpopular with students and masters. But scholastically he was very advanced and able to skip a year, entering his secondary school at 14. By this time, Nathaniel junior had grown in physical resemblance to his father. Tall, of athletic build and graceful movement, his features recalled his father's—but his expression was entirely different.

Whereas Nathaniel senior wore a jaunty look at most times, with a mesh of blonde hair bouncing on his forehead, his son maintained a look of contentious severity and his blond hair was slicked back and firmly in place. At Groton his aloofness worsened, and he began to adopt attitudes hardly appropriate for his age—disapproving of the hilarity of teenage play, critical of lapses in ordained behaviour and all the panoply of youthful indiscretions a fecklessness. In fact, he had become a bore, made no friends and dismayed Sophie whose gregarious nature was the exact opposite of her ward's.

"Nat, my dear, why don't you have some friends over for tennis and tea this afternoon. It's a glorious day and you can't just sit around during your holidays," said Sophie, one summer morning, as she was arranging flowers in the study.

Young Nathaniel looked up from his book. "I have no friends, Aunt Sophie."

"What on earth do you mean? What about your schoolmates?"

"All they think about is having a good time."

"But surely that's what you should think about at your age. There will be plenty of time to get serious, my pet."

"I'm serious now and that's what I want to be—and Aunt Sophie, I'm no one's pet—if you don't mind. Thank you."

Sophie put down her remaining flowers and stared at Nathaniel in amazement.

"Well, I never! You are an odd child. I'm trying to be family for you. I know you are grown up, but young people should be cheerful before taking on the cares of later years."

"I know all about that kind of cheerfulness," said Nathaniel, adopting an angry tone. "I know my father was cheerful and broke everyone's heart and then ran away. I don't want to be like that."

"How do you know that about your father? He loved your mother. Is anything wrong with that?" Sophie was always uncomfortable when the subject of her brother-in-law came up. This was very rarely in the Underwood family. Certainly, Nathaniel had been brought up to believe that his father was permanently far away and perhaps even remarried.

"Oh, they talk about him at school! I know he was a drunk and unfaithful to my mother, that's why you and Grandmama never mention him." Nathaniel picked up his book, seeking to close the conversation.

Sophie was equally reluctant to pursue the subject. Nathaniel's curiosity about his father had increase dramatically with his attendance at boarding school. The story of Nathaniel senior's mysterious and sudden disappearance was well entrenched in the gossip catalogue of Boston society.

As Francis Bramwell had predicted, pressure to supply some narrative grew with the son's years. He had even called at the family lawyer's office seeking information about his father's whereabouts—and general views on his character and history. And it was distinctly Bramwell's impression that the boy had no wish to emulate any aspect of his father's personality but, on the contrary, wished to know more to oppose it—not match it.

The growing concern of Sophie, Bramwell and the Underwood clan in general on how to cope with this inevitable development in the rearing of young Nat Whitmore was resolved—or one might rather say, exacerbated by a sudden and momentous event. Nathaniel Whitmore senior re-appeared after a fifteen-year absence. Francis Bramwell was sitting in his office one September morning when his secretary entered, looking unusually flustered.

"Mr Bramwell! Someone claiming to be Nathaniel Whitmore has called asking to speak to you! I have said we would call back. He's staying at the Ritz-Carlton Hotel in room 104 and 5. What shall I do?"

"Call him back. Miss Appleby—call him back, of course!" Francis Bramwell smiled, indicating his judicial experience and worldly knowledge always anticipated such an event. "Never seem surprised" was his professional motto.

"Olla! Francis, you old sinner—how are the briefs? Still flowing in?" This was the greeting the venerable advocate heard when he was put through to Nathaniel Whitmore's suite at the Ritz. '*Same Nathaniel*,' he thought to himself. '*that silly play on words over my firm's name.*'

"Where on earth have you been, Nathaniel? No! Save that for a meeting, I must see you as soon as possible." Francis attempted a stern tone—which always failed when he was talking to this client.

"What about lunch in my suite here at 1 o'clock? Shall I order you a dry martini, straight up with a twist? You see—my memory is pristine."

Over lunch, Nathaniel told his story. He had gone to Argentina. One of the professionals who came to Myopia for the summer polo season had been his first point of contact.

Then, downing most of the bottle of Chablis, he described the *estancia* he had bought 'for peanuts!', the *petisero* (groom) he engaged, the horses he bought and broke, the *gauchos* on the estate, the *asados* (picnics of roasted lamb), the gallops across the pampas hunting hare, the polo at Hurlingham, the tango night clubs of BSA, the girls of easy virtue, the neighbours of suspicious German origin, the deer stalking and the skiing at Bariloche, the sunsets over the Andes, the resort town of Mar del Plata. He concluded that he had had a 'thundering' good time.

Francis Bramwell feigned rapt attention, but throughout he was thinking; '*is Nathaniel still a light-headed playboy or has he grown up in the last decade and a half?*' He was inclined to the first premise.

"Have you been in touch with Sophie," he asked.

"Not yet," replied Nathaniel. "But she needn't worry—I'm not going to move in at Wellesley; she can keep the house, I won't charge her rent, ha! ha! After all, I suppose the boy is still there."

"But you will go and see your son? He is well-grown and resembles you."

"In every way? I wonder! Well—certainly I will go and see the lad. Is he at school?"

"He is in his second year at Groton." Francis noted the father hardly seemed impatient to see a son he had abandoned 15 years ago.

Francis Bramwell felt uneasy after this first meeting with the returning prodigal father but offered any assistance needed, on the assumption Nathaniel planned to remain and they parted somewhat cooly.

"Where are you going to go?" asked a relieved Sophie when Nathaniel paid his first call on his sister-in-law.

"Oh, I'll find a little place—probably near Myopia. I've got some horses coming from Argentina."

"What about Nat? Shall he stay here with me—of course, with you over his holidays?"

"Naturally! Why disturb the boy? He can do what he likes for school breaks."

"I'm sure you're anxious to see him," said Sophie, thinking to herself that Nathaniel had expressed no such sentiment so far. "There's a parents' thing at Groton next weekend—shall we go down together?"

"Great idea!" replied Nathaniel. "And by the way, I haven't said how grateful I am for all you've done—looking after him, you know—almost mother, in fact. After Ady died, I just couldn't—you know, I was a broken man—as they say. I don't suppose anyone understands."

And in fact, few did—but few had sympathised with Nathaniel Whitmore in the agitated years that had preceded Adelaide's death and his debunking. "What a nerve! Just turning up like that—without a by your leave," declaimed old Mrs Underwood.

Nathaniel and Sophie met first with the headmaster on their arrival at Groton. He described Nat as old for his years, an outstanding student, but strangely humourless and not popular with the other boys. "He's missed a father, I must tell you frankly," said the headmaster.

Nathaniel senior frowned. Their meeting with young Nat was hardly a success, despite Sophie's valiant effort to make it seem like a celebratory reunion.

"Hello," had said Nat.

"Hello, Father—I rather think!" had countered Nathaniel.

"Sorry—I am hardly accustomed to that expression," said the boy—sulking slightly.

"Dr Roydon says you're really good at tennis—you'll be on the senior squad!" said Sophie, trying to sound jolly and positive.

"He has to say something," said Nat.

"But do you like it here?" enquired his father.

"It's OK."

The interview hardly warmed beyond this level. In the car driving back, Nathaniel said, "That boy has ice water in his veins!"

"What can you expect? The boy doesn't know you at all. You are a complete stranger!" Sophie was exasperated.

She had forebodings for the future. Nat had never been an outgoing and affectionate boy and his father seemed unaware of the obvious challenge inherent in the circumstances of the long separation. How on earth were the two going to establish anything approaching a normal father/son relationship? They were chalk and cheese—Nathaniel was a 'good time Charlie' and his son Nat was—to put it frankly, a 'nerd'.

At first, Nathaniel made an effort. He took up residence at a cottage in South Hamilton near the Myopia Club and spent the first of his son's school summer holidays trying to teach him ride. He had decided that joint equestrian pursuits would serve to bind father and son. His horses had arrived from Argentina, and he went about his tutorial task with gusto and dedication. A *petissero* called Manuel had come with the horses; he took a liking to the lad and happily joined in the effort. And effort it was.

Nat was not a natural horseman, resisted attempts to make him a reluctant horseman and much preferred spending his time on the grass tennis courts at the club where his prowess earned him a reputation. Rather than a source of pride for Nathaniel senior, he resented his son's new popularity. He soon abandoned his efforts regarding his son and took to playing his own polo in a wild and rumbustious fashion, producing complaints of unsportsmanlike like conduct. This further alienated young Nat and by the end of the summer holidays, Nat returned to school no longer on speaking terms with his father.

Rather than seeking fresh conciliatory initiatives from a long absent father to an introverted son, Nathaniel resumed a careless and dissipated lifestyle himself—which further separated him from his strict and rather puritanical offspring. His drinking increased and with it characteristic bouts of violence. Incidents on the polo field brought censure from the Committee and he was banned from play form the rest of the season, the *petissero* went home.

Young Nat, who was much at the club playing tennis, was angry and mortified. Sophie's efforts to mediate between the two were fruitless; young Nat absolutely refused to speak to his father and the latter insulted his sister-in-law when drunk.

Now shunned by the Boston society in which he had grown up, Nathaniel senior took to what he liked to describe as 'a bit of harmless slumming'. This involved an increasing presence in the less salubrious sectors of downtown Boston. But it also led to drunken brawls in Irish bars and appearances before the magistrates. Francis Bramwell was called on to represent him and try to mitigate the penalties involved.

These soon included an occasional short imprisonment, in addition to fines and some publicity—further horrifying young Nat. Now at Harvard and to no one's surprise, he applied immediately for the Divinity School and proceeded to try and gain a BA at the college in three years to qualify for its graduate programme. "What a wimp!" said his father to Sophie, on learning of this.

"And what a useless father you are!" replied Sophie. They were meeting for tea at the Ritz, at Sophie's request, she had not given up entirely. Nathaniel was drinking whiskey and soda.

"I know where I could find him a girl," said Nathaniel with a leer. "That's what the boy needs."

"And I know the kind of girl you have in mind," said Sophie.

"So, what!—I can tell you; I find them a greater comfort than Radcliffe girls!"

Worse was to follow. Nathaniel took up with a blowsy and vulgar widow called Mrs Bridget O'Day (no relation to the jazz singer Anita). Her husband, with a lengthy police record, had been killed in a bar-room altercation—in his own establishment, which had been inherited by his wife. She was jolly and promiscuous, having no doubt practised as a professional in her early years; she had a record for soliciting to prove it.

Nathaniel had become one of her regulars and they soon began to co-habit in her North End apartment. Proud of her conquest of a 'Beacon Hill-type'—as she termed her new paramour, she took it on herself to visit young Nat in his Eliot House rooms across the Charles River at Harvard. "Just to be friendly like," was her stated intention, as she described it to Nathaniel, the father—who she had not notified in advance.

But Mrs O'Day had hoped to effect some sort of reconciliation between father and son, having great confidence in her rather mature but still evident charms. The appearance of this platinum-haired floozy, in a décolleté just short of topless, certainly startled young Nat, who glanced up and down the dormitory corridor before letting her in—as good manners required. Describing Nathaniel Senior as her 'bosom pal'—thereby frustrating Nat's efforts to lift his eyes from her front, she began on her mission.

"Come on, Junior! How about making it up with your old man," she barked, flashing her stocking tops as she sat and crossed her legs. "He's a lot of fun when he's off the hard stuff and you could help me keep him on the wagon."

Young Nat was speechless.

"Listen! Come on down to us and we'll party big time! I've got a couple of gals who'll go for a good looker like you!"

Nat recovered his voice. "Madame. I appreciate the goodwill behind your visit, but I must inform you that I have no intention of reuniting myself with my father, whose style of life is at total variance with my own. You should know that I will soon be studying for ordination as an Episcopalian priest."

"Jesus 'n' Mary!" exclaimed the woman. "Does your own father know? He won't know whether to laugh or cry!"

"I can assure you that I have not the slightest interest in my father's opinion—who, let me assure you, has not the slightest interest in my own existence. Now, if you will excuse me, Madame. I have studying to do." Nat rose and walked to the door to open it.

"Well, I must say! You are a caution! But you sure as hell ain't no fun!" And Mrs O'Day flounced out.

Young Nat, in some shock at this visitation, called Francis Bramwell at his office.

"Is there nothing we can do about this dreadful woman?"

"I'm afraid not," replied the lawyer, "your father has got himself mixed up with some bad and even dangerous company. As you know I have had to represent him before the magistrates twice after serious incidents. I have warned him, as strictly as I can. He laughs it off in that most annoying, characteristic way."

"I suppose the police can do nothing until a crime is committed," said Nat—aware he was stating the obvious.

"It's more serious than just typical bar-room brawls. Mrs O'Day's establishment is at the centre of rivalry between the Irish and Italian criminal gangs, who fight over their territories where prostitution, protection rackets and other criminal activities are rife. Mr O'Day was a leader of the Irish *mafia.*"

"How horrible!" exclaimed poor Nat.

"If it were known that he was in touch with—even under the protection of some lawyer, his life could be in danger. They might suspect him of being an informer. I have had to tell him; I cannot come to his aid again—in the interest of his own protection."

Francis Bramwell paused, while there was silence from his interlocutor.

"Ahem—might you not speak with him?" His tone was hesitant.

"No! Certainly not! I will have no contact with my father as long as he continues to consort with that horrible woman. It is an affront to the memory of the mother I never knew."

Francis Bramwell could not help thinking that this was a singularly unchristian sentiment from a future student of divinity. But he decided that nothing could be gained by so remarking to the distressed son of his old friend and client.

Some weeks after Mrs O'Day's visit to young Nathaniel, that unfortunate lady had struck up an amorous relationship with a young Italian, son of one of the criminal gang chiefs. Perhaps Nathaniel's drinking was blunting his ability to satisfy the harridan's physical needs. When drunk at the bar of 'O'Day's Bar & Grill' in downtown Boston, Nathaniel was wont to refer to the young man—called Angelo Romiti, as "Bridget's Wop toyboy."

This already threatened to set off a fresh confrontation between the rival gangs. Mrs O'Day described herself and her new paramour as "conciliators." Perhaps to remove her from Angelo's influence, Nathaniel took to bringing Mrs O'Day to his cottage near Myopia at weekends. On one occasion, she insisted Nathaniel take her to dinner at the Myopia Club. Of course, he refused. Both had been drinking all day. A strenuous argument ensued. "I'm not smart enough for your Beacon Hill friends. You stuck up bastard!" and more in this style.

When Nathaniel stepped outside, Mrs O'Day telephoned Angelo and told him to come pronto. The argument continued to rage; Angelo turned up; fisticuffs followed; Angelo pulled a knife—a much bigger and fitter Nathaniel grabbed a cushion and pushed Angelo, knife and all, through a window. The young man decided discretion trumped valour and began to run to his car. Nathaniel, in one easy motion, grabbed his Purdy shotgun, stuffed in a single cartridge, and shot at the fleeing Italian, hitting him in the buttocks.

The police, summoned by Mrs O'Day, took all three into custody, but only Nathaniel was charged with assault with a deadly weapon and sentenced to 18 months prison. Angelo had suffered nothing more than some pellets in his backside. Francis Bramwell engaged a Boston-based trial lawyer who cited Angelo's knife as support for a self-defence plea. This failed, but the fact Nathaniel had only loaded one cartridge helped to remove the phrase "with intent to kill" from the charge.

The publicity surrounding this affair was wormwood to the Underwood clan and young Nat became even more hostile to his father, insisting Francis explore means of legally restraining his father for the future. But Francis Bramwell was well aware the situation was hopeless. There could be no grounds for involuntary commitment of Nathaniel to some sanatorium for the mentally disturbed and he was most unlikely to seek treatment willingly.

Of course, the now well-established estrangement between father and son might well account for the father's anti-social behaviour, but remedial action would now be too little and too late.

Francis visited his client in prison accompanied by a psychiatrist friend, but both were dismissed by Nathaniel with a torrent of abuse. Young Nat had categorically refused to even convey a message of consolation. On his release, Nathaniel resumed his dissolute ways. He was now spending most of his days at O'Day's Bar & Grill in Boston's North End. It was presumed he spent weekends at his cottage near Mypia but this was so isolated that no one could observe his comings and goings.

When Francis Bramwell enquired of the daily cleaner, she told him she had given notice after some drunken tirade from her employer. Nathaniel no longer frequented the club or saw any friends and acquaintances. It was as though he had dropped out without leaving the country.

And so when a few weeks later, a headline glared from the front page of the *Boston Globe*: "Society figure charged in North End Murder," the shock was profound. Those who eagerly read on were informed that, "Nathaniel Whitmore, aged 51, of South Hamilton, Mass has been charged with the first-degree murder of Mrs Bridget O'Day, the proprietor and licensee of O'Day's Bar & Grill in Hanover Street, North End."

The facts were simple—or so it seemed. Because of repeated calls to quell riots—prompted by internecine warfare between the rival gangs, the police had imposed a curfew of nine o'clock on O'Day's Bar & Grill. The establishment was frequented by both Irish and Italian contingents, as they often collaborated on major criminal 'capers', but still rival territorial claims over day-to-day prostitution and protection rackets persisted.

It had been a busy Saturday night. Witnesses reported the dispute over Angelo, Bridget O'Day's 'toyboy', still raged—with Nathanial expressing threats against the couple of an increasing severity, the drunker he became. The closing at 21:00 hours was supervised by the genial Irish cop on the local beat and he—and most witnesses, were prepared to swear having seen Nathaniel leave with the others, walk to his car, and drive away. But had he come back?

That block in Hanover Street was almost deserted by then and no one had seen him return. On Sunday morning, a maid coming to collect her wages before going to Mass, found the body of Bridget O'Day in her apartment above the establishment—which was reached by a separate staircase. A police surgeon opined she had been strangled and estimated the time of death as between 10 o'clock and 11 o'clock the previous evening—confirmation to await the autopsy.

The detective in attendance considered Angelo Romiti and Nathanial as prime suspects, but Angelo had not been present that evening, the police drove out to South Hamilton, found Nathaniel, and questioned him. He claimed an alibi but would not give any details. He was taken downtown and further questioned—with the threats he had uttered the night before and his recent conviction for violence deemed sufficient to charge him. He complied with the Miranda offer to silence and offered no further defence.

Nathaniel was held overnight in the Suffolk County Correctional Facility and visited first by Francis Bramwell and secondly by his son Nat, who was with him for a good half hour. Unbeknownst to anyone, young Nat immediately drove to his father's cottage in South Hamilton, made sure he left fresh tyre tracks in front and placed a crumpled note in the pocket of a tweed jacket, thrown casually on a chair in his father's bedroom.

On Monday morning, the young man returned to the police station where his father had been questioned and swore out a statement that his father had been with him in the South Hamilton cottage from 9:30 until around midnight on the Saturday evening. At the arraignment the next day, Nathanial was bound over for trial. The County prosecutor argued he should be held without bail in view of his previous conviction for violence.

The attorney who had represent him then, one James Gardiner, cited the alibi furnished by young Nathaniel and argued unsuccessfully for release under his own cognisance, pointing out the prisoner was unlikely to abscond before his son's evidence had been given under oath in court, as it was so clearly exculpatory. Nathaniel was transferred to the same prison in which he had been previously incarcerated.

The press had a field day. The case had all the sensational ingredients so beloved by the Third Estate: love and sex, violence, gang warfare, class distinctions, society dropouts. The Underwoods and their friends groaned in embarrassment and dismay. Neither Francis Bramwell nor young Nat visited the prison, leaving it to James Gardiner to prepare the defence with his client.

The veracity of the alibi provided by the suspect's son was a preoccupation of all concerned. The police had gone over Nathaniel's cottage in South Hamilton with the proverbial fine-tooth comb. The found and examined the tyre tracks, comparing them successfully with Nat's car—but could not determine their exact age. The found the crumpled note in the pocket of Nathaniel's tweed jacket. It read:

"Dear Father,

We must meet. It's time we talked. We cannot be divided forever. I am intending to join the priesthood. I must tell you why. I will come to you at your cottage at about nine o'clock this Saturday evening. Please be there.

Your son Nathaniel."

The handwriting checked; there was no envelope or date with the note.

Young Nathaniel was summoned for further questioning, with solemn warnings of the consequences of lying to the police. He refused to change a word of his sworn statement, His father had been at home when he called at about 9:30 on that fateful evening and they had remained talking until near mid night.

The questioning went on for hours.

Why had he suddenly decided to make up with his father after a lifetime of estrangement?

In preparing to begin at Divinity School he had been reflecting on Christian values, the Commandments and so forth.

When, where and how had he delivered the note?

On the Thursday. He had dropped by O'Day's Bar & Grill and left it in the tray by the hat and coat check booth.

Had anyone seen him?

He didn't know—he didn't talk to anyone; he knew his father spent most of the day there. He was bound to find the note or have it given to him.

138

Why didn't he just go in and find his father?

He didn't want their reunion to be in a public place.

Did anyone see him leave or return to his rooms at Eliot house on Saturday?

No. His roommate was away for the weekend.

Did he tell anyone he intended meeting with his father?

No—he could not be sure if the meeting would be successful.

What did they talk about?

Everything.

The questions were repeated *ad nauseum*, in typical police style. Young Nathaniel was unshakeable. Francis Bramwell held several meetings with him, and they were polite and courteous versions of the same questioning.

"You realise you will have to testify to all this under oath?" Francis insisted, close to losing patience.

"Of course," replied Nat. "I have already sworn to it."

"You know the penalties for perjury?"

"There is no point in bullying me, Mr Bramwell," said Nat, testily. "I have told my story and I am sticking to it!"

Francis did not believe him. James Gardiner did not believe him. The police did not believe him. But the jury did. They returned a verdict of not guilty. The trial was a sensation as one of the first in Massachusetts to be televised. Young Nat's performance was worthy of an Academy award. The State's Attorney General, as prosecutor, was warned several times by a sympathetic judge not to cajole the witness, Nathaniel senior was not called to testify.

Meanwhile, the police continued their efforts to find other suspects. Angelo Romiti had a watertight alibi. Various gang-related rivalries and personalities were examined. The circumstances surround the violent death of Mr O'Day were re-evaluated. All leads went nowhere. The police were not only frustrated, but they were also angry. They were certain Nathaniel Whitmore had murdered Bridget O'Day in a fit of jealous rage.

After his acquittal, Nathaniel left for Argentina where he sold his *estancia* and quietly drank himself to death. He had not bothered to contact his son before leaving and had no further communication with him whatever. Nathaniel Underwood Whitmore, who never put 'junior' after his name, was ordained a priest of the Episcopal church, and ministered to one fashionable congregation after another. He never married. Many years later, he had occasion to dine alone with a fast-ageing Francis Bramwell at the Somerset Club. They were at a quiet corner table. The conversation finally turned to the past.

"I have often wondered, my dear Nat, why you were willing to put your life and career at such extraordinary risk by committing perjury to save your most undeserving father."

Francis Bramwell took a sip of his wine and waited some moments for an answer.

The Reverend Nathaniel Underwood Whitmore smiled sweetly-

"The Fifth Commandment, my dear Francis—the Fifth Commandment!"

"But what about bearing false witness?"

"That is only the Ninth Commandment—I have taken them in order of importance." The Reverend Whitmore now adopted a serious mien, well known to his parishioners.

Francis Bramwell could not help thinking: '*once a nerd, always a nerd!*'

FINIS

The Gentle Tennis Pro

Massimo Balluzzi was a citizen of the Republic of San Marino, a tiny country of some 25 square miles, tucked away in the northeast corner of Italy. Founded by Saint Marinus in AD 301, it claims to be the world's oldest constitutional republic despite having a very imperial looking crown sitting atop its cost of arms. Its population is just over 33,000 and a good many will have served as one of the two co-heads of state, known as Captains Regent, as these are elected by the Grand and General Council for a six-month term.

One wonders what other business that legislature can have with head-of-state elections twice a year. Massimo Balluzzi was proud to have served a term as a Captain Regent whilst still in his 30s. He was even prouder to be a member of the Crossbow Corps, a military unit founded in the 13th century and consisting of 80 volunteers. Their duties are largely ceremonial—but then everything about San Marino is largely ceremonial, which accounts for its success as a tourist destination.

The Balluzzi are an old San Marino family—but then most families in this miniature republic could be so described. Massimo's main claim to fame was the five years he had spent as a professional football player with Lazio, the second team in Rome. His career had been closely followed and celebrated in San Marino and it was thought he had ended it prematurely. But Massimo had observed many players declining in speed and skill for having hung on for just a year or two too long.

On returning, he had quickly been engaged as a teacher and sports master at a leading secondary school. In that capacity, he turned out students who pursued sporting careers abroad in a larger number than the population of their home country might justify. Although San Marino had its own football team, its leading players were often tempted by greater financial rewards available with other Italian and foreign teams. But here it must be noted that for a San Marinian,

Italy was a foreign country. A unique language—Romangnol, was a second official language (or dialect—if you must) in San Marino.

When Massimo Balluzzi became immersed in San Marino's world of sport, he was surprised to find that an Olympic bronze medal had been won by a couple of compatriots in an unusual sport—trap shooting. The competition is divided between men, women and mixed—each having a different number of targets. Massimo had been aware the sport existed in San Marino—and also in Monte Carlo, where he had seen it when playing football there.

He decided to take it up—not with Olympic ambitions for himself but to train his son Antonio. He soon became adept and won some competitions at the club where skeet and trap shooting were practised.

Antonio was an only son who had lost his mother, virtually at childbirth. The beautiful Angelica had been discovered and courted by Massimo when she was an Alitalia stewardess, often on the flights from Milano to Rome, when Massimo was playing for Lazio. Sadly, the caesarean birth of Antonio had produced an infection and Angelica had responded to no antibiotic. Massimo's sister, married to a doctor, took charge of the baby, as the distraught father was still largely in Rome.

Naturally, Massimo doted on his son Antonio. Nothing could be or would be, too good for him. The lad had inherited his mother's looks and his father's frame and coordination. This was very satisfying and indicated sporting potential in general. Massimo soon took him to the trap shoot at the club having acquired a second 'over and under' shotgun made especially for trap shooting by the great makers Berretta. Massimo's very first lesson was the most important and its principle would stay with Antonio for the rest of his life.

"The first thing you must learn, *mio figlio*, is that in trap shooting you point— you do not aim. There is a big difference between pointing and aiming—and pointing is more natural. Let me show you." And Massimo held up the palm of his hand and began to move it around erratically.

"Now, put your forefinger against the middle of the palm of my hand with a light touch."

And Antonio began to do just that—and even as his father moved his hand faster and faster in all directions, he never failed to place his forefinger immediately and accurately.

"Perfect!" said Massimo, "and you see you are not looking at your finger, you are looking at the target—the palm of my hand."

Soon they were on the range with a friend at the control of the trap. And Antonio was instructed to say, "pull!" a few times without shooting—just to watch the flight of the clay pigeon.

"Now, imagine you have a rigid stick coming out of the barrels of your gun and you are going to tap it on the target and then pull the trigger," explained Massimo. "Shooting is in your mind—not in your arms and trigger finger. In fact, forget about the gun—concentrate entirely on the target."

And so the lesson went on and within a short time. Antonio matched his father's skill. Everything he heard, he retained. They talked these principles at home.

"When I was shooting at goal in my days at Lazio," said Massimo, "I wasn't looking at my foot or at the ball, I was looking at the side of the net. Shooting a penalty, the goalkeeper would just guess and lunge to one side. It was amazing how often he guessed wrong."

Massimo wasn't encouraging his son to take up football—although he was highly proficient on the school team. He had the Olympic trap shooting medal in mind. But soon it became clear that Antonio was going to go in an entirely different direction.

There were three tennis courts at the school; the girls used them rather more often than the boys. With a friend, Antonio began encroaching on the near-feminine monopoly of court usage. If the girls were the original attraction the game quickly took over. Antonio decided he had found his sporting niche. Massimo could but only encourage him.

And so Antonio played and played; he won the school tournament and then the inter-school tournament and then the junior national tournament and then the senior national tournament. At 17, he was San Marino's Number 1 with a ranking in the ITF (International Tennis Federation).

Observers noted his great speed on court and perfect footwork—but not all noticed an unusual aspect of his style. Quite simply, he was using the lesson his father had taught him. He found he could place his ball with extraordinary accuracy. He imagined a straight dotted line between his racquet and the spot on the opposing court and, instead of watching the ball as he struck it, he watched it incoming but in the last seconds, he took his eye off the ball and concentrated on the imaginary dotted line to the spot where he wanted his shot to land.

He did this with his serve and overhead smash. He also struck observers as having a seemingly casual attitude in tournament play. Massimo had found a retired tennis professional called Frederico Bellavista, who had worked in Italian country clubs teaching children, and he did his best to keep up with Antonio's meteoric rise.

"I don't know how he keeps his concentration," Frederico said to Massimo one day. "He seems to be dreaming half the time."

"That's his nature," said his father. "It all comes naturally to him."

"Let's hope that continues when he turns professional—which he should," responded Frederico.

And it happened quite soon. Antonio reached the quarterfinals of the Monte Carlo Open and was approached by a representative of IAM 360, a leading professional sports agency.

"We train you up and get you a sponsor," said the lady, a retired former champion, ridiculously called Miss Playfair.

"Ask you father and family lawyer if you like, to look over this contract."

"My father was a professional football player with Lazio," said Antonio, somewhat offended. "We don't need a lawyer to look over a sports contract."

"I am so sorry!" said Miss Playfair.

"What fees!" said Massimo, as he perused the 12-page document, "these people are certainly not cheap. But it's a percentage of your earnings, so they have every incentive."

And so it came to pass that Antonio went off to one of the many tennis camps in Florida—this one near Fort Lauderdale, where hopefuls from every corner of the globe undergo strenuous training. Now, Antonio had never been to boarding school and at first, he felt confused and intimidated by his new environment. As a good Catholic he was also shocked by the degree of promiscuity which existed amongst the student body despite very strictly separated quarters.

He was soon called 'Tony' and subjected to unexpected advances by a few of the girls. But his tennis skill level was quickly established, and this made him popular and was regarded with some awe. One of the more senior coaches took him in hand.

"But you are not looking at the ball when you strike it. You might have great instincts—but that's not right."

"But I don't need to see my racquet hit the ball," explained Antonio, "I need to see my target first."

"Well, let's see about targets," said the coach and he took several ball cannisters (which used to be made of tin but are now cardboard) and placed them at random around the court. "OK! Get as close to each as you can—in any order," and standing in the middle on the service line, he began stroking balls at Antonio.

"Plonk!" went the first cannister, then the second, then the third and so on, until each cannister was lying on its side. A little knot of students that were watching broke into applause.

"OK, Tony—you've made your point—but the rest of you kids, don't try it. Keep your eye on the ball. You should have the exact dimensions of the court burnt into your mind and eventually we are going to play in the dark with luminous balls and every return has got to be in." And the coach winked at Antonio.

And so the training went on. Antonio never discovered what was meant by that wink. The coach did not try to alter his habitual technique. Was he suggesting that Antonio had a secret weapon that he should preserve? Or was it that he would eventually recognise the error of his ways and then conform? Antonio certainly noticed that a certain uniformity of style quickly emerged within the camp. When his class had first gathered and rallies among them began in warm-up sessions, their standard was roughly at the same level, but there were considerable variances in style of play.

For example, some utilised the two-handed backhander, some did not. The coach soon explained that this school did not favour that practice, which was most prevalent amongst the girls. "Try it one-handed for a while—you can always go back later," he addressed those few with that technique. And for the service, all were soon bouncing the ball several times with their racquet free hand before tossing it the air. This was deemed important to maintaining concentration—and gave time for a decision on where to aim.

Antonio had never engaged in this bouncing although he had seen almost all other players on the circuit doing it. He would decide at the last minute which of the dotted lines his mind entertained he would follow. Almost everyone rocked back and forth once or twice, holding the ball against the face of the racquet, having completed the bouncing, before throwing it in the air.

Antonio just placed his feet on the back line carefully to avoid a foot fault and tossed it up straight away. The crouched receiving stance, feet spread appropriately and rocking back and forth, soon became standard. Antonio adopted a more relaxed stance and stood still, ready to spring into action to either side.

"OK, Tony!" barked the coach one day, "let's just see who gets away more quickly. I want some of you kids—yes—say, you three to start with. Line up in front of each other on one side of the court, on the line, but outside—Tony, you at the back. That's right—leave enough space between you. OK—all adopt your receiving stance. That's right, Tony, your favourite stance. Now when I yell 'go!'—make for the other sideline—quick as you can. Let's see who gets there first. Ready?—GO!"

Needless to say, Antonio won by at least one pace. He did again against another three. Speed on court had been his forté since the beginning. He now achieved greater popularity as his studied differences in technique became a sort of traditional eccentricity for the training camp, supported as it was by leading excellence at play.

But his divergence became even greater when 'attitude' training began. This was provided by a different, specialised coach with degrees in various branches of psychiatry and psychoanalysis. He wore a goatee beard and sported a small pot belly, standing out in a crowd of clean-shaven, fitness examples.

"Now all you people have been playing tennis long enough to know the role the mind plays in this game," he began his opening address to the students sitting in a small bleacher next to the No. 1 court. "You are here getting physically fit to play set after set with the same energy reserves, to perfect your strokes and to move around the court. I am here to train your minds to win. Yes! To win! That is the sole and overwhelming objective of your profession. Don't fool yourself into thinking you can pick up sponsors because you are charming and beautiful or photogenic.

"No, it's your capacity to win which is your route to the big money and if there is anyone here that doesn't care about big money, raise your hand! (Antonio almost did—but checked himself), Here are the three mental conditions you must learn to develop and then maintain: One—concentration—anyone can concentrate for a minute, for a half hour, but can you maintain your concentration for five sets?

"Two—anger—yes—anger. You must be angry at yourself, at the ball, at your racquet, at your opponent, at the umpire, at the spectators and your goal is to relieve your anger by winning. You don't like being angry—and that's why you are angry at yourself. As soon as you win, your anger disappears and you love yourself, you love your opponent, the umpire, the crowd, everything and everybody. Think what a relief that will be!

"Three—superiority—yes, you are superior, you are better, you are stronger than that weakling, that lousy player on the other side of the net. If you don't start the game absolutely convinced you are the better player (forget about the rankings), you reduce your chances of winning.

"Everybody out there, most tennis fans, they just assume the winner is the best player. Let me tell you the winner is usually the angriest, most completely self-confident player with the greatest concentration."

Antonio listened to this with rapt attention and with a sinking heart because he knew, with the same degree of self-confidence just described—he knew, without a shadow of a doubt, that he could not possibly and indeed, would not want to adopt the mental attitudes this specialised coach had just propounded. That night, Morpheus deserted him. He agonised over a proposition he had not entertained for even a second during his entire tennis career to date: should he quit?

After a night of tossing and turning, he rose with a final conclusion. No! He would not quit, He would not let down his father, and He would not let down the Republic of San Marino. He would continue to play, and he would play with a smile. He would love his opponent who sent him returns allowing him to visualise his straight, dotted line and place his ball exactly where he wanted. And he would have no difficulty maintaining concentration because that was how he saw his straight, dotted each time he went to strike the ball.

Of course, his unique pose was quickly noticed, and the attitude coach reprimanded him severely.

"Where do you think you are Balluzzi? At some weekend house party with a bunch of debs you're trying to impress. Wipe that smile off your face and get serious! This is not a game. It's a business! If you don't understand that, you don't belong here."

Antonio understood perfectly; he ignored the attitude coach and easily won the inter-tennis camp tournament. Miss Playfair from IAM 360 was busily introducing potential sponsors, who were filming candidates at play—and even viewing them with field glasses from the side lines, so as to verify details of their playing styles. Antonio found himself ignored by the main tennis clothing and equipment sponsors.

But with a touch of sarcasm in her voice, Miss Playfair introduced him to another lady representing a recently launched social media channel branded 'luv'em.com', with a heart-shaped logo on which was imposed a white and black hand shaking over the new, circular symbol designed to indicate male, female and the third gender (whatever you may choose that to be).

The target audience was courting couples about to be or already engaged. The title and logo designer had naturally discarded 'luv him/her', after a long discussion about which order to put 'him/her'—or maybe 'her/him'. Antonio heard Miss Playfair briefing the luv'em.com agent.

"He's a brilliant player but he has the attitude of a flower child of the 1960s."

"Sounds just right for us. We're in to *love,* big time!" said the agent, who had the new heart logo tattooed on a forearm. And so, Antonio, now known as Tony, signed with luv'em.com. One of the many clauses in the contract required him to use his new first name exclusively during the life of the contract. Soon a supply of shirts and shorts arrived with the new logo patch.

As a new member of the world tennis tour, Antonio continued to astonish. His father soon joined him as a tour manager and much enjoyed both seeing the world and watching Antonio play. He was also amused and gratified when another joined the Balluzzi team. In an impromptu imitation of his father, Antonia met an Alitalia air hostess named Sophia. She was a compatriot from San Marino, and they might certainly have met before within a population of only thirty-odd-thousand but for the fact that her father had been head chef at the Savoy in London.

A wise young couple, they soon agreed that their whirlwind romance should lead to a lengthy engagement until Antonio had secured a more assured income from playing tennis. But Sophia, who had the polished manners of an English public-school girl, resigned her job at Alitalia and joined the touring Balluzzi team.

To say that Antonio was causing a sensation would be to understate. An article from *World Tennis* said it all, "Tony Balluzzi's rise from triple to single digits in the ITA rankings in the space of two years beats Ken Rosewall's record way back then. But what makes Balluzzi the tennis story of the year is not just his speed on court or the amazing accuracy of his shot-making—it's his attitude or, as some would say, his lack of attitude.

"Jimmy Robins, Sandy Peskov's veteran coach put it well in a recent interview: 'Tony always looks as if he was playing house party tennis on a lazy summer day.' Right on Jimmy! Balluzzi wears a permanent smile, which never fades regardless of the score. He shouts, 'good shot!' across the net when his opponent makes a point and 'great serve!' for an ace—pretty rare, as Balluzzi's return capacity is incredible.

"On the even rarer occasion when he makes an unforced error he can be heard saying 'sorry'. You won't get a clenched fist out of Tony Balluzzi or even a frown when he loses a point. And to top it all, he has even taken to jumping over the net after a win to shake hands. We haven't seen that since Don Budge. Some in the tennis world reckon this is gamesmanship. But those who know him well insist it's perfectly genuine. That tiny Republic of San Marino has certainly bred a giant."

Privately, Antonio would explain, "People don't understand. If I get mad, I lose my concentration. If I lose that, my technique collapses—I don't see that magic dotted line." A few who heard about the 'magic dotted line' tried to find it themselves—and when they couldn't, they got mad.

One thing was certain. His sponsors luv'em.com could not believe their luck. They rushed to protect their logo in countries where it was not properly registered. They tried to talk Antonio into backing a TV series entitled *The Tennis Luvs of Tony Balluzzi and*, yes—that was the spelling they were going to insist on. And, of course, all the tennis shoe and apparel labels approached him for co-sponsorships.

But Antonio scorned the series idea and would not re-negotiate the exclusive clause in the luv'em.com contract. "It would not be fair—they came forward when no one else would," said Antonio. And both Massimo and Sophia agreed.

Antonio's success made waves everywhere. The Captains General of San Marino awarded him the Republic's highest honour. Not to be outdone by its diminutive enclave, Italy awarded him the Medal for Merit in Culture and Art. A new tennis camp teaching what they claimed was the 'Balluzzi method' was set up in Sarasota, Florida. The Pope referred to 'The excellent Catholic love and charity of Antonio Balluzzi' in a communication to a delegation of representatives of Sport. Miss Playfair at IAM 360 was promoted and given a substantial rise in salary. Antonio appeared on the cover of *Time Magazine*.

Massimo was concerned all this would go to his revered son's head. The wise fiancée Sophia countered, "My dear Papa-in-law to be, the main thing about Antonio (she eschewed calling him Tony) is that it won't. Never have I known someone whose modesty is not only natural—but cannot be shaken."

The meteoric rise of Antonio Balluzzi prompted some in the tennis world to question whether he could also prevail on the grass courts of Wimbledon. In fact,

Massimo, ever focussed on his son's career, had anticipated this very question when Antonio was just finishing his term at the tennis camp. An old family friend was not only the Consul General in New York for the Republic of San Marino, he was a partner of Lehman Brothers and a member of an exclusive Long Island country club with several grass tennis courts maintained in perfect condition.

Guest member facilities were arranged, and Antonio spent a week working with the local professional to accustom his game to grass. He, therefore, arrived at Wimbledon well-prepared and reached the quarterfinals on his first appearance and the semi-finals the following year.

But then came the culminating event in Antonio's brilliant career to date. He made the finals at Wimbledon. He had beaten a previous winner, the great Spanish superstar Juan Gonzales in the semi-finals and his opponent was to be Alexander 'Sandy' Peskov, who had won easily over a fading Swiss player—a four times Wimbledon winner, now having difficulty outrunning advancing years. A claque assembled for this momentous event.

Obviously, Massimo and Sophia were in close attendance. A recently appointed physical education coach was there to share in the excitement—so was Frederico Bellavista, his old coach. the CEO of luv'em.com—a gorgeous lady free of tattoos, the Lehman Brothers partner, Miss Fairplay of IAM 360 and the chairman of the San Marino Tennis Association.

The Ambassador of the Republic of San Marino to the Court of St. James had been invited to sit in the Royal box—but he courteously declined with profuse thanks and joined the little knot of Antonio's supporters in the front to row of Centre Court. How many of the 33,000 citizens of that miniature republic were also there was impossible to estimate.

But things did not go as expected. It is probably best to listen to the commentators, rather than rely on this author's inadequate descriptions of play, "Well, how about that, Frank! Two love to Peskov in the first set! When's the last time we saw Tony Balluzzi lose his serve?"

"I certainly can't remember, Bill. But this is beginning to look like one for the books! What do you think Tony is up to?"

"I'm not sure Bill, but something's wrong here. Are you watching Sandy Peskov?"

"I sure am, Frank—and something is strange."

"That's a typical Balluzzi return—love fifteen, but I'll tell you what it is. Peskov is smiling! What's going on here, Bill?"

"And I heard him say 'nice shot!' in the first game. It's as though he's doing a take-off on the Balluzzi attitude. But. Frank, I think it's putting Balluzzi off his game."

"Way over the back line—that return! You're right, Bill! We're not watching Tony Balluzzi here—he's definitely looking unsettled."

I believe it is superfluous to continue quoting the banter of the commentators. As the match progressed it became clear to all what was happening. Peskov had decided to engage in an extraordinary piece of gamesmanship and the unexpected change in his manner was destroying Antonio's concentration and blurring or omitting his famous straight dotted line.

Peskov, who Antonio had played with countless times on the World Tennis Tour, was known for an attitude which would have delighted the tennis camp coach whose lesson Antonio had rejected—but never forgotten. Peskov played with a permanent scowl on his face. He shook his fist in triumph even when his opponent made an unforced error. He threw his racquet down in frustration at his own mistakes. He barked at the ball boys and girls. He objected to line referee decisions as often as possible—and scowled, even more, when the television replay went against him.

Now, suddenly Peskov was smiling, thanking the ball boys and girls and complimenting Antonio on his shots. He was even bouncing the ball before serving only once compared to his usual half-a-dozen bounces. At one point, he objected to a call—but in Antonio's favour, "Oh, I believe that was in!"

It was also so unexpected that the crowd was hushed, the commentators couldn't get over it, Antonio's clutch of close supporters sat downcast, unbelieving, whispering to each other—as the camera panned onto them. Almost every aspect of Balluzzi's game was off and unrecognisable. From sheer willpower, he staged some sort of recovery in the second set which went to a tie breaker—which he lost 7/6. He lost the third set 6/2. It was devastation.

At the presentation of the silver by the Duchess of Kent, the two opponents stood together, Peskov smiling and Antonio just looking bewildered. The world watching on TV heard the following exchange as the runner-up prize—the Venus silver rosewater dish, was handed to Antonio.

HRH: "I am so sorry—I've seen you play before, Signor Balluzzi. I think I was not the only one somewhat surprised."

AB (now smiling broadly): "*Grazia mille*—many thanks, Your Royal Highness. I can only say, M'am—I hope I have made a convert."

There was little exchange when the great silver cup was handed to Alexander Peskov. But Antonio gave him a big hug before the photographers started shooting.

FINIS

The Girl with a Limp

I noticed immediately that she walked with a slight limp. But it didn't mar the grace of her walk, and this struck me almost more than the limp itself. I saw her first whilst on horseback; she was coming towards me down the slight hill which emerges from some woods and leads to the valley where I was riding. She was clad in a royal blue, cotton blouse, faded blue jeans and old-fashioned tennis shoes.

On her head was a wide-brimmed straw hat and so I could not see her face until we crossed, but I could observe her motion from the vantage point on my mount, rather like watching a dancer on stage from a loge on the side. Her motion was fluid despite the limp, and I could not tell whether the foot or the limb itself was its cause.

There was something almost balletic in her gentle stride—purposeful enough but also strangely retiring, as someone who knows their path but is wary of an unexpected encounter. Her arms swung evenly at her sides, despite the merest variation in her gait and the forefingers of her hands were just extended a touch, like in a dancer's gesture.

As we crossed, I touched the brim of my flat cap, and she raised her head to look at me and then gave a slight nod. My glance at her face had been so brief that, illogically—with no chance of seeing it again, I stopped and turned to watch her walk away. I hoped she might hear that my horse had stopped and turn herself, but this was also foolish, as everything I had so quickly noted about her told me she would not be so forward.

We began to meet in this way, usually at the same point in our little valley. Realising that she was keeping to some schedule, I timed my own rides accordingly, to the satisfaction of my girl groom, surprised at my new punctuality. I longed to enquire as to the identity of the girl with a limp. But was embarrassed to do so—perhaps by respect for her minor disability. But then, how was she to know of my curiosity?

I realised that my feeling was not simple curiosity and I feared I might disclose a sentimental interest. Finally, as casually as I could, I questioned my girl groom, who usually knew everything about everybody in our neighbourhood.

"I don't really know her," said Debbie, with a hint of disapproval at the girl being outside her full acquaintance. "She lives with her invalid father in that cottage on the Quenington road—you know, opposite the Sidelands covert."

This explained the course of her walk. She was taking a shortcut, through the valley, to the village to shop at the little general store cum post office and would have used a little lane separating my house from the stables to do so. I wondered how I could have missed her—surely an encounter should have been inevitable, given my own movements around our small village. But in the meantime, we continued to meet as at first and I soon chanced a "Good morning," partially doffing my cap.

She lifted her head and replied simply, "It is"—a rather curious response but given with a quick smile. Remarkably, the smile was with her eyes—or if her mouth did move, I did not notice it, so taken was I by the expression of her eyes. They enlarged very slightly, and it was if an inner light had been switched on— a light of welcome for my entirely mundane greeting. I now saw her face illuminated for a millisecond as though the light of her eyes had served as a photographer's flash bulb incorporated within the subject.

The picture developed instantly in my mind, and I saw a simple, slightly freckled face, topped with light brown hair—as in 'Jeannie' of the song and the whole dominated by hazel eyes—not by their size but by their unusual brilliance. Her mouth I hardly noticed, and it seemed to have uttered its short reply to my greeting without moving—but I certainly noted that the corners turned up. As I rode on, my immediate and offhand summation was 'a pretty girl with a beautiful expression' and I was never to part with that shorthand description, even as I discovered the hidden depths of her personality—and her true beauty.

After a while, a small incident transformed our passing acquaintance. For context, I should mention I am an artist, but not a very good one in my opinion— an opinion which is expert rather than humble. I earn my living from portraiture commissions, supplement by a small legacy from a maiden aunt which allows me to live quietly in the country and hunt. My profession or trade, if you will, has honed my appreciation of facial characteristics and taught me that expression, rather than symmetry of features, is the key to feminine beauty.

It is thus that I noticed the upturned corners of the mouth of a creature I had seen but a few times in passing—a sure sign of a positive disposition. I was now to have an opportunity of examining that face more closely.

I own two horses—an 8 year old mare called Florence and a 6-year-old gelding called Gladstone, their breeder having 19th century tastes in names. I was on the mare one morning at my appointed time to enjoy watching my girl with a limp descending the little slope which brought her into my view from the woods at the top of the valley. That now familiar movement, so light and without contrivance, almost like a feather floating to earth, with a subtle combination of purpose and lassitude, always increased my heartbeat.

As she neared, I could see her face, blurred by the remaining distance between us, but sharp in my mind's eye. Her light hair under the straw hat was drawn back in a ponytail. Her forehead was smooth, her nose unremarkable, with some freckling, her eyebrows full and gently arched, her mouth slightly open with lips not too full and the turned-up corners banishing any sternness. But the eyes were paramount—eyes of a soft hazel shade, eyes that seemed prepared for a multitude of expressions, to reflect a richness of mood and thought. I realised I was falling.

She was still a few yards from me when my mare slightly stumbled and then walked on—the near side fore clearly lame. I dismounted and the girl moved quickly towards me, bent down and lifted the horse's leg, felt under the hoof, put it down and said, "Hold her, will you?"

The voice was soft, authoritative but not commanding, matter of fact but with just enough urgency. Suddenly breathless, I did as I was told and she went to the side of the path, picked up a dry twig and broke a piece off.

"She has a stone in the frog of her hoof," she said, coming back to me. "I don't suppose you have a pen knife?"

"I don't," I replied, my voice catching.

"So!—you didn't go to pony club camp!" And she suddenly broke into a real smile—her eyes exuding humour. She was displaying the competence of my groom Debbie, but without a hint of bossiness. She picked up the hoof again and, on her knees, slowly and gently prised the stone out of the frog with one hand, put the leg down, rose, patted the mare on the neck and handed me the sharp, rectangular, little stone. I put it in my pocket.

"You don't have to keep it!" she said, her eyes laughing.

"A souvenir."

"Of what?"

"Meeting you at last."

She said nothing but bent down with her hands fixed to give me a leg up to remount. I wanted to keep her talking—to hear her voice.

"You wouldn't like to ride her for a bit—I'll walk along." I was amazed at my courage.

"How kind! But maybe another time. What is she called?"

She had straightened up and was patting the mare's neck.

"Florence—and my name is Charles Wooley—er, Charlie, I mean." I was stammering.

"I am Evangeline Forbes—Evy—as you would have it. And I live with my old father back there on the Quenington road."

"I know. My groom told me—I mean where you live—not your name."

"Debbie, isn't it? We've chatted. I've seen her out also on that bay gelding of yours. Well, I'd love to ride with you sometime—we don't keep a horse anymore."

I could hardly believe my good fortune. In such a short span, our passing acquaintance had moved to a condition of newly made friendship. We were to ride together. I wondered if her ready acceptance of this mild intimacy indicated she regarded it as entirely casual—of no possible romantic significance. I set out for our engagement in two minds. Should I hint she already meant something more to me? Or had I best leave it as a simple follow-up of our experience with the stone in Florence's hoof? The day fixed, I offered to lead a saddled horse to her cottage, suggesting I might pay my respects to her father.

"No—Papa never goes anywhere or sees anyone—there's no point," said Evy. "We'll meet in the yard at ten—I'll do my shopping early. Let's go the other way—towards Ablington, It's a nice part of the valley."

Here was decisiveness and confidence—talking to me as if we were old friends. In the yard, she chatted with Debbie, who had saddled Florence for her.

"No further trouble from the stone in the frog, Debbie?"

"None, Miss—you did a fine job. I've known 'em get infection from a rusty nail, though."

Debbie had let the near side stirrup strap down for ease of mounting and I watched Evy holding on to the strap, having noted this.

"Thank you!" she said, "but fortunately it's my right leg that's bad—otherwise I might have had to train a horse to be mounted from the off side." Saying this, Evy mounted quickly before Debbie could give her a leg up.

I had pretended to be wholly occupied mounting Gladstone, but my ear had been cocked to the little exchange between the two girls. It was the first time I heard Evy make reference to her limp. As she adjusted the stirrup straps, I couldn't resist looking to see if they might be fixed to different lengths—but of course, I couldn't tell. The buckle holes are only a few millimetres apart on the straps—I hated myself for wanting to observe some sign of her lameness.

We rode out of the yard and on our way in silence for a while. It was obvious she was an experienced horsewoman. Her seat was perfection—not stiff and stilted, as with girls who have competed at dressage, nor was it aggressive, as with hunting ladies whose chins stick out as they lean slightly forward, straining to hear a hound open. It was natural and entirely genuine—in keeping with everything I had noticed so far about Evy's manner and personality. Genuine! That was the word I had sought in my mind and would use if I was to describe her to a friend. I realised I was staring at her and decided to break the silence.

"Have you someone to help with your father?" I asked.

"Only our daily, Mrs Day and her handy man husband who does the firewood and heavy stuff in the garden. The District Nurse looks in from time to time. Shall we trot on for a bit?" She looked at me and smiled—perhaps indicating she was not trying to evade my questioning.

In fact, as soon as we were back at the walk, she began.

"Papa is a broken man—a ruined man as well. He was wiped out in a Lloyds syndicate. But he has not recovered from two shocks in his life and each has grown in importance over the years, ruining his health—never really good and now with some senile dementia, he's in bad shape—poor dear."

"Your mother?"

"She died giving me life, so I never knew her, but she left a legacy that has stupidly haunted my father. She was a Gordon and Papa was *persona non grata* for marrying her. The old Clan chief refused to have anything to do with him. Malcolm, the current one, has been trying to put that right."

"The Forbes and the Gordons are clan enemies?"

"Absolutely! For over a dozen generations—goes back to some slaughter in fifteen hundred and something. I can't remember who slaughtered who—the subject has bored me for so long that I've tried to forget the actual history."

157

"I find it amazing, in this day and age. I wonder if it's kept alive just out of a respect for tradition. But what was the other shock?"

Suddenly, with a slow gesture, Evy put her hand on my horse's mane, not on my arm or shoulder and paused before answering me.

"Papa dropped me on a stone floor when I was a baby, injuring my right leg—and the surgeon botched an operation to put it right. That's why I have a gamy leg."

"And your father took the blame and has kept it?"

"Exactly! With Mummy dead, I was brought up by Nanny and a sweet maiden Aunt, who had dedicated her life to simply being a Forbes. She was my grandfather's much younger sister—so really Papa's aunt. The tartan was all over the place in her cottage. I've never been to Balmoral but in pictures you see the Royal tartan's all over the house there.

"Anyway, Aunt Mathilda never tired of telling my father, that it could so easily have been her or Nanny who dropped me and he was not the surgeon who made it worse. 'But I chose him,' Papa would answer. There was simply no way of getting him to see reason and treat it as an accident that could have happened to anyone. I sometimes believe Papa has almost enjoyed keeping and savouring the guilt."

We rode on in silence. I felt that Evy had told me all about herself she was prepared to do at this point. But I wondered how often she had told the story of her limp—and whether always so candidly. I felt I should say something about myself but couldn't think what.

"I've only been here about three years—I was in the army for a while." I thought how off hand this was as a response to her trauma.

"Yes, I know," said Evy.

"You know?"

"Mrs Smith-Bingham told me about you."

"Oh, did she? I painted her portrait last year. I didn't much like it—but she did."

"I suppose that's what counts. Why did you join the army? They don't have artists in peace time."

"Someone told me I would have more free time to paint than in any other occupation—and they were right! It's all about hurry up and wait."

We returned from our ride promising to repeat it and each time we rode in every direction but the one back to Evy's cottage. Sometimes, she left a bicycle at the yard and once a Morris minor. We swapped horses each time and talked of everything but ourselves. I was increasingly smitten and struggled not to show it.

For reasons I could not explain, I was certain any amorous advance would put paid to our friendship. Finally, I asked her to dinner, and she accepted, but insisted she would meet me at the pub in Barnsley—recently taken over by a gastronomic couple, fortunately with limited ambitions. It remained a pleasant and quiet venue for dinner.

Now, Evy spoke more freely of herself.

"Papa was afraid to send me to school because of my limp. How foolish! Poor Papa—fortunately Aunt Mathilda was an extremely well-educated woman, and she took my home schooling in hand. I had a companion—a quite distant cousin called Alistair Forbes whose parents were in India.

"He lived with my aunt and was with me until he went off to prep school. We lived in an old farmhouse, rented from a cousin of my mother—a hated Gordon, but Aunt Mathilda though her kinsmen's attitude ridiculous. She taught us French and German and had an amazing library. When I turned up at Hatherop, I was well ahead of the other girls."

"How come you went to Hatherop?" I asked.

"My father had a lady friend in London—a divorcee. I liked her. I hoped something would come of it. I told Papa I liked her—but no—always stubborn. 'I won't visit my pain on her,' he said. 'But Papa,' I said, 'she'll take your pain away!' He said, 'Nobody can do that' it was hopeless.

"Anyway, she had a daughter my age, who I liked as well—and she was going to Hatherop. At least Papa was persuaded to send me as well. They had a country place quite near here in the Cotswold country and the lady offered to keep me at school holidays, but Papa said no—he would move here and I would be a weekly boarder. I have to say Hatherop School for Young Ladies is fine for girls training to marry rich landowners, but I can't say it impressed me."

"So your father never re-married?" It was a stupid question.

"No—and I don't think I should tell you who the lady is. You may know her. But, the daughter was a great friend—she's gone off to America. Papa bought me a hunter, which my friend kept at her place, and we hunted with the Cotswold."

"I have the occasional day with them. I promise I won't try and guess—you are very discreet."

My mind was racing—trying to think who it might be amongst my limited acquaintances from the Cotswold country.

As our friendship grew so did my unrequited love. I fought it to some extent by trying to find faults in the girl with a limp. The limp was certainly not one of them. On the contrary—and I wondered whether, in some fetishist manner, it added to my attraction. I was seriously disturbed by my growing passion and distracted. I had an almost finished canvas on my easel—a portrait of a local great lady, ready to be coated and signed and I could not even look at it.

I have had a normal if relatively uneventful love life. I have avoided marriage for fear of failure. I'm a Catholic and unhappy with divorce—I believe in the oath taken at the hymeneal alter. This new condition, prompted so suddenly by the girl with a limp, required a degree of introspection and even retrospection, which I had never undertaken with my previous, few romantic attachments. There is always the problem of distinguishing lust from love and vice-versa.

As a sort of frame to the multi-faceted images which were contained in Evy's expressions, there was a look of innocence. Perhaps I could better describe it as a feeling of innocence. Nothing could be more disturbing, because lurking as an evil undertone to the riot of my emotions was an unspeakable desire to corrupt that innocence. There was no great difference in age between us, but I still felt a degree of discomfort which I could not account for—nor could I see how to eliminate it without a far greater degree of intimacy than that which I currently enjoyed with Evy.

I had never propositioned a young lady. Where a relationship had led to bed, it had been at the behest of my paramour. Even those couplings with professional ladies, which army postings inevitably provide, had found me in a rather passive mode, unlike the traditional image of the libidinous soldier. I could imagine no circumstance under which Evy herself would suggest we sleep together, no matter how regularly we saw each other.

And we did see each other regularly. We walked, rode, lunched and dined together. Evy came to see my studio but did not ask me to her cottage, which we even rode by once or twice. But I understood. It was not that she was ashamed of her father—she had become accustomed to protecting his self-imposed isolation. In the village, we were soon considered an 'item'.

Debbie made horse talk with Evy as if she was almost mistress in the yard. We began to be invited as a couple by my few friends and these few were friends because the hated country gossip. Through all this Evy maintained a perfect poise—a mixture of proximity and distance, in no way cold or forbidding, but strangely reassuring and still frustrating. In turn, my love continued to intensify like a knot being twisted and tightened.

I took comfort in the fact that my love was not entirely physical. Evy's personality shone with the same brilliance as the light in her eyes. Our tastes were not the same as mine but compatible and complimentary. Her view of life was realistic but benign. She gave no hint of complaint about her infirmity, or the isolation imposed on her by her father's condition.

She had a keen sense of humour, free of any malignity towards others. She saw a joke even before it was fully apparent, and her eyes would signal an imminent sense of mirth. Her laughter was harmonious variations on the musical score which was her voice. Her Aunt Mathilda had clearly emphasised general culture in her home-schooling curriculum and Evy's appreciation of history and the arts had not been dulled by the mundane nature of Hatherop School for Young Ladies.

After much useless deliberation, I decided I would offer to paint Evy's portrait—but I quickly corrected myself, "I mean, I'm not offering—I'm asking your permission to paint your portrait," I said one day, in my usual awkward manner.

"That's better!" said Evy with her little, teasing smile, "My father taught me never to accept portraits from strange men."

"Am I a strange man?"

"I'm joking, my dear—when, where and how do you want me?"

It turned out to be a greater challenge than I imagined. Despite the hackneyed tradition of artist/model love affairs, I had never felt the slightest amorous inclination to the ladies I painted—several young and beautiful. We were to be in my studio in natural morning light. I posed Evy seated, at a slight angle and with her straw hat on a little table next to her. I find a small 'prop' like this gives the portrait a more natural look.

She was a good model. Stillness was a component of her soft and entrancing character. She was like a small pond, gently fed by a little, almost silent stream. But her pose, with its freshness and, yes!—dare I say it even to myself, its innocence, made my longing for her surge to such a point that I could hardly paint. And when an alarming consequence of my excitement became visible and caused me dismay, Evy clearly noticed my discomfort and broke her silent pose.

"Go outside and take a couple of deep breaths, Charlie," she said—smiling her mirthful smile. "I think you need a break."

I was embarrassed but relieved it by laughing—perhaps a little artificially.

"I'm so sorry—but—" I was stammering again.

Evy quickly interrupted, "Don't worry—I guess you paint a lot of girls—maybe the odd nude?"

"Certainly not!"

"Just wondered."

We both went outside and walked around the garden. Evy dead—headed some geraniums.

"I hope this portrait is not a mistake, Charlie—I don't want to cause you distress." She had taken my arm and looked at me with serious, enquiring eyes.

"No, no!" I quickly responded. "Loveliness can hardly cause distress." I hid my emotion behind a courtly pose.

"Always the perfect gentleman," said Evy and we went back in and resumed.

I did manage to finish the painting and it wasn't bad at all—on the contrary. Evy was the best model I have ever known. She seemed to project her beauty to my hand. Her tones blended with those on my pallet as if by an invisible force. Her eyes followed my mood and focused my brush as if they were commanding my every action. The result was extraordinary in relation to my modest gifts as an artist. It required no post pose touch-up and left no sense of the usual slight imperfection.

We carried on as before, apparently a happy couple to an outside observer, who might also assume a natural, marital consequence to our relationship. I could see no such inevitable *dénoument.* Soon the dreaded expression 'all good things—' began to permeate my unconscious.

One day, Evy took both my hands in hers and said, "Charlie, my dear, we are about to suffer the pangs of 'sweet sorrow'—as we must part, for a while at least. Papa is dying and wants to go home to die. Suddenly, home for him has become Castle Forbes in Aberdeenshire, where he has certainly never lived. But I told you I've been in touch with my cousin Malcolm—he's the current Lord Forbes and Clan chief—his father was the nasty one who snubbed poor Papa. Malcolm wants him to come back and live at the Castle—a typical castellated mansion built in 1820. I must go with him. We'll see what happens. I won't sell the cottage yet—maybe rent it."

To add to this collection of hackneyed phrases, I said to myself, '*It's now or never.*' Courage overwhelmed me.

"Evy, I love you. Will you marry me?"

She kissed me on the cheek.

"Thank you. But men don't marry girls who limp."

"Nonsense!"

"Alright, Charlie—put it this way. Men don't marry *this* girl with a limp."

"Even bigger nonsense! Evy, I love you."

"The answer's still no, my sweet—for too many reasons to go into. Please, please Charlie, let's stay friends!"

She looked at me with such pleading eyes, with such extraordinary sincerity, such genuine emotion—that every feeling that had summoned up my courage now melted away. I kissed her hands, turned, and walked away.

Evy came back some months later. I read in the *Times* that her father had died. She was selling the cottage and would live in Scotland. We had lunch together and it was like old times—a perfect friendship, dulled on my side by the pangs of enduring love.

A year later she wrote me from Switzerland to tell me a surgeon had been found who could fix her leg—some bone grafting was involved. Next, I had a letter from her in Scotland, enclosing a photograph of her in front of Castle Forbes. She was standing very straight in a tartan skirt. She said her leg was almost perfect and she no longer limped, just needing a thin extra innersole in one shoe. She also told me she was to marry her distant cousin Alistair Forbes and please could I be at the wedding.

I wrote congratulating her. I explained I could not make it to Scotland but was sending her portrait as a wedding present.

FINIS

The Oak Tree

He lived alone, in semi-dotage, in a little cottage in a Close in a suburb of Cape Town and his only companions were the flora and minimal fauna that graced his small patch. The grey squirrels and the goldfish in two little ponds were the wildlife. One squirrel, which he named Cecil after Rhodes, had tempted him to supply unsalted hazelnuts and come daily at the same time.

But he caught him entering the house if he happened to miss the appointment and so he desisted—facing a brief period of angry stares from Cecil, on his hind legs. The goldfish would gather in a corner every morning for a sprinkle of goldfish flakes. The label on the cardboard tin listed an astonishing number of ingredients, including fish meal and claimed total nutritional value—even enhancement of the natural colour.

Each pond had a stone fountain from which the water was recycled through an urn carried by a carved putti. From time to time, he heard a frog croaking in them. These were the live things which rescued him from total solitude.

The garden was very rich, having been designed by the lady predecessor of the property who was keen on diversity of shape and colour. There was a tidy sward of lawn in the middle and the borders were filled with shrubs, small trees, and flowers of every variety, providing a display that changed with the seasons but was always satisfying and soothing to observe. His own horticultural knowledge was nil and he had failed to note the names of the plants when the lady had given him a brief tour as he was taking possession.

She had left him her Xhosa gardener named George, who fortunately took a proprietorial interest in his garden charge and was industrious, if not expert. But master and gardener were unable to communicate adequately as one had no Xhosa and the other very little English. In extremis his housekeeper Zoe, also a Xhosa, but quite fluent in English, acted as interpreter. She came daily and gave George his tea.

Sometimes, George would simply say, "compost." This was the signal for a visit to the garden centre, where he would push the trolley and George would select the plants. This was noticed as unique, for with the other customers, the gardener was pushing the trolley and the white boss lady was making the choices.

But his pride and joy, his favourite horticultural companions were his two giant European oaks. They were oddly placed and must have been on the lot when his bungalow was built. One was in front, at the very corner of the house—almost touching the wall. Inside was his bedroom and he could reach out of a window and caress the gnarled trunk.

The other was behind, also at a corner of the property—just beyond the wooden deck outside the French doors on the other side of his bedroom, in what constituted a back garden. European oaks—and the English variety *Quercus Robur,* had been imported to the Western Cape in the earliest days. A governor of the Cape, Simon van der Stel, had begun to make wine at Stellenbosch, the town named after him in the 17th century and had quickly determined that no local wood made barrels as did the English oak.

No doubt the barrels were better quality than the wine, which did not improve in the Cape until the French Huguenots were induced to immigrate. But English oaks were imported in massive quantities—the oldest, 300 years at least, is at Verschelagen, an estate near Stellenbosch. Thousands were scattered around the suburbs of Cape Town.

He was aware of this glorious history. In fact, he doted on it. For him the oak trees were a sacred forest, even though now greatly dispersed. As he gazed daily on his own two English oaks, he fancied spirits dwelt with in them and, furthermore, he believed he had the ability to communicate subconsciously with their arboreal souls. Did not Karl Jung connect all living things, even the inanimate, to his theory of the collective unconscious? If he hadn't, surely, he should have—or his theory could not be complete. And hadn't he read somewhere that the Prince of Wales talked to his plants?

His oak trees had a life of their own and their quasi-permanence separating them from the flowerbeds with the small plants and shrubs George tended and often had to replace. In the wind, the oak trees waved their limbs, groaning and straining, much as his own limbs felt on rising in the morning. The more he looked at his oak trees and the more he felt their omnipresence in his modest garden—the more he associated with their uniqueness.

After all, he reasoned to himself, he was himself a great man in some respect and now confined to a small patch. He had enjoyed a successful career in finance and was often referred to as a 'City Grandee'—and here he was ending his days in a modest bungalow, just as his great oaks, of historic repute, were now confined to a very small garden.

From what a historically knowledgeable friend had told him, he knew they had first been planted when the Close was a majestic alley leading to an important building that was no more. They had been like sentries before a palace of the great and they were now merely a consolation for a geriatric.

Given their location, it was inevitable that some portion of each of the great oaks reached over to the neighbours. The one at the corner of his bedroom—which seemed to be an extension built after the main body of the bungalow, had several important branches hanging over his neighbour's shed—built against the boundary wall.

Some blackening of the leaves produced a noxious deposit after rain and apparently ran into a freshwater tank. The neighbour had complained. Aphids were diagnosed as the cause and the tree was sprayed annually by a taciturn but efficient tree specialist. But prior to one spraying, a major crack near the trunk appeared, threatening an important branch. In fact, the end of the branch seemed to be largely supported by a fir tree standing next to his little wooden 'wendy' house.

He was very concerned and summoned the tree surgeon with anxious haste. A day later he watched, fascinated but with knots in his stomach, as the amputation proceeded. An image flashed in his mid from some film he had seen recently. During the Crimean war, a soldier watches as the leg of his best friend is amputated by the surgeon. He is both fascinated and horrified. For the damaged oak, three men, roped with pulleys, were aloft to section the great branch and avoid damage below from falling material.

Like monkeys, they swung from the other branches, with motor-driven chain saws fixed to their belts. Their boss stood with him, nonchalant, chatting with him, as if—like the military surgeon in a raging battle, the operation was run of the mill, the identity of the stricken patient barely noted. Finally, the ordeal was over, the pieces of the amputated branch neatly loaded into the van, twigs and leaves swept up.

The tree surgeon then delivered a prognosis which left his client in shock, "As you can see that branch was hollow—that's why it broke. Doesn't surprise me—much of the tree might be hollow, they get that way eventually, you know, these great English oaks. All different—some can carry on for a while. You could top it a bit, but that doesn't always help. In the end, they all have to come down."

He was struck dumb. Half of him screamed for more detail, but a dominant half was too frightened. He heard himself thanking the tree surgeon, seeing him off, acting casual. He sat down on the veranda and stared at his tree. It seemed unconcerned, not suffering from post-wound trauma, its upper branches swaying as usual in a gentle breeze. But could it be possible—even conceivable, that his oak tree would have to be cut down during his own lifetime?

He knew European oaks were a protected species. Permission from the Council was required before they could be cut down. But this might be granted if a tree was perceived to be a danger. Might his neighbour petition for such a consent? Surely, the tree could last his own lifetime. That was absolutely his minimum requirement. But how old was the tree? People guessed with these great trees, some more accurately than others.

One would only know for certain by counting the rings on the severed trunk—just as teeth were used to establish the age of a fossilised skeleton. He had been told his house might be some 70 or 80 years old. How big had been the tree when the extension containing his bedroom had been added? The trunk of the tree almost touched the wall.

Sprouts on the trunk had to be trimmed by George. He himself was in his eighties. The tree could easily be as much as 100 years old. It must have been there before his house. It had two fellow oaks in the Close in which his bungalow was located. They looked like contemporaries. He had looked for other old trunks as there must have been what the French call an *allée*. There were nonapparent. He must know its age to help determine which would survive—the tree or its owner? This was the burning question.

He decided he must seek an actuarial determination from his own physician and from the tree surgeon or a disinterested expert, the tree man was obviously looking for an assignment to remove the tree. He must find another, summon them to a meeting and then put the question, insisting on an honest and unbiased answer. Could the oak tree be reasonably expected to survive—in other words, exploit its protected status long enough to witness his own demise?

This was the issue. He could not rest until it was resolved. He cared not what might happen to it after his death. His property might be sold and a new owner unconcerned with the fate of the oak trees.

But his doctor would not take him seriously. "For goodness' sake! Just look after yourself properly and forget about the tree; you've got plenty of time left."

Forget about the tree? How could he? These oak trees were the soul of the garden and, therefore, his as well. He made some effort to find another expert, but his research on the internet suggested that there existed such a range of possibilities that he was unlikely to get a definitive opinion. It seemed that with a partially hollowed-out oak—and he saw many as he wondered about his immediate area, it was a question of the balance of weight carried from existing limbs and branches. If the pruning required for safety's sake left the tree lopsided—it might break at the trunk and fall over.

The oak tree in front became an obsession. In fact, the one behind the house was just as old and was already substantially hollowed out near the base. There had been a bees' nest inside the cavity at one point. But most of the upper branches were over the neighbour. If she insisted for some reason, he would not be so reticent to its removal. But the one in front was a different story. He took to monitoring it carefully.

On windy days, he stood observing the swaying of its branches and even swayed himself, imitating the movement of the oak and testing the stability of his own stance. He would caress the tree, carefully pruning the little shoots that emerged from its trunk where large branches had been previously sawn off and satisfying himself as to the apparent health of the leaves. George found him hugging the tree one morning and was surprised he had assumed this garden chore.

At night, he dreamed of the oak tree. He remembered a Disney cartoon where the trees in the forest came alive and the gnarled branches sought to capture the hapless children. That night he relived the scene in his dreams. He had remarked to his dermatologist that the age patches on his skin were similar to those on the bark of old trees. Now he noticed that his wrinkled arms duplicated the furrows on the bark of his oak tree. He studied from a ladder the large and heavy branch that hung over his bedroom. On no account must that be pruned for fear of unbalancing the tree.

He was painfully aware that his neighbour posed a risk to the future of his oak tree. He might well have a case to put to the council, seeking consent to the trees removal. He took to calling on him. Was he happy the tree was no longer shedding the noxious substance? Should he have the tree sprayed again? Of no, all was well—once a year should be enough. Was he concerned about the branch hanging over his shed with the corrugated iron roof?

Not really, he kept an old motorcycle and some garden tools there—he didn't think there was much risk. The neighbour wondered about these visits. Surely the concern was a bit overdone. But after a particularly windy day, a branch from one of the other oak trees lining the Close fell onto the road surface. What if a car had been passing?

He worried even more and now observed the wind condition in his daily consultation of the weather forecast. His dreams were dominated by trees. In one he was the tree itself and he felt his arms spreading out and watched spellbound as leaves sprouted from his fingers. Now he lost interest in his own health and his doctor expressed concern. He summoned the tree surgeon twice in one month, only to receive a shrug of the shoulders and an assurance that there was no need for further pruning. He was disappointed in this diagnosis. But that evening he hugged the tree again.

One day, a particularly violent windstorm was announced. He could not sleep that night and listened to the wind howling as he lay in bed. Finally, he rose, put on his dressing gown and went outside. He stood in the garden, as twigs and leaves scurried around him. Then he heard a violent crack, as if from lightning— but here was no thunderstorm. He could not see. The branches of all the trees and tall shrubs around him were in great motion.

The next morning, his worse fear was confirmed; a large branch had fallen on his neighbour's shed. He rushed over to find his neighbour surveying the damage. The corrugated roof was bent under the branch and a supporting wooden post had broken, falling on the motorcycle.

"You'll have to get your tree man back. I think he needs to cut the tree back again—maybe even top it a bit. I'm happy to share the cost." The neighbour was very friendly.

A month went by. The tree surgeon with his assistants armed with power chain saws hanging from their belts had come and gone. The neighbour had come over to watch. There had been a discussion—but he had been too upset to participate fully. One morning George arrived and found his boss lying at the foot of the oak tree. He was dead. From the bits of tree trunk on the inside of the pullover, it seemed he had been hugging the tree when his heart failed.

Amongst the papers found on his desk was a note from the neighbour. It read, "I think we're all agreed that we should ask the Council to allow us to cut down that oak tree—but if they agree, let's wait for a convenient time when you are away—to reduce the disturbance."

He was now away.

FINIS

The Spectacles

The heat hung heavily, like a shroud in the starless night on the last remnants of life struggling to breathe. In an upper bunk of a Quonset hut barracks, Marcin Wosczinskiewicz lay sweating in his skivvies and listening to the night sounds. The crickets provided a non-stop background outside and the groans and singing bed springs of the occupants inside signalled struggles to sleep. He wondered what thoughts brightened or darkened the minds of his fellow recruits as they awaited the relief of sleep—a condition demanded by tired limbs but delayed by the heat.

His own ruminations were bound to be as different as possible. Was he not from another world? He let his mind savour in fleeting glimpses the debutant balls and fading strains of dance music; the early morning discarding of evening clothes to fall into delicious slumber, in the happy expectation of more parties and leisure activities the following day. But what about the slum kids from New York—a significant portion of his recruit platoon?

They were mostly of Italian origin with one or two Puerto Ricans. Did they dream of knife attacks and swinging bicycle chains; of flights down dark alleys from the police breaking up gang battles; of warm but worried mom's waiting up for them in tenement flats? Or that other contingent of farm boys from the middle west; high school football heroes, many with Swedish names, who had enlisted in the Marines to impress their girlfriends.

Were their thoughts of roaring crowds at the football games, encouraged by pom pom bearing, mini-skirted and buxom cheerleaders; locker room victory celebrations; twirling the girls at the senior year prom? Surely theirs were happier thoughts—rather closer to his own, than the dark memories of the mostly Italian kids from the Bronx. There was a few in the platoon who did not fall into these easily identifiable categories—including even one black boy. There was little occasion to question fellow recruits about their origins.

But Marcin, with the unpronounceable name, was the only 'college boy'—an expression much in use when only a small minority of the population could afford to finance their children's higher education. It was miss-placed to an extent in Wosczinskiewicz's case as, after being sent down twice, he had no college degree.

Still, for the three drill instructors of Recruit Platoon 115, Company A, at the U.S. Marine Corps Recruit Training Depot, Parris Island, South Carolina, he was immediately recognised as hailing from another class of society. His fellow recruits understood this when he was appointed squad leader of the First Squad. The three 9-man squads in the 27-man platoon were arranged by height and he would have been in the middle squad if he was not marching alongside the first, comprised of the tallest farm boys.

This early promotion to the lowest rank of recruit society, generated no jealousy as he might have feared since he was spared none of the physical strain and brutality of much of the training regime. So all-consuming of time and attention was the curriculum, that there were insufficient periods of rest to allow grudges or dissents to develop within the platoon.

There were the usual three drill instructors assigned to Platoon 115 and Marcin was amused at the extreme diversity they represented. The chief DI was a Master Sergeant Murphy, a 'redneck' from the Deep South, with the hue and bulk typically found among the bayous and cotton fields of Dixie. Loud and super confident, he pursued his mission of creating Marines from the chaff sent to him by over-enthusiastic recruiting sergeants—particularly the one stationed in Times Square, who he was convinced delighted in collecting the dregs of urban society solely to inconvenience drill instructors at Parris Island.

Sgt Murphy had immediately moved to eliminate the Puerto Ricans, who he considered particularly hopeless raw material. They had been marched against the corrugated metal sides of the Quonset hut until their knees were bloody and then sent off to Sick Bay with a recommendation of immediate discharge for physical infirmity.

Miraculously, two fresh replacements had arrived to fill the quota. Marcin also noted an early example of favouritism of an unexpected nature. He overheard another DI saying to Sgt Murpy, "You sure seem soft on that nigger boy," and the chief DI's reply, "Yup, he's a nigga—but he's ma nigga!"

The inquiring DI was a Staff Sergeant McKensie, a genuine Scot and Marcin wondered what strange events or motivation might have caused a Scotsman to join the United States Marine Corps. Despite his apparent concerns over Sgt Murphy's apparent solicitude for the black recruit, Sgt McKensie was himself the mildest of the three DI's. He was the least inclined to address the platoon as 'maggots' or, more frequently 'mother fucking maggots'.

It was a convention at Parris Island that recruits were never addressed as Marines until the successful completion of their basic training—and they were not even entitled to be addressed as 'recruits'. Marcin also quickly noticed that the jargon popular with both drill instructors and their recruits was extensively punctuated with that expletive which suggests an incestuous relationship by the subject with his mother.

Of course, he was immediately aware that the accents of his fellow recruits, flavoured with regional tones, differed significantly from his own—but then so did their language. The schoolboy swearing, he had grown up with at his exclusive New England school was much milder than what he was now hearing in his new environment. And the constantly recurring use of that same expression led him to suspect that incest was far more prevalent in the broader American public than he had ever suspected.

Sergeant McKensie allowed more frequent breaks on the parade ground where the surface seemed on the point of melting in the heat. He was also the most likely to declare "the smoking lamp is lit"—a Marine expression dating from the time when the old square riggers maintained a whale oil-fed lamp near the fo'c'sle from which sailors could light their pipes in calm weather, thus limiting risk of fires on board. At drill, Sgt McKensie was particularly concerned with posture and would admonish, "don't stick your neck out like a turtle!"

In marked contrast to the two senior DI's, little Sergeant Lacorbiere was a sadistic French Canadian who had done embassy service in Paris—a memorable posting, as his French—even of the heavily accented Canadian variety, had enabled a success with the girls which had been the envy of his colleagues. His severity was such as to bring some degree of restraint from Master Sergeant Murphy and Staff Sergeant McKensie, who both outranked him.

Sgt Lacorbiere had somehow discovered that Marcin spoke French, He now addressed him as 'Frenchman' and only occasionally in anger as 'mother fucking Frenchman'. Individual recruits were never addressed by their surnames, and, in any case, Marcin's would have been too difficult to attempt. At evening parade, when the platoon was in ranks and in their skivvies, the order would ring out from Sgt Lacorbiere: "Frenchman! Sing the Marseillaise!"

The main concern of recruits at this ceremony was to avoid slapping a mosquito, hundreds of which settled into a pleasant feed. Should an attempt at a surreptitious slap be detected, the culprit was required to first find the dead insect, then take his entrenching tool and bury it. Marcin found that singing the anthem at the top of his voice seemed to deter the blood-sucking predators, but perhaps it was the diversion of his attention. In any case, Marcin was clearly favoured by Sgt Lacorbiere for his Francophile gift, but still, this did not cause retributive reaction from his fellow recruits.

When the platoon moved from one site to another it was always at the run—often accompanied by a chant and a stamp of one foot on every other stride. The only time it was at the walk was when drilling. To and from the mess hall, the parade ground, the exercise field, the classroom, the swimming pool, the hand-to-hand combat training gym, the obstacle course, the parachute jump simulation structures, to church call—the platoon was always on the run.

The underlying theme of every training exercise was instantaneous obedience to orders. As Master Sergeant Murphy expressed it more than once, "When I say 'duck!' if you don't duck, you get your mother fucking head blown off!" The emphasis of immediacy of reaction to orders was amply illustrated when one day Marcin was ordered to convey a message to company HQ.

As he wheeled around in preparation for starting his run, Sgt Murphy barked: "Back so soon! What took you so long?" Sgt McKensie, standing nearby, laughed politely. Apparently, this was one of the senior DI's favourite jokes. But its point was well taken. Immediate and unquestioning reaction to an order could save your life.

Marcin enjoyed a moment of respite and pride when he was selected as 'recruit of the day'. This involved acting as an enlisted ADC to the Commanding General. Marcin never learned what was the process by which each day a recruit amongst the thousands was so chosen. Suitably uniformed in summer khaki, he reported to the Commanding General's headquarters.

There he found three BAMs engaged in secretarial duties. Women had been accepted in the Corps for some time—but restricted to non-combative roles. They had soon become known in the vernacular as 'broad-assed Marines'—BAMs—an extension of the American slang term for women: 'broads'. One of these approached Marcin to put an armband on his right arm—red with the legend Recruit of the Day in gold letters.

Marcin was overwhelmed at this sudden aura of female presence and began to feel the need to resist shaking. This intensified when the BAM went to her desk for some nail scissors and returned having spotted what is known in Marine parlance as an 'Irish pennant'. This is a tiny thread that has come loose from a lining and stitching somewhere on the uniform. Marcin struggled to control shaking as she delicately snipped the offending thread. He knew she was enjoying the reaction she was getting from her recruit victim.

After being photographed shaking hands with the General, Marcin was assigned to sit in front with the staff sergeant driver with the General and his Lieutenant ADC in the back. A wide-ranging inspection tour got underway, affording Marcin a view of Parris Island he had not seen. At a remote corner of the parade ground. A DI was drilling his platoon. The car stopped at some distance, but the DI spotted it.

He halted his platoon, ordered then at ease, and told them to take a drink from their canteens. There was an evident pause and a recruit spoke up, but his words were not distinct. Behind him, Marcin heard the Lieutenant say—almost in a whisper "their canteens are empty." The General said: "Take his name" and the ADC got out of the car and walked to the DI, who was now at strict attention and saluting.

Marcin was aware he was witnessing an extraordinary scene. The staff sergeant driver was smiling, Marcin noticed the Lieutenant had not put the DI at ease. A *soto voce* conversation was taking place. The lieutenant returned to the car and said merely, "two ten." Marcin realised he did not want to mention the DI's name in front of a recruit and so just gave the platoon number. The staff sergeant driver leaned over to Marcin and said: "You haven't seen this."

"Sir! Yes—I mean No, Sir!" Marcin replied, in best recruit fashion. In a friendlier tone, the General leaned forward from the back and said to Marcin, "Wouldn't happen in your platoon, would it?"

"Sir! No! Sir!" said Marcin.

"Drive on," said the General.

Each recruit platoon had a guidon topped with a red pennon on which was the platoon number in gold. Normally, the guidon bearer is the ranking NCO or the senior enlisted man—but in the recruit platoons, where there was no NCO and all were of the same seniority, it seemed to Marcin that the smallest recruit was chosen as the guidon bearer. He marched at the right of the front rank of the first squad.

The three squad leaders marched on the left side, two paces from the centre of the squad. On the successful completion of each phase of training a streamer in a colour reflecting excellence in the particular phase was attached under the pennon. As the programme evolved platoons became ranked according to the number of streamers on their guidons. But it was made crystal clear at the outset, that platoons were in competition for excellence and the DIs were undoubtedly betting amongst themselves on the ratings of their platoons.

This was much discussed within the platoon during the few moments when unsupervised conversation was allowed. No one believed DI pride was the sole motivation behind their extraordinary concern with the success indicators of the streamers attached to platoon guidons. Perhaps it was just military records, suggested one naïve recruit. A chorus of cynical dissent followed. "It's mother fucking money changing hands," said the diminutive guidon bearer.

No phase of training was more critical than the last, which took place on the rifle range, where the platoon was billeted for a full two weeks. Marines are riflemen before anything else. Marksmanship is their most important attribute. It is at the origin of this branch of the military. Marines oversaw ship security but their most important battle role in olden days was in the rigging as snipers, as they sought to take out the sailors manning the enemy ships in close combat.

Prior to the march, with full kit, to the rifle range barracks, there had been a full week of marksmanship training known as 'clicking in'. This consisted of small targets, set at distances to simulate real targets, at which one aimed an unloaded M1 rifle and learned how to squeeze rather than jerk the trigger. The exercise was closely monitored by the DI's and Marcin became aware that one of his platoon colleagues had difficulty with this process—and was also clumsy in handling his rifle in general. Marcin had seen his name—Wilson, on his locker and had even addressed him as such, having identified him as being from a somewhat similar background. From his accent, he guessed the Middle West, but he seemed distinctly urban. He had been one of the few raising his hand when, on arrival at the swimming pool, Sgt Murphy had asked, "how many of you maggots can swim?"

To Marcin's amazement most of the platoon could not—even the farm boys from Minnesota. Those few who could had been ordered to assist a Marine corporal swimming instructor and this duty had brought Marcin in some contact with Wilson.

The other distinguishing feature of Wilson was that he wore glasses—the only recruit so handicapped. Interestingly, Marcin had been surprised to find the commanding general wore glasses. Beginning a training session in the pool, Wilson had handed his glasses to Sgt McKensie. He explained to Marcin that they were government issue, replacing his own which, with all civilian clothes and articles, had been posted home after arrival at Parris Island.

Of course, he didn't need glasses swimming—and goggles were issued. Perhaps this condition had already affected Wilson's difficulty 'clicking in'. Marcin noticed him, a few places down the line, first taking his spectacles off, then putting them back. He seemed to be uncomfortable either way.

Finally, Platoon 115, set off on the 10-mile march to the rifle range at the far end of the Island—a satisfactory number of multi-coloured streamers flying from its guidon. On the day preceding departure, Sgt Murphy, his two deputy DI's standing either side, had delivered a stern lecture to the platoon, opening with the now familiar phrase: "Listen up, you mother fucking maggots!" The gist of his talk was simply that no previous phase of our training came close to rivalling in importance the forthcoming session on the rifle range.

To himself, Marcin reflected on the interesting hand-to-hand combat sessions when they had been taught how to kill an enemy with bare hands. He wondered when that might emerge as more useful than marksmanship. Meanwhile, the DI droned on, reminding all the history of the Corps, the importance of marksmanship and the rewards available pointing to the shooting medal that topped the row of ribbons on his uniform.

The Marine Corps is unique in awarding iron medals for shooting, in order: crossed rifles against laurel leaves for 'expert', a Maltese cross for 'sharpshooter' and a square target for 'marksman'. According to our individual scores, we 'maggots' would be entitled to wear one of these in the unlikely event that we would emerge successfully from recruit training and could actually be called Marines. But the honour of the platoon was at stake and the most important streamer for excellence awaited us if we performed. Most of the platoon interpreted this as confirmation that the DIs had placed large bets on our results.

As training got underway, involving firing at targets in lying, sitting and kneeling positions, with extra rifle range-based DI's scoring through field glasses and platoon members taking turns changing targets—it became obvious that Wilson was having difficulty. A range DI was assigned to coach him. He began adjusting Wilson's position, suggesting he try with and without his glasses—he seemed to do better without in the lying position but not when sitting.

"Look away and stare at the green grass for a few minutes," Marcin heard the DI say—he was two positions away and tried it himself. It was very therapeutic. The sight blur that concentrating on the target for a period caused, seemed cleared away. After a few days, Marcin's own performance improved considerably, and he soon topped the list of individual scores posted in the barracks every evening.

"You're on your way to a fucking expert medal, Frenchman," declared Sgt Lacorbiere. Sadly, Wilson fell to the bottom and stayed there. The gap with the second-lowest score was considerable and the platoon average was bound to be affected.

One evening, after the platoon had returned from the range, Marcin was summoned to the DI's room. He reported in the proscribed fashion, "Sir! Recruit Wosczinskiewicz reporting as ordered—Sir!"

He fully expected to receive the habitual rejoinder, "Recruit? You're no mother fucking recruit—you're a mother fucking maggot!"

It was Parris Island's custom to train recruits in Marine forms of address whilst reminding them of their lowly status prior to course completion. But to Marcin's surprise, the usual rejoinder was omitted and—even more amazingly, Sgt Murphy ordered, "At ease, Wosczinskiewicz—and listen up!"

This was unprecedented. He had been called by his name! The DI's must have been rehearsing its pronunciation. Marcin sensed they had been in conference.

It was Sgt Lacorbiere who then spoke up.

"You've got a mission, Frenchman. That mother fucking maggot Wilson is dragging your platoon down. He's gotta go! Here's how. Tonight, in the showers you take his glasses, you put them under your pillow. We'll recover them before roll call tomorrow. Repeat the order."

"Sir! Tonight, in the showers I take Wilson's glasses and put them under my pillow. Sir!"

"That's right—those specs are government property, understand?"

"Sir, yes Sir!"

"Dismissed!"

Marcin snapped to attention, wheeled in the correct fashion and walked out.

Back in his barrack room, all were engaged in cleaning their rifles. Marcin set out to do the same.

"What did they want?" someone asked.

"Nothing much—just first squad to the right of the range tomorrow."

Marcin had told his first lie. He reckoned it might not be his last. The enormity of the crime he was being ordered to commit began to sink in. But he had little time to reflect further. There would soon be a quick rifle inspection, then a line up prior to evening showers—added to the usual regime because of the heat. He had frequently observed Wilson putting his spectacles on a shelf just outside the shower enclosure. If Marcin was quick to shower first, he could grab them and be back in the barrack room before Wilson had finished.

And this is how it happened. His heart was in his throat and his stomach churning. Marcin had Wilson's spectacles under his pillow by the time the hapless victim entered and said, "Has anyone seen my glasses?"

There followed groans and denials and a few volunteers went back into the shower room to help search further. That night Marcin lay wide awake, suspecting that Wilson, a few bunks down, was also awake; thinking how he was going to report their loss, perhaps hoping it might not be noticed immediately—but still realising, with a sickening sense of certainty—that such was impossible. Marcin imagined he could feel the stolen spectacles burning under his pillow.

He thought about how stolen items were described as 'hot' in crime annals. He felt a surge of sympathy for Wilson. It was hardly his fault he was a poor shot. Perhaps he should not have enlisted in the Corps. Marcin had no idea why he had done so. He had not been on terms of confidential friendship with Wilson. Did he have a girlfriend and parents who would feel disgraced by his being subject to disciplinary action? But need they know? Was it after all such a serious problem? Marcin struggled to mitigate his growing sense of guilt.

At the following morning's roll call. Sgt Lascordiere walked up the first rank inspecting rifles. He reached Wilson.

"Where are your fucking glasses, maggot?"

"Sir! Lost them. Sir!"

"Lost them? Why haven't you reported that?"

"Sir, I told my squad leader, Sir!"

"Is that right, Frenchman?"

"Sir! I heard him tell the platoon he couldn't find them. Sir!"

Marcin felt a sudden sense of relief. He had not been forced to lie.

"You mother fucking maggot!" Sgt Lacorbiere continued, his face inches away from Wilson, who was shaking slightly and looking straight forward. "You know those fucking glasses are the property of the United States Government?"

"Sir! Yes Sir!"

"Repeat after me, maggot: 'I have lost property of the United States Government'."

"Sir, I have lost property of the United States Government. Sir!"

"Fall out and report to DI Murphy, maggot."

As far as Platoon 115 was concerned, that was the last we saw of recruit Wilson. He was not immediately replaced but our platoon rifle range score, calculated on average, earned us an excellence streamer on our guidon and presumably some monetary gain for our drill instructors. We learned that Wilson had been disciplined, sentenced to a week in the Brig, then assigned to another platoon and issued a new pair of spectacles. We all knew a stint in the Brig was no picnic.

Marcin found he had little peace of mind as his recruit training neared completion. In the final week, he found Wilson again; his new platoon was engaged in mess duty. As Marcin pushed his tray along the line, there was his victim, doling out the mashed potatoes. Wilson gave him a half smile.

"You took them, didn't you?" he said.

To his great shame, Marcin couldn't answer and, looking away, passed on. The incident revived his sense of guilt which had begun to wane. Now he could not stop thinking about it. At night, a repeating dream haunted him. Wilson was standing behind the lunch counter, pointing his rifle at him and repeating: you took them didn't you? Took them, didn't you? Took them, didn't you?

Marcin would wake in a cold sweat. He tried to say to himself—after all, there was Wilson, apparently having survived his week in the brig, still on his way to being a Marine. And that half smile! Might that not be playful irony? But why had he not stopped and said, "I'm so sorry—I was ordered to take them."

No! He had aggravated the crime by his insolent refusal to apologise.

Marcin Wosczinskiewicz was nearing a prime moment in his life as a Marine. He should have enjoyed a feeling of accomplishment. He would have some leave before assignment to a company in the 2nd Marine Division at Camp LeJeune, North Carolina. He would return home in full summer uniform, with a sharpshooter cross on his left breast. But, in fact—he was miserable. He could not get Wilson out of his mind. He had a sudden thought.

He was, of course, a Roman Catholic—but not a very active adherent of the faith. Of course, he had attended Mass at Church call on Sundays. The US Marine Corps depends on its parent, the US Navy, for its medical corpsmen and its chaplains. Marcin decided to go to confession. Sgt Lacorbiere, RC himself, of course, looked a bit quizzical as 'Frenchman' requested leave to see the chaplain, but directed him as to where to report.

There was a sort of multi-faith centre on Parris Island, which was not the chapel where Platoon 115 had gone for church call—on the run, of course. But Marcin had no difficulty finding the Catholic chaplain, a Lieutenant Commander by Naval rank.

"Follow me, son," had said the chaplain when Marcin explained he wanted to confess, and should he come at a different time? They went to a small, consecrated side chapel.

"Not at all, Marine—you are welcome now," and Marcin's morale shot up as he was indicated the entrance to the confessional booth. He had said, "Sir" at first, but now he said, "Forgive me, Father, for I have sinned—" and continued on with the familiar words, mentioning the rather long-time lapse since his last confession.

Finally, he recounted the tale of the spectacles, in some detail and explaining how he had seen Wilson in the mess hall and failed to ask his pardon.

"And the Drill Instructors specifically ordered you to take the glasses?" said the priest after a pause.

"Yes. Father."

"You know you are here to learn how to follow orders, which is an absolute requirement of a good Marine?"

"I know, Father."

The chaplain paused again, and Marcin wondered if he should say something else.

"You know your Bible—the New Testament? You learned your catechism?" resumed the chaplain.

"Some time ago, I'm afraid, Father."

"In the Gospel of St Mark, it is told how some disciples showed Our Lord a coin, with the head of Caesar engraved upon it. They asked should they pay taxes? Our Lord said, *Give unto Caesar that which is Caesar's and give unto God that which is God's.* Well, my son, let me tell you this: Give unto the DIs for the Marine Corps that which is the Marine Corps' and give unto God that which is God's.

"Now—you are in lapse as a Catholic having failed to go regularly to confession. That is a menial sin. Say the Act of Contrition with me and then three Hail Marys as your penance. And as a Marine—follow orders. Bless you, my son."

Marcin Wosczinskiewicz knelt outside to say his penance, left the little chapel and ran back to his barracks, smartly saluting two officers along the way. He was unsure why, but he had suddenly decided to become a career Marine.

Epilogue

Wosczinskiewicz was assigned a secondary MOS (military occupation speciality) as a French interpreter in the 2nd Marine Division at Camp LeJeune. There he met Wilson again and they became friends. He 'shipped over'—re-enlisted on the expiration of his first service term. He was in Vietnam in Military Intelligence as a Staff Sergeant. On his way to interview a retired French rubber planter, he was killed by a roadside bomb. Wilson completed his term as a Lance Corporal and retired from the Marine Corps. He went to Wall Street where he made a considerable fortune. Wilson was greatly saddened when he learned of Wosczinskiewicz's death in Vietnam.

FINIS

The Utility Bill

From: edenroc@hotel.co.fr
Lady Faultyspouse
To: felix@faultyspouse.com

Darling—have had a tiny reversal on that wretched wheel at the casino (surely it's fixed!). Can you send me ten thousand pounds from my account? I know you arranged to access it when I'm away. Send it to the branch in Salon—Armand will drive me there to pick it up.
   Love and xxx
   Cecily

From: salome@bigbank.co.uk
To: felix@faultyspouse.com

Dear Sir Felix
I'm sorry but Compliance does not accept the City of Cape Town invoice you sent as proof of residence for Lady Faultyspouse, as it only has your name on it. The passport copy and ten-page form signed by her are all satisfactory. Once we have a utility bill in Lady Faultysouce's name, you will be able to access her account on the internet banking service.
   Kind regards
   Salome Gregorivana
   International Premier Account Relationship Manager

From: felix@faultyhouse.com
To: edenroc@hotel.co.fr
attn Lady Faultyspouse

Cecily—what on earth are you doing at the Eden Roc? When you told me—without a by your leave, you were pushing off with that smarmy gigolo Armand, you said you were going to his Granny in a house in Antibes. And since when is ten thousand pounds a "tiny reversal?"

Felix

From: felix@faultyhouse.com
To: salome@bigbank.co.uk

Dear Salome—the invoice is in my name as the house is in my name. You have always accepted this as proof of residence for both of us. Our address is on Lady Faultyhouse's account with you. If you don't believe she lives there—why do you send her statement to that address? Compliance is being unreasonable. I need to access her account—she is travelling at the moment and can't access herself.

Felix

From: edenfroc@hotel.co.fr
Lady Faultyspouse
To: felix@faultyspouse.com

Don't be such a meany, my sweet! It was so boring at Antibes. We could only play bridge with Armand's Granny and her old butler (I owe them 200 Euros). And I don't like your bitterness about nice Armand. I think I've been very reasonable after your roll in the hay with my maid Lulu. Please hurry with the money.

Love and xxx
Cecily

From: felix@faultyspouse.com
To: edenroc@hotel.co.fr
attn Lady Faultyspouse

What roll in the hay? I already explained to you that having come home late and a touch squiffy, I went to bed in the dressing room so as not to disturb you and that stupid little maid of yours sneaked in and assaulted me—I should have had her charged with rape—but the police here wouldn't understand that. You will engage these girls with silly names from French farces. The last one Fifi was a disgrace—always flashing her frilly knickers at me. I'm working on the money, but the bank is throwing red tape at me. Stay away from the casino!

Felix

From: salome@bigbank.co.uk
To: felix@faultyspouse.com

Dear Sir Felix

I'm afraid Compliance can be a bit awkward. I would suggest you have the title deeds altered to include Lady Faultyspouses name so that the utility bill can be in both names. This would be a great convenience to you when the utility bill was needed for proof of residence in the future.

Kind regards

Salome Gregorivana

International Premier Account Relationship Manager

To: salome@bigbank.co.uk
From: felix@faultyspouse.com

Dear Salome

You must be joking! Are you suggesting, I should give half my house to my wife solely for the purpose of having a utility bill in both names? Apart from the gift tax implications and probate problems on the death of either of us, the whole process would take at least a year. I have never heard of such an impractical suggestion! What about other invoices to her at this address?

Kind regards

Felix

From: edenroc@hotel.co.fr
Lady Faultyspouse
To: felix@faultyspouse.com

My dear sweet lambkin! I'm afraid your story didn't wash when you first tried it on. Why was Lulu in tears the next morning? I would hate to think you disappointed her! Darling—some big, nasty men in black suits are after me. Armand says they are from the casino. They want their money. We're having to move back to Granny in Antibes. I'm in hiding! Please hurry with the money. I'm going to use Armand's laptop—don't worry—he has no idea how it works— the lovely man! But use this address: armandlesuave@gmail.com

love and xxx

Cecily

From: felix@faultyspouse.com
To: armandlesuave@gmail.com

Cecily

You have got yourself in a mess and I'm having to pick up the pieces! At least you are out of the hugely expensive Eden Roc. I can't imagine what the concierge thought of our correspondence. Can't Armand borrow the money if he doesn't have it himself? Surely, he knows you will pay him back. Your maid Lulu is a liar and consummate actress—but that's by the by. Bigbank is saying the CT rates/utility bill is not proof of your residence because it's only in my name.

They suggest I give you half the house to put the title and so the utility bill in both names! I'm trying to find a solution. If the granny and her butler play bridge for stakes, maybe she can lend you the money—but don't play to try and win it yourself!

Your bridge isn't up to it.

Felix

From: salome@bigbank.co.uk
To: felix@faultyspouse.com
Dear Sir Felix

I have passed your suggestion concerning alternative invoices in Lady Faultyspouse's name and address to Compliance at Head Office where it will be considered at the next Compliance committee meeting. In the meantime, if Lady Faultyspouse needs funds while travelling, I suggest debiting your own account and reimbursing from her account when she is home. You may use the internet banking service.

Kind regards

Salome Grigorivana
International Premier Account Relationship Manager

From: armandlesuave@gmail.com
To: felix@faultyspouse.com

Dear sweet cuddly bear—you know poor Armand hasn't got a centime. Surely you suspected that when he pinched your gold cigarette case and tried to sell it. And were you grateful when I stopped him? No! You just became old grumpy bear!

As for borrowing from Granny—I'm afraid that's a bit awkward. Armand and I are down 2000 Euros to her and that shark butler. I'm afraid we were vulnerable when I doubled their 6 spades. I was so sure Armand had the ace.

Armand says giving me half the house isn't a bad idea. He knows it will take a while, but we can wait. But please do something, my love—we've spotted those nasty men in black in town. They didn't see me as I'm now dressed like a French matelot—striped shirt and all. It must be an effective disguise because a rather camp English tourist propositioned me. But I hate to think what will happen if they catch me.

Love and xxx
Cecily.

PS The concierge at Eden Roc was a sweety pie. He thought we were a scream. I gave him a small diamond brooch as a tip.

From: felix@faultyspouse.com
To: salome@bigbank.co.uk

Dear Salome,

I have decided to advance the funds from my own account—I logged on to the internet banking service but of course, there must be a receiving account at Salon where she can pick up the funds. Can you help?

Kind regards
Felix

To: armandlesuave@gmail.com
From: felix@faultyspouse.com

Cecily—Did I not tell you to stop gambling? And don't you know doubling when vulnerable is dangerous? How many points did you have? Despite your appalling conduct and hopeless bridge, I'm going to send the money from my account. I thought I would put your diamond neckless in my safe as security because I know I'll have to wait till doomsday for you to pay me back.

But when I looked in your jewel case, I found it almost empty. So you must have something with you can hock—did you not think of that? Anyway, time and the men in black suits are pressing so I will arrange for the money to be at the Bigbank branch in Salon—but it needs arranging with Salome. I can't do it on the internet. Wait for me to get back to you. Don't play any more bridge and keep out of sight—or if you must go out, perhaps you can borrow from the next gentleman who tries to pick you up.

Felix

From: salome@bigbank.co.uk
To: felix@faultyspouse.com

Dear Sir Felix,

I have spoken to the Bigbank Manager in Salon-de-Provence. Since you are a Premier Customer, he can arrange a suspense account in your name and on your further instruction, I will debit your account and forward the specified amount. Please note that this will not give you an opportunity to confirm any rate of exchange involved. I am attaching a form which please complete, sign, scan and send back to me. It absolves Bigbank from any responsibility regarding a market exchange rate.

I hope this will be convenient for you and Lady Faultyspouse.

Kind regards

Salome Grigorivana

International Premier Account Relationship Manager

From: armandlesuave@gmail.com
To: felix@faultyspouse.com

Darling poor possum—don't be such a scold! Really, you are an old grouch. And here I am in great distress. Aren't you a teeny-weeny bit sorry for your loving Cecily? All right, so I only had four points—but Armand had opened one club so he must have had 12. Anyway, Granny and the butler are being nasty—they won't play more unless we pay up. Of course, I took my diamond neckless, my sweet. Did you expect me to go to the casino in an evening gown and a naked neck? And you wouldn't want me to go to a nasty pawn shop. Really!

How absolutely famous of you to lend me the money—of course, I'll pay you back. You are a suspicious old fox, my love!

Let me know when we should go to Salon. Armand says there's a slap up three-star restaurant for lunch on the way.

Love and millions of xxx Cecily

To: salome@ bigbank.co.uk
From: felix@faultyspouse.com

Dear Salome

Please debit my current account and transfer Euro 15,000 (fifteen thousand Euros) to the suspense account in my name at Bigbank Salon-de-Provence with instructions to hand the same in cash to Lady Faultyspouse. I am attaching the signed document you sent.

Kind regards

Felix

From: auguste@ bigbank.co.fr
To: felix@faultyspouse.com

Dear Sir Felix Faultyspouse

I hope this message finds you well. Allow me to introduce myself. I am Auguste LeBrave, General Manager of the branch of Bigbank France in Salon-de—Provence. I have spoken of you with my esteemed colleague Madame Salome Grigorivana from Bigbank in London. Funds have arrived for a suspense account in your name, but before I can activate the account and credit the funds, international money laundering regulations require that I receive a copy of your passport and a utility bill as proof of residence.

In anticipation of the honour of receiving a communication from your good self, I beg you to accept the sincere expression of my most amiable sentiments.

Auguste LeBrave

General Manager, Bigbank France

From: felix@faultyspouse.com
To: auguste@bigbank.co.fr

Dear M. LeBrave

As the funds come from your own Bigbank in London, where I have banked for over thirty years, I think you can make a reasonable assumption that they are not laundered monies. Nevertheless, I enclose a copy of my passport and of a recent utility bill—which you will note is an invoice from the City of Cape Town which incorporates property taxes, water and electric utility services—a convenience which does not exist in La Belle France, no doubt because it would limit the number of civil servants employed.

As Mrs Grigorivana has informed you—once available the funds are to be handed to Lady Faultyspouse who will identify herself of course.

Kind regards

Felix Faultyspouse

From: felix@faultyspouse.com
To: armandlesuave@gmail.com

Cecily—I would go and pick up the money tomorrow. Of course, I had to go through a process. The manager's name is Auguste LeBrave—don't laugh. He expects you. I don't think lunch on the way is such a great idea. In any case, make sure one of you is sober to drive after lunch.

Felix

From: armandlesuave@gmail.com
To: felix@faultyspouse.com

Darling! You are the greatest hero! I kiss your feet—and everything else. We'll be there with a paper bag to hold the loot. Don't worry about lunch. We'll have a nap after—an *al fresco siesta...* mmm! Do I tip M. LeBrave? No—I suppose not. He might kiss me on both cheeks like a general presenting a medal.

Love and xxx

Cecily

To: felix@faultyspouse.com
From: armandlesuave@gmail

Darling! The most horrible thing! That nasty LeBrave insisted I needed a utility bill in my name as proof of residence! My passport wasn't enough. I tried everything and was even unbuttoning my blouse—but there were customers around. It was so embarrassing!

A gendarme appeared and Armand scarpered around the corner. LeBrave finally suggested he could send it to Granny's bank in Antibes but would need fresh instructions from you. We've had to drive all the way back. Granny laughed when we told her the story. I didn't like that laugh. Anyway, here's her details. I couldn't believe it, Madame la Comtesse Desflaux de la Boudrière (imagine that old witch has a name like that!)

Credit Agricole, 10 Place du General de Gaulle, Antibes
Code Bancaire: CX4759
Code Guichet: 275
A/C No: 43088613

So, darling—be a dear and do send the order right away. Now that she knows she is going to get her bridge winnings, she has become quite chummy, and we are great friends. She tells me she married her husband for his title, but it turned out to be phony. Aren't people dishonest! Anyway, she kept it because it helps booking tables.

Love and hundreds of xxx

Cecily

From: auguste@bigbank.co.fr
To: felix@faultyspouse.com

Dear Sir Felix

I am very desolated to tell you we have had to refuse to provide the funds to

Lady Faultyspouse because she was not armed with a utility bill as proof of domicile. I have asked Madame Grigorivana why she did not warn you of this requirement so that in turn you could warn her Ladyship who was, unfortunately much distressed, having motored from Antibes. My colleague explained it was a very long story.

We discussed a solution which would require your sending the funds to the bank of the estimable lady where your own lady wife is staying in Antibes. I ventured to say that had this alternative been contemplated in the first place it would have saved the voyage of Lady Faultyspouse and her chauffeur. Your new instructions will be executed as soon as received.

Please accept the expression of my most cordial complements.

Auguste LeBrave

General Manager Bigbank France

From: felix@faulryspouse.com
To: auguste@bigbank.co.fr.

Dear M. LeBrave

To relate the story of Lady Faultyspouses's non-existent utility bill would require a volume and since neither you nor I can expect to reform the eccentricities of Bigbank's compliance functions, I suggest we consign the story to legend. Please debit my new suspense account and transfer Euro 15,000 (fifteen thousand Euros) to, Madame la Comtesse Desflaux de la Boudrière.

Credit Agricole, 10 Place du General de Gaulle, Antibes

Code Bancaire : CX4759

Code Guichet : 275

A/C No: 43088613

Thank you,

Kind regards

Felix Faultyspouse

From: felix@faultyspouse.com
To: armandlesuave@gmail.com

All right, Cecily, Granny can go to her bank—but make sure you go with her—and tell her not to forget to take a utility bill in her name together with her passport! I do expect this saga, which has been very inconvenient for me, to finally come to an end.

Felix

From: armandlesuave@gmail.com
To: felix@faultyspouse.com

Dearest—or should I say old grumpypuss! You *are* a stuffy bear—but I love you still! This will be a <u>long</u> message because the most surprising things have happened—but your loving Cecily is OK! Isn't that the most important thing? I went with the Comtesse to her bank, but she said they knew her since she was a girl (must be pre-war) and she wouldn't need a utility bill. We have become very confidential, and it turns out the house is in the butler's name—and so is the utility bill—and he is actually her secret husband!

Secret, because she wants to keep her old name for booking the best tables. It's just like *Sunset Boulevard* and Eric von Strohiem! Well, she got the money and counted out what we owed her for bridge on the spot. Turns out it's 3000 Euros so we're short for the men in black suits. But Armand said he had a plan. It's another disguise. So, he fitted me out like a tart (if you say that should be easy, I'll kill you!), mini skirt, fishnet stockings and knee boots—the lot.

I must say I looked quite fetching. The plan was, I should go down to the Marina and hang about wiggling my bum and see if I can't cage an invite on to one of the yachts.

"But Armand," I said, "I'm not sure I want to go that far and what would Felix say?" You see, my sweet, I was thinking of you! "Don't be silly!" said Armand, "you ask for the money upfront—it's usual. You stuff it into this plastic thing we've put in your string bag—and then you pop overboard. I will have been tracking you the whole time. I'll know which yacht you are on, and I'll hear the splash. You swim to the nearest shore—it's not far from the dock moorings and I'll be there with dry clothes. Well! I thought I'd better not have the knee boots—so we found some spike-heeled, open toed shoes, easy to kick off. Took a while to paint my toenails purple."

Darling! You won't believe how good I was! I mean, Bette Davis—eat your heart out! And it didn't take me long. A very stout gentleman in a blue blazer, white ducks, and a big cigar, ambled down his gangplank. "Looking for a good time?" I said. "How much?" he said. "5000 Euros," I said, "Done," he said. If

I'd known it was so easy—we might have spared you all the bother, my poor lambkin!

Well, the water was surprisingly warm, although it smelt of diesel a bit. But—my dearest, sweetest Felix—all the best plans and so on—when I got to shore there was Armand all right, but also two gendarmes! What a row we had! They were going to arrest Armand for pimping and me for soliciting! I persuaded them to take us to Granny's house (or the butler's—it seems) so I could show them my British passport and I demanded the right to contact the British consulate.

Well, Granny put on her best Comtesse act, Armand looked sheepish—I was a bit worried because one of the gendarmes said, "don't we know you from somewhere?" But Granny said, "Perhaps because my grandson is a good friend of the *Commissaire*." Anyway, I finally got a hold of the Consul in Nice and you'll never guess! It's Reggie Everitt—your chum from Eton!! Well, you can imagine! A bottle of champers was opened for the Gendarmes who said they would pick up the men in black suits—seems they are known to the *flics*.

Reggie says I should go home. But my darling, I think I had better own up about one thing. You wondered why I hadn't popped my diamond necklace. My sweetest of understanding husbands—because it's paste! I had to sell the real diamonds after that terrible night at Aspinall's when we were entertaining the Goodman twins—remember?

I lost a packet at *vingt et un.* You see, the twins were betting huge stakes, like there was no tomorrow and I felt I had to keep up. I am sooo sorry!! Well, I think perhaps I should go home. Can you call the travel agents and book me Nice/Heathrow/Cape Town? Armand is going to stay with his Granny for a while—he says her nerves are a bit shot.

Love and a million xxx
Cecily

From: everittnice@gov.uk
To: felix@faultyspouse.com

Hi Felix
I've just got Cecily out of a bit of a scrape down here. To be frank, old sport, I don't think you should allow her to gallivant around with unsuitable chums.

We all love Cecily, but she can be a bit irresponsible. She said it was all because of some utility bill! I'm sure she will explain it to you when she gets home.

Do let me know if you come this way.

As ever

Reggie

FINIS

The Wisdom of Youth

I have always been annoyed at the tyranny inherent in well-known aphorisms, sayings, proverbs, and *bon-mots*. Perhaps the origin of my annoyance is childhood when mother or nanny, but particularly the latter, used such sayings to make one eat up one's porridge or clean one's teeth at night—or whatever. The soul of a child rebels against the ruthless logic incorporated in such sayings as "a stitch in time saves nine" or "fortune favours the brave."

Like most children, I had an enquiring mind, and I hated the smugness and confidence with which adults pronounced on matters I was still exploring. I wanted to find out for myself whether courage always equated with financial success or expedition in repair avoided total breakdown.

Even as a young adult, I hated the final conclusions so present in ordinary small talk; for a long time, I insisted that conversation was meant to be a means of enquiry into the mysteries of life. As a result, I now realise, I was a terrible bore. People are not always prepared to pronounce on great metaphysical issues; they often find it more relaxing to deal in proven certainties. Even exceptions give rise to that most dreadful of aphorisms: "the exception proves the rule."

I was thinking of a particularly pernicious platitude one Monday evening in September, sitting in a basement flat with some friends. We were drinking a rather indifferent champagne which served to underscore the modest surroundings, as it was neither cold nor dry enough. The platitude in question which was buzzing about in my head was that concerned with the energy of youth and the wisdom of age.

There is no succinct expression of this generality in English. But in French, the phrase is: "*si jeunesse savait et veillesse pouvait.*" If youth knew and age could. I have long suspected that observation. Perhaps I have not known many young people lacking energy. I have certainly known some old fools. Wisdom is not an inevitable by-product of age and now I was listening to two people—a young girl and a much older man and that dreaded rule-proving exception sprang to mind.

The girl was called Faith. It was her basement flat in which we now sat. The décor was an overall jumble but striking in one regard. One half of the large room was simple and tidy—a three-seat sofa covered with an attractive loose sheet of India material; in front was a wicker and glass coffee table. A simple standard lamp with a plain parchment shade stood on one side and on the other a round table with a piece of gingham material draped over it and an earthenware pot made into a lamp with a single bulb-holding device stuck in the tip of the pot with a thick piece of cork.

The shade on this lamp was clearly from a child's room; it showed scenes from Winnie the Pooh, with Christopher Robin and other characters. If this side of the room, where Faith now sat quietly sipping her champagne, gave the impression of modest order and simplicity, the other side of the room looked as though a moving van had dumped its contents unceremoniously. The sole seating provided was a ram-shackled canvas director's chair in which now sprawled the third member of our party, a scruffy lawyer called Septimus Naylor, normally shortened to 'Sep' or 'Seppy'.

Surrounding him were packing cases, piles of files and books, a half-empty suitcase with ties, belts and other items trailing over the sides, a bag of golf clubs, some polo sticks, assorted tennis and squash racquets, a compact disc player with wires dangling and piles of CD's and other paraphernalia—all suggesting a recent and hurried move.

Seppy was talking. He was a man in his fifties. I had known him for only a short time but as I sat listening to his monologue, I reflected on the change in his physical appearance—not progressively over the whole span of our acquaintance, but in the last period. Originally, a man of obsessive correctness and careful grooming, Seppy now spilled out of his clothes, wore his hair unkempt and over his collar, had begun to sport a designer stubble and generally appeared to be engaged in a theatrical sketch of a tramp.

"D'you remember those twin girls we went to stay with down in Wiltshire?" Seppy was now asking Faith.

"Of course—I was at school with them for a year," Faith answered in her quiet voice.

"I've always wondered about twins—you know, about their sex life."

"You wonder too much about that sort of thing."

"No! I mean really," Seppy persisted, "let me tell you a true story that will shed light on what I'm getting at."

I looked at Faith who had adopted an air of patience. Seppy was always declaring 'true stories' that were, in fact, inventions of his own. This storytelling had become a central feature of the new conversational style—adopted to match his new bohemian look.

Seppy took up his tale.

"This chap I knew at school was amazingly good-looking—but in a very girlish way. Of course, he was used to being ragged and stories would circulate about him and the head of games type that he fagged for. But he certainly wasn't queer—he was a decent but quiet chap and I got to know him quite well. Now you know how they say that everyone in this world has an exact double somewhere.

"Well, I somehow doubt it—I don't think the law of averages works that way. Anyway, some people believe it and you do hear of people running into the double. Don't the Germans have a word for it? 'DoppelGanger' or something. Well, one day my friend ran into his exact double—only she was a girl. He described the shock to me afterwards. She was an identical female version of himself—same colour hair, eyes, bone structure, skin type, the lot.

"As he explained it to me—she was him, except with boobs and hips. They were both bowled over by the co-incidence or whatever it was. If they had been born identical twin brother and sister, they couldn't have been more alike. In fact, they were the same age but born in different months and they couldn't discover any family connections.

"Well, they started seeing each other a lot and one thing led to another and before they knew it, they were engaged in a torrid affair. This went on for a while; they used to spend the whole weekend in the sack—neither could get enough."

Faith began to fidget a bit, as I noticed she always did when Seppy embarked on his stories. "All right now—we're getting on to the twin bit," I intervened—hoping to hurry to the conclusion, as I could see that Faith was uncomfortable.

Seppy held up his hand, in a mock dramatic gesture.

"Only partly, only partly," he repeated. "One day, my friend told me that he was breaking up with that girl and leaving the country as he just couldn't take it anymore."

Seppy paused and looked at Faith and me, one after the other, as though asking us to guess his ending.

"You see," continued the narrator, in the absence of any comment from us, "my friend explained that he was overwhelmed by this feeling of guilt. He realised that the affair with this identical double was either masturbation or incest and possibly both."

Seppy leaned back in his director's chair to drain his glass of champagne and then got up to refill it, looking at Faith to judge her reaction to his story. It was clear that the story had been told largely to provoke a reaction from Faith and equally clear that she was practised in avoiding the issue. I was just annoyed, as I was frequently now with Seppy because he seemed to tell stories with no real point—but simply to test Faith's reaction.

It had not always been so, to say the least. Seppy had begun his relationship with Faith by placing her on a pedestal—excessively so in my view. I should explain that I had known them both separately at first and was now condemned to be the observer of an increasingly flawed relationship. I should resist the temptation at this early point of my narrative to complain. It was a pain to watch two friends destroying themselves for different but associated reasons and to be a confidant to both—a referee and arbiter, but with no power at all to change the course of events.

At some time, we have all known someone on the brink; we take a certain morbid pleasure in this process, if we are honest with ourselves; will they jump, or won't they? I have never been involved in that most hackneyed of incidents: the suicide threat on the window ledge. The crowd below watches in fear; there is a collective intake of breath as he or she moves slightly. It could be a high wire at act at the circus. How often has this scene been a comic device in a Hollywood movie?

There is usually one person who crawls out on the ledge, pleading with the unstable subject—ready to catch him or her at the last moment as they do jump. I did dream that Seppy was in just such a situation. In my dream, Faith was at the window with me and I crawled out onto the ledge. I remember just before waking thinking to myself that I was just as likely to push him off the ledge as I was to drag him back inside. Even after waking, I still couldn't decide in my own mind which I would have done if the dream had gone on.

I first knew Septimus Naylor as a lawyer. He was a solicitor, in fact, but liked to adopt the pose of a supercilious Queen's Council. He was tailored to the nines, never without a stiff collar and a monocle dangled from a black silk cord around his neck. His manner of speech was a cross between Noel Coward and Robert Donat: "that is indubitably so," he liked to say when replying to some simple fact raised in conversation.

He was methodical, precise, punctual, and scathing about any irregularity of behaviour which ordinary mortals are prone to. We met first quite by accident whilst waiting to have our haircut at a traditional establishment in St James's Street. On the second occasion, we realised that due to a mix-up in appointments, we were both waiting for the same barber.

"Have the Times," he said, as he rose to take the barber's chair. "It's barely ruffled. I have only read the law reports." In this short exchange, a few things were revealed to me about Septimus Naylor. In the first place, there was no question as to who would take the first opening with the barber of mutual choice.

Secondly, my new acquaintance was so fastidious that the idea of a rumpled newspaper was distasteful and finally, he was in the legal profession and uninterested in ordinary news. We would next meet at a cocktail party when we were formally introduced and exchanged only a few words before our hostess moved one of us on. We then met again a few months later at the same hair cutters in St James's Street.

"Are you free for lunch afterwards?" asked Septimus, as he allowed his jacket to be removed prior to settling in the barber's chair. "If so, join me at Boodles, we shall be before the rush and certain of a table."

As it happens, I was and, after an errand nearby, I returned, and we sauntered up St James's together. Septimus informed me that he much preferred the Garrick as there were too many solicitors at Boodles. Indeed, the Garrick is the club of literary and theatrical types, journalists and barristers. I assumed from his general manner and this early reference that Septimus Naylor was at the Bar, a Q.C. in all probability (he was around 50 at the time).

At luncheon, he talked generalities and made a series of stuffy remarks which made me think he might be mocking me. I should mention at this point, that I happen to be a hereditary peer of the Realm. I was educated abroad, my father having died in the war and my mother was remarried to an Italian living in Switzerland.

In neither appearance nor manner do I correspond to most people's traditional view of an English aristocrat. I have a quite prominent chin; my English is slightly accented, and I am not interested in field sports. Our country seat has long been a hotel; our acres sold, our townhouse bombed in the war and now the property of National Car Parks. I live in a three-room flat in Notting Hill gate and work for at an advertising agency.

But I have a very well-known name; Septimus in those days was socially upwardly mobile—as they say. At any rate, at lunch on that day, he carefully avoided asking me any questions about myself, what I did or even who I knew, so that we might discover mutual friends. I felt that he might be reluctant to talk about his own background and so I reciprocated his lack of curiosity. Much later in our acquaintance, He amused himself by pointing out that I was not a 'practising peer'—I don't think he meant in the sense of attendance at the House of Lords.

Septimus and I became friends after this. I'll call him Seppy from now on. I asked him to lunch one day and soon afterwards I was invited to a dinner party at his house just off Kings Road. His wife turned out to be exactly as one would expect the wife of a successful, socially proactive solicitor to be. A compact brunette, impeccably turned out in a mixture of Sloane Ranger and County lady in town, she enthused about everything, giving one the impression that an ordinary dinner party was a special occasion.

The other guests were clearly clients or prospective clients—at least one City type and a literary agent, who I realised it was to have been the guest of honour until Seppy told his wife that I had to be on her right because of my rank. Although she was very polite to me and clearly enjoyed introducing me to the rest of the party, I sensed that that Seppy had added me to an event already planned (I was an extra man).

Mrs Naylor's conversation was very focused on coincidences involving people and their relations. She prefaced her interventions with the phrase: "it's absolutely amazing!" With the middle 'a' in the word 'amazing' drawn out and further emphasised by a widening of her large brown eyes. As she chatted (inevitably about mutual acquaintances) it transpired that my eldest sister, who with her schoolmaster husband ran a boarding school in Lucerne, mostly for diplomats' children, had looked after a cousin of Mrs Naylor's for two years. Mrs Naylor turned back to the literary agent on her left.

"It's absolutely amazing!" she drawled, "but Lord Wister's sister looked after little Cecily in Switzerland for two years!"

"Please call me Gerald," I pleaded, for the third time that evening.

Suddenly, Seppy intervened.

"Little Cecily was abandoned by her parents in a most reprehensible way whilst they were in gauged in an acrimonious and, as it proved, disastrous divorce." He boomed this from the other end of the table. He had an ear tuned to his wife's conversation.

"My name is Gerald, and my sister is called Evangeline," I said, somewhat hopelessly.

"But it's absolutely amazing!" said Mrs Naylor. "My best friend at school was called Evangeline."

The evening wore on in a similar manner and I remember thinking to myself as I left, that Seppy was pompous and his wife shallow.

Soon afterwards, I introduced a client in need of legal services to Seppy. It was not a major affair: a question of the rights to a photograph which had been used in an advertising display. My photographer friend, on whose behalf Seppy acted, was bemused but uncomplaining. Apparently, Seppy treated the matter as if it were an affair of state. He seemed far more interested in procedural issues than in matters of substance, but the case was resolved in favour of his client and the fee was reasonable.

Seppy and I continued to meet on and off, but I never considered that I had become an intimate friend. Some of my city friends knew Seppy and I was not surprised to find that he was considered stuffy and pretentious, but adept at circulating. He was a partner in a relatively minor firm but attracted business through his many contacts rather than because of the standing of the firm. One day, I was lunching at the club table at Whites when I overheard a snatch of conversation between two other members.

"I hear Seppy Nayler's making an ass of himself over some young thing," said one.

"Well! I wonder how he will handle that since he is so scathing about divorce," said the other.

I thought little about this, until I ran into Seppy again at our mutual haircutting establishment.

"I say, Wister," said Seppy who, at this stage in our friendship still refused to call me by my Christian name, "I'd rather like a word with you about an awkward situation. Can we lunch?"

We did. Seppy had never seemed more ill at ease. I had suggested a quiet Italian place in the Kings Road, rather than a club.

"I've met this girl," said Seppy, after some small talk—no doubt summoning up the courage to embark on a full conversation. He gulped vigorously at his gin and tonic whilst looking off into the distance.

"I'm absolutely smitten, old boy—the problem is she is 20 years younger than I am."

I immediately wondered how Seppy could have met someone of another generation. The Naylers had no children and seemed engrossed in their own set or in the cultivation of clients which didn't involve young people. Apparently, an aunt of the young lady in question had been referred to Seppy by a friend. As a courtesy, Seppy had called on the lady, a semi-invalid and then met her niece, who was called Faith and aged about 23.

By the end of our luncheon, Seppy had detailed his personal anguish, discussed various options, marvelled at his ability to conceal the affair from his wife, speculated on the cost of a conventional divorce, expressed concern over the impact of the affair on his professional reputation, but said nothing about Faith. I was not comfortable being taken into Seppy's confidence. I was surprised that he had no more intimate friend in which he could confide.

A faint but persistent feeling of injustice began to invade my general reaction to the whole story. I was annoyed that I should be dragged in. I felt certain that Seppy was taking advantage of this girl in some way. Although Mrs Naylor had not inspired my sympathy or respect, on the few occasions I had met her, I felt she was bound to be mistreated. In all his confidences to me, which were destined to be frequent and numerous, Seppy was never concerned with anyone but himself.

Seppy talked to me at least three times in the following month to report on his affair with Faith and the early stages of his separation from his wife—and yet I still knew nothing about the young girl who had so dramatically entered his life (at least this was how Seppy liked to put it—as though the initiative had somehow been hers). It was with some relief that I accepted an invitation to dine *à trois* in a restaurant on the Thames one evening in late June.

The establishment was expensive and pretentious; one of the first English restaurants to be granted three stars by the Michelin guide. The clientele was comprised of celebrities and well-heeled American tourists. As menus were handed around, an elaborate description of the featured dishes was presented by a cockney head waiter with a poorly executed, phoney French accent.

The chef/ proprietor appeared at a certain moment in a white stainless chef's uniform with his name elaborately embroidered on his left breast and greeted certain favourite tables. I realised, as my acquaintance with Faith blossomed into friendship, it was just the sort of place she hated.

I did not learn much that first evening as Seppy dominated the conversation. I did notice a change in his style and manner. He had suddenly become rather loud and expansive in his gestures. It was as though he had had a few drinks beforehand. I wondered why he was making our table somewhat conspicuous with loud guffaws and an overdrawn discussion with the chef in bad French.

Faith was a remarkably quiet, calm and gentle person with none of the flirtatiousness or verve one associates with a pretty girl. It was on this occasion that I began to note the conflict in personality between them, which was to grow, almost as if consciously planned, as the affair progressed or, rather—to be more accurate—regressed.

Faith was beautiful. I could not put it more simply, but it was a kind of beauty not everyone would identify. It was a far cry from the model girl, popular actress or society girl type of beauty. She had been born with a facial flaw: an eyelid which drooped—perhaps because of some dead nerve on the left side of her face. As soon as she reached the age when girls become particularly conscious of their looks, she had taught herself to adjust the normal eyelid on the right side, so that it matched its pair.

The result was a distinctive, sultry look—what one might describe as 'bedroom eyes'. Since she could not move the other eyelid except to close it, she kept the half lidded, slightly sleepy look with all facial expressions, dropping her guard, so to speak, only at times of emotional distress. I was to see Faith in this condition more than once.

The underlying beauty was so dominant that even the skewed look, resulting from her failure to adjust her a good eye, produced a striking, rather than an odd effect. Her beauty was largely generated from inside. It was the consequence of an inner peace which resisted external turbulence and was always strong enough to maintain an aura and expression which, together with the more mundane aspects of composition of features, constituted exceptional beauty.

Faith had been born in Africa and this could be ascertained in her movement. One suspected she had watched Africans and animals as a young girl and unconsciously adopted their grace and languor. Her father was a younger son of an impoverished family of Devon squires. After an undistinguished war in a regiment of Yeomanry, he had gone to seek his fortune in Rhodesia, married the daughter of a Cape Town judge, taken up tobacco farming, failed; tried Safari camp management on the Zambezi, failed again, then went through a succession of jobs, moving to Kenya as an hotel manager and finally to Cape Town as an overseer on a wine estate.

He was good-looking, charming, well-mannered, a born storyteller, always popular, but fundamentally lazy and unreliable. With a wife to motivate him, he might have succeeded in a settled occupation, but Faith's mother died in childbirth, and he never could face remarrying. His daughter was first raised on the tobacco farm by a series of African nannies under the occasional supervision of a neighbour's wife.

The failure of the tobacco farm required that Faith be placed in a convent boarding school in Salisbury. By now, she was seven years old. Holidays were spent at her father's Safari camp or with the tobacco farm neighbours. Then came the failure of the Safari business and it was decided that Faith must be sent to England to the charge of a series of maiden aunts, who would look after the balance of her education and return her to Africa for holidays—whenever her father's resources would permit.

As I got to know Faith in those later years, I began to appreciate that this deportation from Africa had been a major heartbreak for her and that she regarded her subsequent life as an exile. Two of the maiden aunts lived in Brighton and another, from Faith's mother's side, lived in Tenby—all in genteel poverty, surrounded by mementos of a once affluent, land-owning, county existence. There were days when the monotony of their lives was relieved only by letters sent to and received from relatives scattered throughout the Empire. Cousins resettled in Canada, Australia, India, and Africa were in receipt of long and wordy letters, commenting on political events, the Royal family and reminding each other of their glorious Norman antecedents. Replies were desultory and not always regular, but no less eagerly awaited.

Faith was placed in a second-rate boarding school where she had difficulty forming friendships with girls of a non-colonial background. Her father's resources diminished each year and holidays at home in Africa became less frequent, condemning Faith to periods of extreme sadness at Brighton or Tenby, in rooms with peeling wallpaper, musty and soulless, dried out like the old sachets left in the bureau drawers.

The aunts were kind and as generous as their limited means allowed, but they were from another world. They could talk of Africa because of their lifelong correspondence with relatives living there, but this would just increase Faith's sense of loss. They had no friends with other children of Faith's age. She spent her school holidays taking long walks along the leaden seashores.

She would blot out the sights of the tawdry resort clutter she encountered in her walks and would look down at her feet, imagining that they were bare or sandalled and that she was walking over the red earth of Africa, on tracks lined with Jacaranda, listening to the sounds, inhaling the smells. Passers-by would see a girl looking through them with her sultry but seemingly sightless eyes. She did not see the aged folk or provincial trippers that populated her places of exile.

She saw Africans walking back to the compound from the lands, the women with their washing on their heads, the children with their soulful eyes, rounded bellies and best Sunday school greetings. Faith was physically in England in these years, but her soul was in Africa and her heart was dormant. She was sometimes invited by school friends who tried to pair her off with brothers and discarded boyfriends, but these found her distant, closed and forbidding. The bedroom eyes seemed to promise, but her manner was ethereal—almost religious in its cool calmness and poise.

Faith heard irregularly from her father; he only wrote when he could report some positive development in his erratic career, and this became increasingly rare. She knew she must forgive him his feckless decline. She felt this must be due to the early loss of her mother. But she could not forgive his refusal to have her with him—whatever his circumstances. She would have lived in a rondavel and cooked his meals on an open fire to be with her father. She was successful at school and interested in most subjects but only Africa and things African really stimulated her intellectual curiosity and she never dreamed unless it was of the bush and the people and animals who lived there.

I later thought that this distancing from her father and from Africa which, if it is truly the mother continent of mankind, was for Faith the father continent; this tear in the fabric of her girlhood, was the reason Faith reciprocated or, rather, did not resist the attentions of Seppy. He was certainly a potential father figure at the outset, with his stuffy but kindly solicitor's ways. Then, as he began to go to pieces, I realised that he was unconsciously emulating her father. But for Faith the key difference was that she was with him. She couldn't 'mother' her father as he sat, unshaven, shabby, and brooding on the veranda of his bungalow at the

206

Cape—drinking his dinner. But she was with Seppy and he needed her. Mother, daughter, sister, wife, mistress—there is an element of each in every woman, of course and it is men who are simple-minded enough to think that they always know exactly which role the woman in their life is playing.

I had my first evidence that this new chapter in Seppy's life was to be his undoing when he rang to tell me that he was leaving his firm to set up as a 'business/lawyer'.

"What's that when it's at home," I said.

"You know—an entrepreneur with sound, legal training. I'm fed up with picking up after other people while they make a bundle. I'm going to make some serious money myself, for a change. I've got alimony payments staring me in the face, you know."

"But surely now is the time to play it safe—not take risks—you're doing that in other ways."

"I presume you are referring to Faith. She wants me to have a complete change of lifestyle—she understands what I'm doing."

"So, you are abandoning prudence in order to have faith?" I said. I couldn't resist it.

"If that's the sort of humour you find in the tearoom of the House of Lords, I'm not surprised you're considered redundant. But if you want to hear my plans, let's lunch."

Seppy joined me for lunch at a fashionable Italian eatery in Beauchamp Place, where the food was expensive, and the paparazzi hung about the entrance because pop stars went there. He was wearing a polo shirt under a patched tweed shooting coat and grey flannels. His hair needed cutting, he looked somewhat rumpled, and he ordered two vodkas on the rocks for himself before the menus were brought. He explained that he was planning to join with a partner in the business of property conversions in Mayfair and surrounding 'desirable areas'. According to Seppy, there were countless run-down residences—flats, maisonettes and small houses which just needed a facelift and could then be sold or let at fabulous prices to young marrieds, Arabs, Hong Kong Chinese, Italians et etcetera.

"What do you know about residential property?" I asked.

"Listen, I can do conveyancing in my sleep—also, I've got the contacts. I give the project a respectable face."

Seppy was indignant at my doubts. I wondered whether he could be confronting clients dressed as he was now.

"But guess what my other news is? I'm taking up the game of polo!"

"Can you ride?"

"No, but this chap at Windsor is teaching me everything. You start sitting on a wooden horse and you learn all the strokes."

"Wouldn't it be better to learn to ride first?"

"All in good time, my man says. It's very exciting. Of course, Faith has her doubt. She thinks I'm not very fit. But there are people still playing polo at the age of 70."

"I dare say they live in the country and ride every day."

"You're a spoilsport. I'm just starting to live."

I had more than a vague premonition at this point that Seppy's new lifestyle would end in tears, but I didn't think too much about it. In fact, Seppy was beginning to bore me.

One day, I ran into Faith in Peter Jones of all places. I was there to buy a suitcase and she was wondering among the multi-coloured cushions.

"Septimus is moving in with me," she said quietly and with no hint of embarrassment. "I suppose I need to smarten up my little basement flat."

"Everything going smoothly, then?"

Faith paused and looked around as if expecting another acquaintance.

"There used to be a coffee shop here somewhere. Would you like some?" She took me by the arm.

We went up to the top floor and found a depressing cafeteria. Faith looked at her cup with her hooded eyes and her head slightly cocked to one side. She was dressed in beige linen trousers and a sort of safari-style jacket with the sleeves rolled up.

"Seppy is being very silly," she said, throwing me a glance with the bedroom eyes before resuming the examination of her cup. "I probably shouldn't be talking to you about him—I don't know how old a friend you are. I don't expect you to do anything. Please don't talk to him but there is no one else I can talk to. I hope you don't mind."

The bedroom eyes turned on me again. She took my silence (I couldn't think of what to say) for encouragement.

"He's thrown up his job and started some strange thing with a man I don't trust. He's drinking much more than he used to. There is this idea of polo which seems foolish at his age. He is also being remarkably nasty to Jane (Seppy's wife) and that's not like him. As a lawyer, he knows perfectly well what Jane is entitled to. It seems wrong and foolish not to do the right thing by her. But there is something else he's not telling me. I know it—but I don't know what it is."

I listened to this and more which followed not so much interested in Seppy's transgressions and personality change—I was expecting this—but fascinated by Faith's approach to it all. She talked to me openly even though she hardly knew me and, in any case, presumed me to be his friend.

She was calm and seemingly unemotional—the trained eyelid remained in control. It was difficult for me to relate to this conversation to the knowledge that she was presumably in love with this man who had left his wife and career to live with her. She might have been another mutual friend of the couple in question, sharing impressions with me of the negative turn the affair was taking.

After a while, we seemed to have exhausted the Seppy issue, mostly because I could think of nothing to say by way of consolation or advice. It was then, over a second cup of undrinkable coffee, that Faith told me of Africa. It was then also, that I realised the degree of her exile. She was a grounded aviator, a sailor confined to shore—no world existed for her but the land of her birth and childhood. All the rest, including Seppy, I imagined, was a purgatory to be endured before she could once more be readmitted to paradise. I felt a sudden urge to take her by the hand, partly as one might with someone sleeping—but also to show that warmth, life, and acceptable reality could still exist in a place of exile.

We parted with the hope that we could meet again to exchange confidences without hurting Seppy and I suddenly felt an uncharacteristic and unexpected pang of jealousy. I was none the wiser as to what to do about Faith and Seppy's falling star not having yet developed the father figure theory.

It was some months before I saw Seppy again. In the interval, I heard vague and general comments, all negative in tone, suggesting that his business interests were not prospering and his wrangle with his wife was unresolved. All the commentators sided with his wife. I saw him again suddenly at Annabel's, an establishment I rarely frequent producing a particularly expensive evening when I do go, if one includes the annual subscription.

On this occasion, I had clients in tow and so my firm would reimburse the evening's cost, at least. Of course, the computerised reservation system, including, I suspect, a photograph of the member, ensures that one is greeted as a regular, even if two years have elapsed between visits. This impresses one's guests.

"Good evening, Lord Wister," said the maître delete, who resembles a bishop, on our arrival. "Mr Naylor is here this evening and has asked after your Lordship."

I was taken aback. I could not imagine why Seppy would assume I would be at Annabel's on this evening. We were shown to our table by the head waiter who, like all the staff at Annabel's, has been trained to work in the dark. I tried to pierce the obscurity with a room-scanning gaze, but I could see no sign of Seppy. Between the courses, a sudden outburst of Latin American music made it impossible for me to avoid dancing with my lady guest, a Brazilian whose fingers were already playing bongo drums on the tablecloth.

We rose and threaded our way to the floor to begin the contactless gyrations and rhythmic convulsions which passed for modern nightclub dancing. A couple on the floor we are locked in a lascivious embrace, almost as an act of love whilst upright on the dance floor. When they spun around at one point, I recognised Seppy. He was certainly not with Faith. When a natural break occurred, I suggested to my partner that we return to our table and lingered long enough to pass by Seppy's alcove, where he and his date were also re-gaining their places.

"I bet you wondered how I knew you would be here," said Seppy grinning.

"This is Samantha," he indicated his escort but singularly failed to mention my name and so it was hardly an introduction.

"Pleased to meet you," chirped Samantha, who was probably called Sharon, hailed from East London, and worked for an agency that answered telephones by day and sent its employees out by night. Perhaps my suspicion was ungenerous, but I was shocked to see Seppy in these circumstances.

"I think I'd rather not know," I said, probably looking rather severe, "but can I call you tomorrow and arrange a lunch?"

"Oh, oh, I think I'm being carpeted. He's a very upstanding member of parliament—upper house, of course, my girl." Seppy addressed these remarks to his cosmetically advantaged companion, and I left with what I hoped was a polite nod to both.

When I met Seppy some days later, he was even more bombastic than usual. "Faith won't go to Annabel's so, bloody hell, why shouldn't I hire some stuff who will? Anyway, Annabel's is more fun with a floozy in tow."

I was not really interested in Seppy's sex life but more concerned that Faith was going to be abandoned unceremoniously. As usual, Seppy talked only about himself. His business venture had collapsed, but it was his partner's fault.

That should have taken him off the hook to some extent with his wife, but Jane and her lawyer pursued Seppy for an appropriate settlement, based on the conviction that someone with his previous business rectitude could not possibly have allowed his present condition. Apparently broke, drinking heavily and looking increasingly like an overgrown dropout—all this must constitute some elaborate screen to excuse him from his responsibilities.

It was shortly after this brief meeting that I called on Faith and Seppy in the former's basement flat and heard Seppy's lame and pointless anecdote about the twins. Seppy was now doing nothing. A broken collarbone and his almost totally depleted finances had finished his polo—fortunately, it seemed to me. No new prospect was germinating to replace the ill-fated venture in residential property refurbishment. I wondered what he was living on and hoped it wasn't on Faith's meagre salary as a receptionist in an art gallery.

"Let me take you to dinner," I said, noticing that the bottle of champagne was now empty.

"How gracious of you, my Lord," said Seppy, sarcastically.

"Be nice, Seppy," said Faith. "We'd love to, of course."

"Wister knows I'm broke, and I should be taking you both out but there is no reason to rub it in." Seppy was petulant and he now lurched somewhat unsteadily to his feet as Faith collected the glasses. They both disappeared for a moment behind a curtain of plaid which cloaked a small kitchenette, and I could hear Seppy grumbling about something as Faith rinsed the glasses.

We dined in a noisy basement restaurant in a neighbouring street as Seppy embarrassed as both by carrying on a jocular and suggestive dialogue with the harassed student waitress. I reflected on how unamusing Seppy he had become, only partly because of drink. Of course, he had never really been amusing except perhaps as a caricature of the drunken university student.

But his seedy middle age and his lack of aptitude for the frivolous banter of youth produced a result which set the teeth on edge. As always, I noticed Faith's reaction. It was one of extraordinary patience and compensating solemnity. She sat with grace, deftly moving Seppy's wineglass from the path of his gesticulating arm and quietly sympathising with the long-suffering waitress.

When Faith looked at Seppy, with her hooded eyes, her expression did not denote arrogance, long-suffering, or sadness. She seemed rather to be observing an inevitable process, as one might watch demolition work on a building, with some regret for that landmark being destroyed, but even greater interest in the process. We parted outside the restaurant. Faith set off holding Seppy with two hands—whether, in support or affection, I could not say.

A month or so later, I was awake and at around three in the morning by Seppy on the telephone, sounding sober but asking for my urgent attendance at a police station near Southwark Cathedral. No, he was not under arrest, but he had been involved in an 'altercation' and the police required confirmation of his status as a solicitor and a respectable citizen. This did not surprise me.

"Can't I just speak to the sergeant in charge?" I asked.

"No, you must come down here—Please, Gerald, give me a break for Faith's sake—Also, I don't have any money to get home."

This was the first time that I could record Seppy addressing me by my Christian name. The reference to Faith also motivated me, I realised. I told him I didn't know how easily I would find a cab but that I would be there as soon as I could.

I found a cab cruising past Notting Hill gate tube station almost immediately and gave the address Seppy had given me.

"Going to bail out a chum, Guv?" The cabdriver knew the address as a police station. I tried to imagine the circumstances which had led to set his current predicament and thought mostly of Faith, asleep, I hoped or perhaps waiting for Seppy to come home to her little basement flat near the Portobello Road. Having been bored with Seppy, I realised I was now getting angry with him.

I found Seppy sitting on a bench facing a glum-looking police sergeant filling in forms. A few feet from him sat a flashy-looking black man with gold rings and bracelets, wearing a purple satin windcheater with the words 'Tigers' written in bold script across the front. Tight white jeans and what appeared to be sharkskin cowboy boots completed his outfit.

There was dried blood on one ear, and he appeared to have suffered some contusions on the side of his face. The other ear was adorned with an elaborate gold earring from which both a cross and a star of David dangled. Seppy was dressed in khaki trousers and scuffed suede shoes. His old tweed jacket had a torn lapel and his striped, pink shirt collar had blood stains from a cut on his neck. As I entered, Seppy rose to his feet with a hand outstretched.

"Sit down! Sir," said the sergeant and he resumed his seat with an expression which reminded me instantly of school. But for his age and appearance, he could have been a boy outside the headmaster's study. I had already decided that, for Faith's sake, I must play the part expected of me by Seppy.

"I am Lord Wister," I announced to the sergeant in my most plummy voice, "I am well acquainted with Mr Naylor and can give you every assurance that he is a solicitor in good standing and a most respected member of his profession. I am at his disposal and yours, to assist in any way. Of course, I am in entirely unaware of the circumstances behind his presence here, Sergeant. Perhaps you would be willing to enlighten me."

"Well, my Lord, you might say it's a bit of an argy-bargy over money. Could you just step this way a moment?"

The sergeant led me to the far end of his rostrum, seemingly out of your shot of the two disputants.

"Would Mr Naylor be a married man by any chance, my Lord?" enquired the sergeant.

"Separated," I replied.

"Well, that might account for it I suppose. The fact is that well-tanned customer over there has three priors for living off immoral earnings. Those two were brawling outside the Rose and Thorn, an establishment much frequented by working girls, if you know what I mean, my Lord. Now, I'm pretty sure Sambo there had a knife, but my constable couldn't find it anywhere. Either your friend wouldn't pay one of his girls the right money or he got annoyed when he saw the girl hand over the money to her pimp. Obviously, the girl had scarpered. Now I don't want to be bothered charging either of them. I'll get the pimp eventually because he beats up his girls and one of them will finger him one day. But, my Lord, I would like you to take your friend away and tell him the next time he goes slumming, to stay off my patch." The sergeant gave me a slightly mocking salute and then pointed at Seppy.

"You can go now, Mr Naylor."

"Come on, Seppy," I said.

"Why didn't you ask him to call us a cab?" was the first thing Seppy said to me as we walked away from the station.

"Have you never heard of not pushing your luck?" I spoke. I was exasperated.

We walked towards a large thoroughfare in silence. After a while, I heard the familiar diesel engine noise behind us and looked around to see a cab with the welcome light on top, apparently following us.

"The station gave me a call, Guv—you two gents need a cab?"

We got in and I suggested to Seppy we go to my place. He nodded and said nothing for a while.

Finally, he spoke, "I shall be complaining about that sergeant. A clear case of assault with a deadly weapon. The constable must have seen the knife in his hand. I cannot imagine how he got rid of it. Apparently, that rotter is a known criminal. Instead, that ridiculous policeman started threatening me—me! Can you imagine? Something about 'accessory to illegal solicitation'."

I said nothing. I was not going to comment until we had reached my flat and I had regained some degree of objectivity. Seppy continued to the mumble to himself, "Bloody cheek!" and so forth. We reached my abode in Notting Hill. I paid and tipped a bemused cabbie. Once inside my small flat, Seppy asked for a stiff whiskey and went off to the bathroom to wash the cut on his neck which was superficial enough to have stopped bleeding.

When Seppy was settled in a chair holding a wadge of paper handkerchiefs to his neck and slurping his whiskey I began, "Now, let me make it clear that I couldn't care less what you do or where you go. If you want to go pub crawling to pick up hookers, that's your affair. But I'm dammed if I'm going to watch a nice girl get hurt or worse, catch some nasty disease."

"You've got a bloody nerve," interjected Seppy. "What is she to do with you?"

"If you are going to get me up at three in the morning, I am in entitled to a hearing. Let's face go. Move to your own digs. If you want to ruin your life, do it on your own. It's not fair on her."

Seppy was quiet. I don't think he'd ever been spoken to before in this manner. He looked totally defeated. He put his empty glass down and started to shake his head slowly from side to side. He pounded one arm of his chair with a clenched fist as though keeping time to a piece of music. Then he got unsteadily to his feet and began to pace up and down.

"I know, I know," he grumbled. "I can't understand what's wrong with me. I love that girl, you know, I really do. It's not just sex. That part was easy. But I've never really had her, you see. She is with me, but she isn't. I can't work her out. I can't get to the bottom of her—her soul, I mean, her real self. I know I'm inadequate. She is so far above me, on another planet, it seems. The more inadequate I feel, the lower I want to get. It doesn't make sense but it's the way I feel. She's an angel and that makes me want to be the devil. She's on a cloud and that makes me want to wallow in the mud."

Seppy stop pacing and looked at me imploringly. I could think of nothing to say. I asked him if he wanted another drink. He declined and I showed him my very small spare room and gave him some pyjamas and toothbrush. Embarrassed, we said good night and I went to bed but couldn't sleep. I thought of Faith. I saw her hooded eyes looking at me, not questioning but trying to share something. I felt her hand on my arm.

I tried to rehearse a speech I would make to her. I heard myself trying to comfort but sounding patronising. I tried to begin again. It was no use. No approach, no attitude seems right. Perhaps I had no business intervening at all. I thought about extricating myself completely from the whole affair. I had no reason to stay in touch with Seppy. I would simply fail to return his calls.

There was no need for me ever to contact Faith again. I dozed finally, just conscious that my last reasoning was not tenable. When I awoke, later than usual as my alarm had failed, Seppy had gone, leaving his bed made and the pyjamas folded.

Several months past, during which I needed to make no effort to avoid Seppy. He seemed to have passed out of my life. That he no longer frequented the hairdressing establishment where we met was no surprise. I was not often at Boodles and no doubt nor was Seppy, as no one talked of him or had any news when I once enquired. But I couldn't avoid Faith's continuing invasion of my thoughts and finally accepted that I had to find out how she was.

I had no telephone number and suddenly realised I did not even know her surname. But I remembered where her flat was and so walked there from the tube station at Notting Hill. But when I reached her entrance, undistinguished in a long line of early Victorian houses with porticoes in entrances, I lost my nerve. The basement flat had only initials 'F. B.' in the small space above the bell.

There was a light on behind the drawn gingham curtains. I stood for a moment hoping Faith might appear but then walked away, having noted the number at least. That night, I wrote a letter addressed to Miss Faith B. at the right address. I tried to make it casual, proposing luncheon at the Connaught the following Monday, if she had nothing better to do and so forth. I gave my office telephone number.

"I'd love to," said Faith's quiet voice with no other greeting after my secretary had announced, "a Miss Bingham for you." And so, I knew Faith's surname for the first time in our acquaintance of over two years. It turned out that her art gallery was in walking distance of the Connaught and so not far from my own office.

We agreed to meet in the bar at 1 o'clock. As I walked to the hotel from Berkeley Square, I suddenly spotted Faith walking slowly down Mount Street, looking in the shop windows. She was dressed in a black and white hounds' tooth trouser suit with a black turtleneck blouse and a small shoulder bag which she had slung crossways.

She stopped at a shop window and looked at the display for a moment, her head tilted sideways and then walked on again, swinging her arms. I felt awkward watching her without her knowing and so hurried on to meet her at the entrance. She turned each cheek to greet me, one hand holding my arm. In the bar, she ordered a sherry but didn't drink it. When the menus arrived, she studied hers with a frown, the tip of her tongue showing, as though she was trying to memorise it.

"You start," she said, as the waiter waited.

I ordered a green salad and a grilled sole.

"I will have the same," said Faith holding the menu with a straight arm to hand it back to the waiter. When we were finally settled at our table in the old English atmosphere of the Connaught dining room, we had unfolded the starched linen napkins and Faith had thoughtfully realigned the rows of silver forks and knives flanking her plate, I turned the conversation from the commonplace exchanges of our first moments.

"How is Seppy?" I began.

"Oh, much as usual." Faith toyed with her salad.

"Is he doing anything?"

"Not really."

"Drinking?"

"Well, yes—I suppose."

"Faith, can we talk seriously?"

She turned her hooded eyes on me as if in plea, then stopped her white wine appreciatively. "It's nice," she said. Suddenly she began to talk of Africa. She started by pointing out that they now made good wine in Zimbabwe, of course, not up to the South African standards which was very high, but still drinkable.

And then, almost without pause, except to take a mouthful of grilled so, which she would choose slowly and thoughtfully, staring ahead with her hooded eyes, Faith talked.

And as she talked, I no longer heard the background noises of the Connaught dining room, the bustle of the waiters, the clink of glass and silver on plate, the hum of mundane conversation, the slightly false laughter. I heard Africa, the cry of the crickets, the varied songs of the birds, the rustle of the wind in the bamboo grass, the drums from the African village, the rain on the tin roof, the chatter of the Africans outside the farm store. Faith was engaged in pronouncing a prose poem on her Africa, the land of her heart and soul, the theatre of her dreams. She described the red lands, the tall stalks of maize growing in rows, the sleek cattle grazing in the lush scrub, the thatched rondavels in the compound, the jumbled rocks and wild wisteria of the hills and bushveld, The purple blaze of the Jacaranda, the majesty of the Massassa trees. She took me through the day on the tobacco farm she had grown up on, from the ring of the 'chalili' to call the men to work to the evening walks to see the duck flighting over the dam and the sunsets red in ermine cloud.

As I listened and looked at Faith's faraway gaze, the very essence of Africa shining through her hooded eyes, penetrating the wainscoting of the Connaught restaurant and the grey gloom of the London streets, I understood Seppy's frustration. The capture of Faith was more daunting than the capture of white rhino for trans-location to poacher-free precincts, more traumatic and unnatural—however, innocuous the darting used to drag the unknowing victim. In the end, it was man exploiting technical mastery over a form of nature, a creature born of generations of freedom.

Faith also spoke to me of her father. Again, I sensed her anger mixed with love, over her banishment, her forced expatriation on the pretext of insolvency. She had no illusions about her father and had never had any expectation he could survive on his own. But she had loved him and still did, even in his now ruined state and she hated herself for her weakness in accepting her exile so placidly.

"I'm afraid I have no energy," said Faith as we set our coffee, "I know I should have gone back and looked after him. I could have been happy doing that, but I have just sat here in London, doing nothing. I am no use to anyone."

She looked at me and smiled. Her manner made it clear that the confession was over. We had spoken no more of Seppy and I sensed it would not be appropriate to raise the matter. I paid the bill and offered to walk her back to the gallery.

During the months that ensued, I made no further effort to see Faith although I did not stop thinking about her. Since she had seemed content with a continuing involvement with Seppy, it seemed wrong to continue seeing her on her own and I was determined to avoid further contact with him. It struck me that I could certainly have been in love with Faith if it had not been for the combination of my early morning session with Seppy after rescuing him from the police station and my subsequent lunch with Faith.

I realised that for entirely different reasons, no doubt, I would have no greater chance then Seppy of penetrating that self that was Faith's isolation. As with Seppy, she would have been with me but, in truth, she was elsewhere, in the world, she could not regain, a Paradise lost, an exile which brought no consolations. Those hooded eyes shed dried tears even when she smiled; her grace was the grace of caged animals—Faith was certainly not Seppy's, and neither could she ever be mine.

Then suddenly, I heard that Seppy had died. I was sitting in my club reading when a friend passed by and said: "Weren't you a friend of Septimus Naylor? I'm afraid the poor chap is dead. There is a small piece in the Times." He had died in a bizarre fashion, falling from London Bridge which was under construction and closed to traffic.

Apparently, Seppy had been drinking at a pub on the south bank of the Thames and had decided to walk back on a walkway laid out for the bridge builders. A foreman saw him fall and when they fished out the body, he was dead with a broken neck. The piece in the times spoke of, "A solicitor prominent in the world of entertainment who had retired recently from an active practice to pursue various business interests." Apart from his membership at the Garrick, I had never been aware of Seppy's speciality as a lawyer. *The Times* gave his age as 55.

It took me no time to decide that I had to see Faith again. Apart from common courtesy, I felt myself subduing my former resolve and wondering whether Faith would not need someone—perhaps myself, for example. But as I walked again from Notting Hill to face basement flat, I could not manage the memory of my own reaction to Seppy's announcement that he was in love with a much younger girl. Of course, he had been married and I was not. But I was also comfortably over 50. I had never married because the girls attracted to me were always the wrong sort and the girls that I was attracted to did not reciprocate. It was as simple as that. But I had a premonition of disaster at that lunch in the Kings Road when Seppy had told me about Faith. I reached her door now, uncertain as to what approach I should adopt.

The door was opened as soon as I had rung the bell and Faith merely said, "hello." She had probably just returned from work. She had never called me by my name, perhaps because she had always heard Seppy call me 'Wister' and had never enquired about my Christian name.

"Come in," said Faith, "I think there's the bottom of a bottle of scotch."

The flat had been tidied and changed around a bit. The only remaining evidence of Seppy was the director's chair he had sat on, some polo sticks and a golf bag leaning in the corner. I sat in the chair next to the lamp with Winnie the Pooh on the shade. Faith gave me a whiskey and water, apologising for the lack of ice. She sat on the sofa and took a small sip from her class before putting it down and looking at it for a moment. Then she turned her hooded eyes towards me, expecting me to speak first.

"I'm so sorry," I faltered a bit. "I'm afraid I'd lost track of Seppy since the three of us met the last time. Although he annoyed me intensely, I had grown quite fond of him." I was conscious that this was a politeness and not strictly true.

Faith gave me an understanding smile, as there she knew perfectly well that I had never grown fond of Seppy.

"You are nice to come and see me," she said. "You know, Jane's lawyer rang me at work which I thought was kind and I did have a nice note from Jane herself which was even more surprising, I suppose."

She took another small sip of her drink and then sat back. She was wearing a stone-coloured a linen jacket with a light blue silk shirt underneath. She sat with her hands on her lap, palms upturned. She had on a dark blue skirt and she had taken off her shoes, no doubt as soon as she had returned from work.

"You know, I hardly saw Seppy these last few months." She sat looking at the palms of her hands, her head tilted a bit in a characteristic fashion. "He was out all the time; he would come back in the early hours and was always asleep when I left for work. He was just a lump lying there. At least, he didn't snore. I sometimes woke to hear him crashing about a bit and he was asleep on the sofa when I got up. I knew he was miserable; we hardly spoke. The only thing I could do for him, was just to be here."

219

"Look here, Faith," I felt myself leaping over a cliff, "Will you marry me?"

Faith looked up at me, her hooded eyes questioning rather than surprised. I could think of nothing further to say. She got up and kissed me lightly on the forehead and then sat down. She covered her face with her hands for a few minutes. I was suddenly conscious of pedestrians walking past on the pavement outside.

"You are sweet, and kind and I am honoured but the answer is no—I'm going back to Africa, to look after my father." Faith put one hand on the sofa in my direction. I leant towards her and took her hand in both mine.

"I love you," I said.

"I know you do, and I would love you as well, but it wouldn't work, I don't belong here, and you would end up feeling like a jailer rather than a lover or husband. I really know what's best, you know."

Faith looked at me as a mother might look at a son and then began to tell me about her father. She let me hold her hand while she talked. It was at this final session that I learnt about her birth defect, how she had trained her other eye, how they had lived on the tobacco farm, the Safari camp, her father's decision to send her to England, the maiden aunts in Brighton and Tenby, the sad holidays by the seashore, the heartache of exile, the longing for Africa.

It was as though she was opening her soul to me as a proxy for giving herself to me physically. She was calm and composed but trembled slightly, I thought, when she described the bleakness of those teenage years with the kindly aunts.

"I can see my father's face when I tell him I could have been Lady Wister." She gave my hand is squeeze and withdrew hers. I got up and she took my arm and led me slowly to the door, her eyes on her bare feet. At the door, I turned and looked into Faith's hooded eyes for the last time.

"Goodbye," I said.

I stepped into the little well of the staircase which led from the pavement to the door of the flat.

"Goodbye," said Faith, and she closed the door slowly, so that first one eye and then the other disappeared with the final click.

FINIS

Printed in Great Britain
by Amazon

37238812R00123